RAY HOGAN was born in Missouri but has spent most of his life in New Mexico. His father was an early Western marshal and lawman, and Hogan himself has spent a lifetime researching the West. He has written over 100 books, including THE GLORY TRAIL, THE HELL BORN, OVERKILL AT SADDLE ROCK, JACKMAN'S WOLF, THE PEACE KEEPER, THE SHOTGUNNER, and 24 titles in the best-selling Shawn Starbuck series, all available in Signet paperback. His work has been filmed, televised, and translated into sixteen languages.

Ⓢ SIGNET BRAND WESTERN

BRANDON'S POSSE

and

THE HELL MERCHANT

by

Ray Hogan

A SIGNET BOOK

NEW AMERICAN LIBRARY

TIMES MIRROR

Brandon's Posse COPYRIGHT © 1971 BY RAY HOGAN
The Hell Merchant COPYRIGHT © 1972 BY RAY HOGAN

All rights reserved. Originally appeared in paperback as individual
volumes published by The New American Library.

 SIGNET TRADEMARK REG. U.S. PAT. OFF. AND FOREIGN COUNTRIES
REGISTERED TRADEMARK—MARCA REGISTRADA
HECHO EN CHICAGO, U.S.A.

SIGNET, SIGNET CLASSICS, MENTOR, PLUME, MERIDIAN AND NAL
BOOKS *are published by The New American Library, Inc.,*
1633 Broadway, New York, New York 10019

FIRST PRINTING (Double Western Edition), SEPTEMBER, 1979

4 5 6 7 8 9 10 11 12

PRINTED IN THE UNITED STATES OF AMERICA

BRANDON'S
POSSE

～～ 1 ～～

It had been one hell of a day so far. Starbuck had risen early after an uncomfortable night in a dry camp, scraped together a breakfast of coffee, fried meat and grease-soaked bread that was as hard as a stonemason's chisel. Then, just as he was about to down the mess, an erratic gust of the persistent wind that had plagued him for three days garnished it all with a generous topping of sand. Disgusted, he had dumped the spider's contents, gulped the coffee and ridden on.

Right in keeping with that inauspicious beginning, the sorrel had been contrary and hard-mouthed and was earning the spurs and the harsh hand on the leathers he was getting as they moved, teeth to the wind, steadily southwest across a vast, rolling mesa.

It was no consoling thought that Santa Fe, his planned destination where he hoped to find or else learn something of value concerning his brother Ben, for whom he'd searched so long, was still many days away—on the yonder side and opposite end of the dark, towering mountains he could see dimly in the dust-hazed distance.

The ashes and charred remnants of Babylon where he had served briefly as marshal of that riotous colony of gambling and women were behind him, as were Dodge City, Cheyenne, Las Cruces, El Paso, Tucson— all the other places he'd visited in his ceaseless quest for the brother who in anger had fled the family home in Ohio a decade ago.

He had found only cold trails wherever he went and very possibly he would fare no better in the ancient

5

capital of the *Conquistadores,* but as always he must
try, must know. Ben was somewhere, and someday he
would find him—and then the search would end. Until
that moment, however, he led the life of a wanderer,
a drifter, one dedicated to hunting for a man he hadn't
seen since boyhood and likely would not recognize
should they come face to face.

A blast of fine sand whipped at him. Shawn swore
irritably, brushed at his eyes and lips, spat. The gelding,
stung also by the dry particles, jerked his head nervously, shied off the faint trail they were following.

Starbuck brought the sorrel back into line, glanced
ahead. They were breaking off the mesa and dropping
into a wide area of buttes and arroyos littered with
rabbitbrush, cactus and other rank growth. Dust devils,
stirred into frantic motion by the capricious wind,
spun across the more open flats, leaped intervening
obstacles and spiraled on toward the limitless prairie.
He sighed. Matters were not going to get any better.

Guiding the sorrel to a break in the low wall of the
arroyo, he swung the big red horse into it. The gelding
started down, felt the soil give way under his front
hooves. He tried to pull back. Instantly a ten-foot-long
section of the bank broke off. The sorrel bunched,
sprang, eyes rolling wildly, ears laid flat. He struck on
bent knees, went down on his left side. Starbuck, barely able to throw himself clear of the thrashing horse,
went full length into a mass of brittle-stalked snakeweed.

Cursing, wrists and face smarting from the scratches
he'd received, Starbuck scrambled to his feet and
whirled to the sorrel. Relief moved through him. The
horse was up, appeared to be unhurt by the fall. Dust-
ing himself with his hat, he crossed to where the gelding waited.

Shawn swore again. A steady dripping sound told
him that his canteen had been caught under the sorrel
and crushed by his weight. It had emptied itself quickly
through a burst seam and now contained only a few
drops.

Unhooking the container from the saddle, he held
it overhead to catch the small amount yet remaining,

and then tossing it aside, took up the sorrel's reins. He moved forward leading the gelding, eyes watching closely for any indication of a limp. The horse showed no signs of having lamed himself. Grunting in satisfaction, Shawn stepped back into the saddle.

He remained motionless, staring out across the windy landscape. There should be a stream, or at least a spring, somewhere along the hills that he could see in the distance—but it would take the remainder of the day to reach that point and by then he would be plenty thirsty. He shrugged, a tall, gray-eyed man not long out of boyhood in years but well into that phase by the reckoning of trouble and experience, and lifted the reins. He'd live through it, he'd make it. Hell, he had to. There was no other choice.

Roweling the sorrel lightly, he moved on into the arroyo, his mood blacker now from one more irritating incident, his impatience heightened by another of the needless, uncalled-for tribulations that were riding him. . . . There were days when a man should just stay in his blankets.

Near noon the wind finally died, and with a show of dark clouds gathering in the west, he halted to rest the sorrel. He decided against eating; with no water it would only increase the thirst that was making itself felt. Restless, he stalled out a full hour for the sake of the gelding, and then climbing back onto his hull, pressed on.

Shortly he was out of the arroyo and again on a broad, rolling mesa sparsely covered with a thin grass that showed gray in its need for rain. But that was due to end, he guessed, once more eyeing the thickening clouds; a storm was in the offing, and with good luck, should strike sometime during the night.

He hoped the hell he'd have reached a town or a ranch by then; he was in no mood to get soaking wet and besides, the way things were going, he'd like as not get struck by lightning or come a-cropper from some other bit of misfortune.

A time later he pulled in the sorrel. A quarter-mile on, squatted along the first hint of rising land that lifted gracefully to the mountains beyond, was a home-

steader's holdings—a sagging, slanted roof shack, two
or three dilapidated sheds, a corral, a small stretch of
cultivated ground and a water well.

Brushing at his cracked lips, Starback urged the
gelding on, pointing for the circle of stones and water
bucket at the side of the bleak little structures. A door
banged in the warm hush. A figure appeared and the
afternoon's quiet was further shattered by the deafening
blast of a shotgun.

Starbuck hauled up short as pellets spurted dust only
a stride in front of the sorrel. Anger rocking through
him, he raised both hands, palms forward and stared.
It was a woman. She was wearing a ragged and soiled
housedress of sleazy gray, and her hair, unkempt and
tangled, straggled down over her leathery face and neck,
but it did not conceal the fierceness and the fright that
filled her eyes.

"Hold on! Just looking for a drink of water," he
called.

"You ain't getting it here—'cause you ain't stopping!" the woman yelled, waving the shotgun menacingly.

The cocked hammer of the as yet unfired barrel of
the old ten-gauge looked as big as a man's thumb. Starbuck forced a thin smile.

"Mean you no harm, ma'am," he said, trying to keep
the edge from his tone. "Horse of mine fell, busted my
canteen. Been most of the day without water."

"Ain't a damn whit to me—keep moving!"

Starbuck shrugged. No one in his right mind would
argue with a frightened woman holding a cocked scat-
tergun in her hands—thirsty or not.

"Yes, ma'am," he said, lowering his arms. "I'm going. Sure would appreciate a little of that water, however."

"You'll find some—about an hour down the way. . .
Wolf Crossing."

Shawn paused. "That a town?"

"Now, what do you think it is—a Sunday sociable?"

"No, ma'am," Starbuck muttered, and simmering under his hat, doubled back to the trail.

Once out of the shotgun's range, he relaxed, took

a deep breath. Anger still plucked at him, but the moments were tempered now by the thought that he was coming into a settlement where he could satisfy his needs and find comfort for the night.

It was a fair-sized town he noted with further pleasure as he rounded a shoulder of rock and caught sight of the structures nestled in the cove of a steeply rising mountain. He could see three or four two-storied buildings, the steeple of a church, as well as a short main street along which business houses stood shoulder to shoulder on either side. Residences were scattered about it all in a loose circle.

A splash of silver behind the structures marked a stream and for a time he was tempted to cut off from the road he was following and go first to the creek and satisfy his thirst, but he decided against it. Better to pull up to the first saloon he came to, get his fill of water and then treat himself to a drink of rye whiskey. Afterwards he'd see to the sorrel, get a room at the hotel and think about a good meal.

Shortly he turned into the end of the street, noted curiously the number of persons gathered in front of a low-roofed, sprawling building that bore the sign SQUARE DOLLAR SALOON, and slanted toward its hitch-rack.

Several men, listening to a dark, thickset individual wearing the town marshal's star, turned to glance at him as he rode the gelding up to the rack and then returned their attention to the lawman. Some sort of trouble in Wolf Crossing, Shawn concluded as he swung from the saddle—trouble he aimed to stay clear of. Brushing at the dust stiffening his face, he glanced idly along the street. . .GRAND CENTRAL HOTEL Wm. Gooch, Prop. . .ORY JONES GENERAL MERCHANDISE. . .STRATTON DRY GOODS & SUPPLIES. . .L. A. MARBERRY, M.D. . . JOSHUA WILLIS LAWYER. . .THE ANTELOPE CAFE. . . .

"Be a cold day in hell when them Paradise Mine jaspers gets any help from this town!"

At the sound of the words coming from a man close by, Starbuck turned. They had been directed to the lawman, who wagged his head slowly while he stroked the thick mustache that covered his lip.

"I'm the law around here. I'm obliged to do my duty."

"You ain't always felt that way about this here duty of yours, Brandon," another voice in the crowd said. "How's it come you're thinking so strong about it now? Been a few times when folks needed—"

"Always done what I figured was right—"

"Sure—right for you!"

"Makes no difference now. I'm asking for a posse—for volunteers."

"You got yourself three," the speaker said, and laughed.

Brandon half turned, cast an indifferent look at the men standing behind him—a Negro clad in ordinary cowhand garb, a slumped puncher with the drawn, haggard features of a sobering alcoholic, and a slightly built, pale individual whose checked suit and small hat marked him as a newcomer from somewhere east of the Mississippi.

"Need more'n them."

Shawn wrapped the sorrel's reins around the crossbar of the rack and turned to make his way to the saloon's porch. The gelding shied to one side. Instantly a man cursed.

"What the hell you doing? Goddam jughead of yours stepped on my foot!"

Shawn rounded the hindquarters of the gelding, faced the two punchers standing there. His mood had improved little since early morning and the edge of his temper was sharp.

"Reckon my horse is begging your pardon," he said drily.

"The hell you say!" the taller of the pair snapped. "How about the jackass that's riding him?"

It was the ultimate, crowning episode of an arduous day. The balled fist of Starbuck's left arm lashed out, caught the puncher flush on the nose. A fraction of a second later his right scored with deadly precision on the jaw. The man staggered, began to sink as his knees buckled. His partner yelled, reached for the pistol on his hip. Starbuck's left hand swept down, came up smoothly. Sunlight glinted off the barrel of his leveled forty-five.

"My advice—forget it," he said quietly.

The rider, half bent, palm wrapped around the weapon still in its holster, glanced about at the hushed crowd and then straightened slowly. His fingers relaxed their grip, slid away.

"Sure," he murmured almost inaudibly, "sure," and shifted his eyes to his partner. "Whatever you say."

Shawn jammed his pistol back into its leather, shrugged and, ignoring the man, moved on toward the porch of the Square Dollar. Wolf Crossing was about as unfriendly a town as he'd ever ridden into—but he guessed maybe it was him; he wasn't feeling particularly neighborly himself.

~~ 2 ~~

The bartender, a paunchy, balding man with round eyes and a trailing mustache, was standing inside the doorway. He turned as Shawn entered, hurried to get in behind the counter which was immediately adjacent to the batwings.

"What'll it be?"

From habit, Starbuck glanced around the semidark room. It was deserted. Leaning against the bar, he nodded, pushed his hat to the back of his head. The edge had not faded entirely from his voice.

"Rye. . .some water first."

The balding man set a stone pitcher and a tumbler on the counter before Shawn, reached for a shot glass and a bottle, covertly studying him all the while. It was as if he were calculating the wisdom of launching into his usual companionable conversation with strangers.

Starbuck solved the problem for him. Downing a second glass of water, he jerked his thumb in the direction of the street.

"What's going on out there?"

The bartender's brow pulled into a frown. "Been a killing," he said, filling the shot glass with liquor and placing it in front of Shawn. "Four men. The marshal's trying to make up a posse and go after the outlaws that done it."

"Not having much luck, seems."

"He won't around here."

Starbuck's brows lifted. "I figured he was the local lawman."

"He is—but he won't be after next month. Folks just

12

plain ain't got no use for Harry Brandon. Election's coming up and he won't get another term."

Shawn stirred. "It's still the law. If he needs help people ought to give it to him."

The bartender's shoulders twitched. "Well, it ain't only that it's Brandon asking, it's the fact that the gold them outlaws took off with belonged to the Paradise Mine, and there ain't nobody going to turn a hand to help that outfit."

"I heard something about that when I rode up. What's everybody got against the Paradise Mine?"

"They had a chance to set up their office here, and do their buying of supplies from the local merchants. Instead they picked a town on the other side of the mountain. Can't nobody forget that."

Voices in the street rose briefly, fell again to a murmur. Starbuck said, "They probably had a good reason."

"Maybe, but they're going to find out right quick that it'd been smart—and a powerful lot cheaper—to've settled here in Wolf Crossing. . . . A hundred thousand dollars cheaper."

Shawn whistled softly. "Lot of money. What happened?"

"They was sending it to Dodge City—some special deal. Usually all the gold goes the other way, to Denver, but this was different, and it was all real secret like. The gold was on two pack mules and they had four guards with them. Was passing themselves off as engineers. Only it didn't work. Somehow the outlaws, was three of them, got wind of the truth about it."

"They pull the holdup here in town?"

"Nope, about a mile east of here. Ambushed them. Brandon heard the shooting, got out there fast as he could, but the outlaws were already gone. One of the guards was still alive, barely. Told the marshal what had happened."

"When was this?"

"Just around noon. Guards had spent the night here, was heading out for Dodge. Brandon brung the bodies in, then sent word to the Paradise people. He's been trying to get a posse together ever since."

Shawn sipped at his whiskey. "Won't the mining company be sending him some help?"

"Probably, but it'll be this time tomorrow at least before they can get here. Them outlaws will be long gone by then."

The sounds in the street lifted again. Shawn listened idly for a few moments. Harry Brandon, he gathered, was still having no luck.

"Your marshal holds off much more himself, he'll be too late, too. Better settle for those three who did volunteer."

The barman cocked his head to one side, smiled wryly. "If you was him, would you be willing to go after three killers with the town drunk, a greenhorn and a nigra handyman?"

"It'd be a mean choice," Shawn replied, shrugging. "I don't know any of them, but seems they'd be better than nobody at all."

"Doubt that. The greenhorn—name's Walt Moody—blew in here a week or so ago. From St. Louis. Got himself some kind of woman trouble. All he's done is mope around, head hanging and acting like he wish't he was dead. The nigra's been working for some cattle outfit west of here. He got laid off. . . .There's something peculiar about him."

"Peculiar?"

'Well, I mean he's sort of had some learning. Talks real good for a nigra, which is sort of funny."

"A colored man can be educated same as a white. I've known a few in my lifetime."

The bartender nodded. "Sure, I know that, only it sort of surprises a man. You just don't expect it, somehow."

"He got a name?"

"Calls himself Able Rome. . . .Third fellow is Dave Gilder. Lays around here drunk most of the time. Now and then he gets himself a job on some ranch where they don't know him, but it never lasts long. I figure he'd make a pretty good man if he was to get his snout out of the jug and straighten up."

Starbuck finished off the rye, refilled the tumbler with water. The bartender looked at him closely.

"You looking for work? I heard Brandon say he was paying five dollars a day and keep. Good chance the Paradise people will come through with a little reward, too, if they get their hundred thousand back."

Shawn drank the water, shook his head. "No thanks. I got a job of my own to do—looking for my brother."

The man behind the counter paused in the process of wiping the varnished surface of the bar. "He live around here? Maybe I'll know him."

"Name's Ben Starbuck. Good chance he goes by Damon Friend, however."

The bartender resumed his polishing in thoughtful silence. Finally he glanced up. "Nope, don't recollect nobody by either of them names. What's he look like?"

"Probably a little like me. Could be shorter, heavier."

"You talk like you ain't sure—"

"I'm not. Haven't seen him in over ten years or so. Ran off from home after a squabble with my pa."

"I see. . . . You got some reason for thinking he's here in Wolf Crossing?"

"No, I'm just passing through on my way to Santa Fe. I make a point of asking about him wherever I happen to be. Been doing it for a long time—all over the country."

"Must be mighty important that you find him."

"It is. Can't settle Pa's estate until I do. . . .The Grand Central Hotel, that the best place to put up for the night? Been a rough day and I can use a good bed."

"It's the only place, but it's good. Best you do your eating at the Antelope Cafe, howsomever. Vittles are a mite better. How long you aim to be around,"

"Moving on in the morning," Shawn replied. "How much I owe you?"

"Two bits'll cover it. . . .You mind me saying something?"

Starbuck dropped a coin on the bar. "Depends."

"About the way you handled them two smart alecks out there in the street. I was standing in the door watching. You—you're powerful fast with that iron of yours."

"A man learns."

"You—maybe, well—could be you sometimes hire out to somebody—"

"If you're wondering if I'm a hired gun, the answer's no."

The bartender nodded, looked down. "No offense."

"None taken, and there's times when I have hired on a job where a gun was part of the deal. But only a part."

"I see. . . .This here brother of yours that you're hunting for, if he ever shows up, what ought I to tell him?"

"Could be you won't have to tell him nothing, Ed," a voice said from the doorway. "Could be I know where he is."

Starbuck drew himself upright, wheeled quickly. Harry Brandon, light filtering in from a window glinting against his star, was facing him.

"What was that?"

The lawman came on into the saloon. Beyond him in the street Shawn could see that the crowd had broken up. The three volunteers for the posse now stood at the hitchrack.

"I said I might could tell you where this fellow—"

"Brother—" the bartender supplied.

"This brother of yours, name of Ben, could be."

Starbuck studied the marshal's weathered features narrowly. Then, "Where?"

"Like as not he's one of the outlaws I'm setting out after."

~~~ 3 ~~~

Starbuck's mouth tightened. Evidently Brandon had been standing in the saloon's entrance long enough to overhear part of the conversation he'd had with the Square Dollar's bartender and was trying to make the most of it.

"Not likely," he said coolly.

"Other way about. It's probably true."

"Ben's no outlaw."

"If you ain't seen him in quite a spell, how'd you know for sure?" the lawman said, coming on into the room and taking a place at the bar. "Give me a whiskey, Ed," he said to the aproned man, and then, facing Shawn, added, "He could've changed. Maybe he was all right at the start, but just sort of slid into bad ways."

"No man just gradually turns bad," Starbuck said shrugging. "Somewhere along he gets a chance to say no to something—and Ben's the kind who would have said it."

Harry Brandon stirred indifferently, took up his shot glass of liquor and tossed it off. "Could be you're right. I'm only telling you that one of them killers is named Ben—and if he's the Ben I'm thinking he is, he's about your size and he's got your looks."

A faint smile tugged at Starbuck's lips. He was buying none of it; Harry Brandon was simply trying to recruit a fourth member for his posse. Still. . .

Ed refilled the lawman's glass. "How'd you happen to know one of them was named Ben? You said you didn't see none of them."

17

"And I didn't. One of them guards wasn't dead, like I told everybody. He recognized a couple of them, give me their names. Ben Snow was one. Another'n was Ollie Kastman. Didn't know the third man. And like I'm saying, if this Ben Snow's the man I've got in mind, he sort of fits the description of your brother."

Starbuck laughed. "Forget it, Marshal. I'm not about to join your posse—if that's what this is all about."

Brandon downed his liquor. "Suit yourself. Ain't saying I wouldn't like to have you with me, but it's up to you."

"You get anybody else, Harry?" the bartender asked.

"Only them three," the lawman replied in a voice filled with disgust. "Don't know what the hell's eating folks around here."

"I expect you do," Ed countered quietly. "If it was anybody but that Paradise outfit, you'd maybe have your posse."

"Maybe."

The saloonman's brows lifted. "Well, you ain't exactly overloaded with friends, Harry."

"No fault of mine. Man wearing a badge has to do his duty. Sometimes tromping on folks' toes can't be helped." The lawman sighed, shoved his glass aside. "Sure is something! It's hell if I do and hell if I don't when it comes to getting my job done."

Two men drifted in through the doorway, sidled up to the bar. Ed moved off to serve their needs. Shawn felt the marshal's hard, dark eyes pressing him.

"I'll ask you straight out—you interested in riding for me? Pay is five dollars a day and grub. Could be an extra hundred or two if the mine comes through with a reward. I expect it won't take more'n three, four days. . . . You in a hurry to reach Santa Fe?"

"No."

"I could sure use you—it's the law saying that. Them I got—hell—there ain't the makings of one good man in all three. A sobering-up drunk, a greenhorn and a black boy—might as well go it alone!"

"Sounds like you know where to find the killers."

"I do—pretty well, that is. Guard said they headed south after that ambush. I followed their tracks for a spell. Was easy. Three horses and two mules leave a lot of prints. They circled town, then cut into the mountains."

Shawn had a quick recollection of the sprawling mass of rock and timber towering behind the settlement.

"Won't be easy tracking through—"

"Easier'n you think. My hunch is they're lining out on the trail that goes up to the ridge and cuts clean through the mountains. Old one—Indians used it when they was running wild around here. It's the only way a man can cross over, and there ain't no turning off once you're on it."

"Where'll it take them to?"

"These here mountains run into the Sangre de Cristos, and then they sort of tail off into the Sandias and the Manzanos that run along the east side of the Rio Grande river. They just keep right on going and they'll end up close to the Mexican border. That's where I figure they're headed for—Mexico."

"They got a pretty good start—five, six hours."

"I know that and it's what's got me in a sweat. They're working deeper into them hills every minute and I sure got to be moving out after them. Just one thing good, they won't be traveling fast. Mules'll slow them down plenty."

The bartender returned hurriedly, evidently hopeful of missing nothing. He squinted at Shawn. "You decided to go?"

Starbuck stared at the backbar moodily. Brandon's attempt to interest him by stating that one of the outlaws could be Ben was undoubtedly nothing more than a ruse. The lawman was desperate and willing to try anything. . . .But on the other hand the dying guard had named the outlaws, or two of them, and one he'd said was called Ben.

That much he could probably consider the truth. The remainder—that the man Ben Snow fit the description he'd given of his brother to the bartender—was likely an outright lie on the marshal's part. Trouble was, there was no way of knowing for sure, and he'd made it a rule never to pass up a lead or ignore a possibility that could take him to Ben Starbuck.

Boot heels scraped in the doorway. Shawn glanced up into the mirror, saw Brandon turn. Able Rome hesitated just within the batwings, then moved toward the bar.

"All right, boy," the lawman said impatiently. "I'm coming. You and the others get your horses, meet me at the stable."

Rome did not slow his steps, continued until he reached the long counter. "I'm ready when you are, Marshal," he said in a soft, slurred accent. "Whiskey," he added, nodding to the bartender.

Ed reached for a glass, filled it and slid it along the counter. Brandon frowned.

"You do much drinking, boy?"

Rome's expression did not alter. "No more than the next man, I expect."

"Well, I want you to get this straight right now, I won't stand for no drinking on this hunt!"

"What I carry will be in my belly," Rome replied and downed his whiskey. He reached into his pocket, produced a quarter and laid it on the counter. Wheeling, he crossed to the doors and returned to the street.

"Uppity cuss," Brandon murmured, watching until the man had disappeared. "Ain't so sure I want him coming along, only I reckon I can't be choicey." He swung his attention to Shawn.

"What about it? I ain't saying Ben Snow is your brother, but I am saying there's a mighty good chance he is. Riding with me is one way you can find out."

Starbuck gave it another moment's thought, shrugged. "All right, I'll go. I'm not believing anything you say about it being my brother, but I'm willing to have myself proved wrong."

"Good," Brandon said, smiling broadly. "Just might find yourself surprised. We'll be moving out right away."

"Going to take me a few minutes. I got to get myself a fresh horse. Sorrel of mine's had a hard day. I need to buy a new canteen—"

"Forget it. I've got an extra you can have. And far as changing horses is concerned, you won't have to. Figure

to make camp at Gold Creek—about ten miles back
in the mountains. That animal of yours can make it
that far."

"I expect I'm ready then," Shawn said, and nodding
to the bartender, turned for the door.

4

They rode out of Wolf Crossing with the dark clouds still clinging to the mountain peaks, seemingly poised and awaiting only the proper moment to open their overloaded bellies and send a flood cascading down the long slopes.

Shawn, though feeling hunger, had passed up the few minutes of grace permitted him while Harry Brandon made his final preparations—time during which he could have grabbed a hasty bite at the restaurant mentioned by Ed, the bartender—and instead made use of them to water the sorrel and see to his gear.

The marshal had said they would travel only a short distance before making camp; he could ignore his need for food until then—and the sorrel was a different matter. He had gone the entire day without water.

Riding beside Brandon, Starbuck glanced back as they broke clear of the town's limits and turned off the well-defined road toward the towering mountains. Behind the lawman and him came Moody and Dave Gilder, their horses side by side and matching each step. Able Rome, his broad face emotionless, brought up the rear. He had not spoken, so far as Shawn knew, since he had been in the saloon.

"Mighty glad you showed up when you did," Brandon said, shifting his holster forward on his leg. "I figured I had to have at least one good man along that I could depend on—and you was him."

Starbuck half smiled. "You don't know me, Marshal. How can you say that?"

"Shows—that's how. I'm a pretty good judge of men, and on you it shows."

22

"Plain guess. Doubt if I'm any more reliable than the men you've got."

The lawman snorted. "You talking about Gilder and Moody and that nigra?"

"I'm talking about Gilder and Moody and Able Rome," Starbuck said coldly.

Brandon turned his head, considered Shawn for a long breath. "Yeh, them. Like I said, they don't count for hardly nothing. Just three bags of corn husks setting on three saddles." He paused, swept the riders behind him with a scornful glance. "Brandon's posse—hell! Best you call them Brandon's misfits."

"Could be wrong about them."

"Wrong—how?"

"All most men need sometimes is a chance, one that'll make them face up to something hard and force them to prove themselves. Somebody once said that a hero was never born, he was made."

"Not them! What can Dave Gilder prove to himself? He can't even keep hisself sober long enough to do much of anything. And about all the proving he could do me is that he could go a whole day without a drink, which I sure doubt.

"And that greenhorn—Moody. What's he got to prove? That he ain't already dead from something that happened to him sometime or other? He's done showed that he wasn't man enough to take it—else he wouldn't be nothing but a walking corpse."

"Hard to know what's in any man's mind."

"Not with them it ain't. Gilder's figuring how soon it'll be before he can get back to town and blow what money he'll make on whiskey. Moody's trying to forget whatever it is that's chewing on his guts, and far as that nig—that Rome's concerned, he's just out to show he's good as any white man. Always the way with them black ones."

Harry Brandon spat, looked ahead. The trail was slipping down into the bottom of a fairly narrow canyon to pick its course along the floor. Pine trees were beginning to be more plentiful, and the lesser growth common to the lower valley and flats area was thinning out.

"They might as well try changing their color," the lawman said, resuming the subject. "That's what's eating them." He frowned, fixed Shawn with his hard, fixed gaze. "You got a special feeling for blacks?"

"I never thought about it one way or another. Just a man like any other—"

"Then you sure'n hell ain't never had much truck with them!"

"I've worked with a few, and we had a couple of hired hands back on the farm that were colored. Never figured them as being anything other than two men who worked for my pa."

"Where was that?"

"Ohio. Place was on the Muskingum River. Town nearby had the same name."

"Ohio," Brandon repeated as if it explained much to him. "Your people still there?"

"No. My mother's been dead a long time—about twelve years now. Pa died two years ago."

"And that's what cut you loose and started you hunting this brother you was talking about."

Starbuck nodded. "I've been at it off an' on ever since. I have to stop once in awhile, find myself a job and get a little traveling money together."

"I come from a farm myself," the lawman said in a thoughtful voice. "Pennsylvania. Wish't the hell I'd a stayed there. Good land, good house and not no worrying to do like I've had since I got out here."

"You always worn a badge?"

"Yep, first job I took was being a deputy sheriff. Up in Colorado. Had a couple others like it—Wyoming, Nebraska, then I got myself elected marshal of this damned hole. . . . Been sorry of it."

Shawn glanced up, surprised. "I understood from that bartender—"

"Ed Christian—"

"Whatever his name is, that you were up for re-election next month."

"He say that?"

"Not in so many words but it's the way I took it."

Brandon laughed. "Yeh, I reckon he'd be thinking that. He's one of the town councilmen—him and Gooch and Stratton and Doc Marberry—and they'd be figuring on me going after the job again. But they got a big surprise coming. They can take the job and shove it because I'm pulling out. Had all of that town I want."

There was a bitterness in the lawman's tone and his features had become grim.

"How long you been wearing the badge in Wolf Crossing?"

"Six years—almost, and that's more'n enough. No help there when you need it, nobody ever willing to back you up. This posse's a good example of how they feel about the law—me. . . . I need support, ask for it and what do I get? Them!" Brandon finished with a sweeping gesture toward the men behind him.

"I expect the fact that it was the Paradise Mine people they'd be helping was the big reason."

The marshal shook his head, spat. "Nah, the mining company is just something to lay it on. Me—I'm the one they're turning their backs on. But I don't give a good goddam no more. Hell of a life, anyway. No future in it. A man gets too old to work, he gets let out, ends up swamping in a saloon or forking manure in a stable. . . . Pay's never enough for him to lay any money aside.

"But I'm beating them at their own game. No little two-bit town's going to do that to me. I'm quitting, getting out while the getting's good. Already made my plans."

"If that's the way you feel about it," Shawn said, "then that's the thing to do. A man only lives once. I reckon he ought to fill his time doing what he likes."

"That's me exactly, from here on," Brandon replied. "Leastwise it'll be after I hand in my star."

Starbuck made no comment. Darkness was growing and he began to look ahead for signs of the creek where they would be making night camp. He'd be glad to crawl off the saddle and have a meal. It had been a long, tiring day.

Brandon, noting his exploring glance, said, "We'll be pulling up in another mile or so. Gold Creek ain't far. . . . I hear you say you was headed for Santa Fe?"

Shawn nodded. He was a bit weary of conversation,

hoped the lawman had talked himself out for awhile but evidently it was not to be.

"Somebody there you know—or maybe you're just hoping to find your brother?"

"I aim to look for him, do some asking around."

"I expect you've seen a passel of places, drifting around the way you have."

"Quite a few, all right."

"Country south of the mountains—the range we're following—you been there?"

"Not too much. Worked around Las Cruces for a time."

"Where's that?"

"Lower Rio Grande Valley. . . . Some call it the Mesilla Valley."

"Ain't that pretty close to the Mexican border?"

"Forty, fifty miles, as I recall."

Off to their right a piñon jay scolded noisily from the depths of a long-needled pine. Brandon listened briefly and then said, "What's back up this side of Las Cruces?"

"A lot of open country—desert, unless you stay down in the valley where the Rio Grande is."

"But east of that, there ain't much of nothing, that it?"

"About right. A few lonesome hills, and a man can run into Indians if he's not watching sharp. Apaches and Comanches both."

"But a man could get through if he was well fixed for grub and water and kept his eyes peeled."

Brandon was evidently thinking about the outlaws they were pursuing, the possibility of their escaping to make their way to the Mexican border.

"That's what they'll need—along with some good luck."

"Which they sure'n hell ain't going to get the chance of using!" the lawman said harshly.

Starbuck's gaze rested on Harry Brandon. There was solid, cold determination in his tone and manner. Overtaking the killers and recovering the gold apparently was very important to him. He guessed he could understand the lawman's thinking; he was turning in his star and he wanted to do it with success crowning the moment.

Perhaps he even hoped the people of Wolf Crossing would suddenly realize their loss and beg him to stay; then he could laugh in their faces and turn them down cold.

"Reckon we're here—"

The marshal's voice brought Shawn's attention to the trail. A dozen strides ahead he saw a narrow ribbon of water sparkling dully in the fading daylight as it cut its way along the foot of a slope. He heaved a deep sigh. A hot meal was going to do him a lot of good.

Dave Gilder cupped his hands over the saddlehorn and allowed his suffering body to rock back and forth with the motion of his horse. Every nerve within his being was crying that all too familiar cry.

He had known it was coming, that the craving would hit him hardest on the third day—and this was the third day, or rather the evening of the third. But this time he was going to lick it. He'd tipped his last bottle and from now on he was going to be master of his own self.

High time, he thought bitterly. He should have done it years ago. If he had, it would be an entirely different sort of life he'd be leading. Likely he'd be in business somewhere, or maybe he would have had himself a ranch or a farm. Hell, he had plenty of ability—he'd proved that during the war when he headed up the quartermaster department of the corps he was in.

But most of all he'd still have Felicity and the three boys. They'd all be together, living and growing as a family should. . . . He reckoned he could forget all that—them. He didn't even blame Felicity anymore for taking the boys and leaving him and going home to her folks in Georgia. He hadn't been a husband or a father, he'd been nothing but a worthless drunk.

Maybe—just maybe, mind you—if he could straighten up this time and stay that way, Felicity would come back. Oh, sure, he'd tried it before, but something always came up to change things and before he knew what was happening, he found himself sprawled in the back room of some saloon or in a flophouse of a hotel sleeping off a three- or four-day bout with old John Barleycorn.

But this time it was different. He had a feeling about it. He'd not slip, he'd stay cold, stone sober and not even think about a drink. . . .Three days now, and while all hell was breaking loose inside him, he'd fight it out to a finish. This time he'd beat it—win.

Walt Moody slid a glance at the man riding beside him. The marshal had evidently just said something about them to that gunslinger he'd talked into becoming a member of his posse, and he wondered if the fellow had noticed. It hadn't been complimentary, that was for sure. The look on the lawman's face had proved that.

Not that it mattered. Nothing did anymore, although he had tried often enough to pick up the bits and pieces of his life and fit them back together into a satisfactory whole. Perhaps he would be better off if he were like Gilder and could submerge his memories and thoughts and lost hopes in a bottle of whiskey. But liquor had never been of any help; indeed, it had only made matters worse.

It did something to his mind, brought into sharp focus all the plans he'd once entertained and the dreams he had sought to convert into reality. But worst of all it called forth from the dark, shadowy corners of his brain a graphic remembrance, a vivid portrait of Rozella in all her haunting, ethereal beauty to stand before him like a vengeful, accusing ghost.

It never entirely faded, simply receded leaving him always aware of its lurking, destroying presence. He didn't know what the answer to his life would be, and for a year now he'd been searching for it. Somewhere there was a solution, a relief from the past and thoughts of all the things that could have been but were not.

Perhaps he would find it on this manhunt; maybe it lay in danger, in the hammer of gunshots, the whir of bullets—the sight of blood. He had looked everywhere else and found nothing. Could it be that death was the key—the final vindication? If so, and the espousers of religion were right, he'd be with Rozella again.

Able Rome considered the heavy clouds hanging low in the already dark sky. It was going to rain, no doubt of it. Maybe not that very night but it would come before sundown tomorrow. A hard rain would make him feel good. It always did. It gave him a sort of cleaned-off, scoured sensation like when, as a boy, his ma had worked him over in a tubful of suds with a stiff bristled brush.

A storm could complicate the marshal's plans to track down those outlaws and the gold they were running with, however. That was good, too; he was drawing five big dollars for every day he put in with the posse. There could be a little something extra, too, the marshal had said, if they recovered the gold for the mining company.

He could use a couple of hundred dollars. It would give his poke a real boost and put him that much closer to owning that place down in Arizona he planned to have.

But he still had a long way to go before he'd be in shape to settle down. Money wasn't easy to come by. He was always the first to be laid off a job, the last to be hired—not because he wasn't a good cowhand; he knew he was better and more reliable than most, but a black man always had to take the leavings.

His pa had been wrong there, even if he had been plenty smart in almost everything else. The personal bodyservant of a New Orleans plantation owner, he had been tutored privately and had learned to read and write—even think—like a white man.

He had passed on his learning to Able, assuring him all the while that education and knowledge was the open door to all things, that by possessing it he would be the equal of any man regardless of where he went. *It's being ignorant that makes the difference,* he had said.

But Able had found it to be untrue. In fact, it

seemingly had just the opposite effect; those of his
own kind shunned him, called him *high-toned,* and as
for the whites, they either ignored him or were
suspicious and hated him.

During the war when he had served with the Union
Army he had attempted to make use of his abilities for
the good of the Cause but his superiors had been
uninterested and he had stayed in the ranks along
with others of his color, doing the same menial tasks
assigned to those with no education at all.

That was when it began to dawn on him that his
father had been wrong; there was more to it than being
able to read and write and talk intelligently. Somewhere
along the way you had to reach a different level of
proof as to a man being a man.

The burgeoning West offered possibilities where it
could be attained, and when the fighting was over he
had taken the money he'd managed to accumulate,
bought himself a horse and gear, and headed for Texas
and points farther on.

Now, eleven years later, he was still searching for
that level of proof, that elusive something that would
provide him with the means by which he could take
his rightful place and be accepted and equal to all
those with whom he came in contact.

It shouldn't really be so important to him anymore,
he often told himself; he was doing pretty good,
actually far better than most of his kind. He had
money saved, plans for a small ranch of his own, and
while he was relegated to that airless, lonely chasm
lying between the black people and the white—a limbo
where he was neither fish nor fowl—he reckoned he
should not complain.

But it troubled Able Rome nevertheless. Just what
was it he must do to attain that intangible factor Mr.
Lincoln had called equality? Just as all journeys must
begin with a first step, he had begun at the knee of
his father; after that it had all seemed to stall and
the goal he sought receded farther into the gloomy
distance.

He shrugged. It was a thing to puzzle a man, and
he for one would like to find the answer. . . . Not
that it really mattered. . . . A wry smile tugged at his

lips as the old, familiar rationalization slipped effortlessly into his mind. The hell it didn't matter! It mattered a lot. The five dollars a day he was to get as a posse member wasn't important at all—it was the chance to prove that he was a man—a damn good man equal to any that walked the earth with him and not just another black—a nigger—with a bit of education.

5

They rode into a small clearing that paralleled the stream, and dismounted.

"All right, boy," Brandon said, crooking a finger at Rome. "I'm appointing you the hostler for this outfit. Look after the horses."

Able Rome, blandly ignoring the lawman's words, turned, began to loosen his saddle cinch. Back up the slope in the darkening trees an owl hooted.

"You hear me?"

Starbuck faced the marshal. "He's got a name. Might try using it," he drawled.

Brandon gave Shawn a contemptuous side glance, spat, bobbed his head. "Why, sure . . . Mister Rome." he said with exaggerated politeness, "I'll be obliged to you for looking after the horses."

Able smiled faintly, began to gather up the trailing reins of the five mounts.

"And you two—Mister Gilder and Mister Moody, start dragging in some wood for a fire," the lawman continued. He swung his sardonic gaze to Shawn. "If you don't mind, Mister Starbuck, you'll do the cooking."

Shawn nodded coolly to the marshal, neither angered nor amused by his broad irony.

"Sack of grub hanging on my saddle. Go light on it. Liable to have to last a few days," Brandon said and, moving to where Rome was picketing the horses, drew the rifle from his saddle boot.

"Taking me a look up the trail. Back in a few minutes."

32

Starbuck watched him stride off and then crossed to get the flour sack of supplies hanging from Brandon's saddle. As he pulled at the cord securing it, he felt Rome's eyes upon him and looked up. The man's features were taut.

"Don't go out of your way to do me any favors," he said in a low voice. "I can look after myself."

"I expect you can," Shawn replied indifferently. "It wasn't meant as a favor."

"I've been bucking up against men like the marshal all my life and I've got my own way of handling them. I don't need you or anybody else horning in for me just because I'm colored."

Rome's words did bespeak some measure of education, Shawn realized, but his belligerent attitude more than offset the asset.

"That wasn't the reason for it," he said and, wheeling, returned to the center of the clearing where Dave Gilder, sweat standing out on his forehead in large beads despite the coolness, was placing stones in the customary horseshoe arrangement.

"I expect the marshal'll want the fire kept low," he said. "He won't want to let them outlaws know we're on their heels."

Starbuck agreed, began to dig around in the sack of grub. Brandon had neglected to bring a large spider or a coffee pot of suitable size, forcing him to fall back on his own trail equipment. Again he was conscious of Able Rome's dark-eyed consideration as he probed his own saddlebags for the necessary items, but the man said nothing and he had no words for him.

A time later Harry Brandon returned. The meal of fried meat, potatoes, warmed-over bread and coffee was under way on the fire. Gilder and Moody, their supply of wood gathered and nearby, had brought in the blanket rolls and placed them about where they would be handy. Able Rome, his charges watered and now grazing on plentiful grass, hunkered in solitary silence at the edge of the glow.

"Ahead of us, just like I knowed they'd be," the lawman said, propping his rifle against a tree. "That grub about ready?"

"About," Starbuck answered. "We moving after them tonight?"

Brandon glanced about the camp, giving it his appraisal. "No hurry—and no point. They can't give us the slip now, there being only one trail. . . . Be a mite risky in the dark, anyway."

Shawn let it drop. It was up to the lawman and he evidently didn't feel it was necessary to close in at once. Besides, the long hours he had already put in on the sorrel were beginning to catch up to him.

Thunder growled in the distance. Brandon glanced at the black sky, murmured, "Reckon it's a-coming," and walked to where Rome had fitted his saddle over a clump of mountain mahogany. Pulling at the tie strings behind the cantle, he freed his brush jacket and pulled it on.

Settling it about his torso, he reached into an inner pocket and produced a pint bottle of whiskey. Making no effort to conceal his actions, he drew the cork and treated himself to a healthy swallow. Then, smacking his lips and brushing his mustache, he replaced the cork in the container and returned it to his pocket, seemingly oblivious of the watching men.

"Grub's ready," Starbuck said, glancing at Dave Gilder.

The shine of sweat was again on his haggard face as he stared into the fire. Raising a hand, he ran his fingers unsteadily through his thinning red hair.

Able Rome, plate in hand, came forward at once, began to help himself from the contents of the two spiders. Brandon, unsmiling, waited until the black man had finished and then took his turn, plainly irritated. Gilder followed and Shawn then looked expectantly at Moody, who had not stirred.

"You're next."

The immobile, sallow features of the man altered slightly. He shrugged half-heartedly, took up a plate and portioned out a small amount of the food. Shawn gave him a questioning smile.

"Either you don't have much of an appetite or my cooking's not as good as I figured."

"Foods fine—just not hungry," Moody said in an apologetic tone. "Coffee's what I need most."

Starbuck pushed one of the containers at the man and turned to fill his own plate. He hadn't eaten since breakfast—and then but little—and hunger was pushing at him.

They ate in silence, all but Walt Moody wolfing down the food, and when it was gone made their way to the creek, where each cleaned his plate and tools. Shawn made more coffee and after storing the remainder of the supplies where mice and other small animals could not get to them, moved back to the fire and settled down on his folded blanket.

The others were there before him, sprawled in the warm glow. Gilder had produced a pipe, was puffing at it nervously. Both Rome and Moody had built cigarettes, and Shawn dug into his shirt pocket for his sack of tobacco and papers.

"Ought to have a better fire than that," Brandon said cheerfully. Gathering up an armload of dry limbs, he dropped them onto the low flames. "We running short on wood or something?"

Gilder glanced up at the lawman. "I figured you wouldn't want them outlaws to spot us."

The lawman dismissed the thought with a motion of his hand. "Makes no difference. They know—and there ain't nothing they can do about it."

"Except move on," Starbuck said, finishing his smoke and hanging it in a corner of his mouth.

"Not them—not while it's night. They've got two pack mules they won't chance losing. Be daylight before they'll pull out. . . . That there fancy belt you're wearing, does it mean you're a champion fighter or something?"

"No," Shawn replied, looking down at the silver buckle with its superimposed ivory figure of a boxer. "It belonged to my pa. It was given him by some folks back where I came from. He was good at boxing, but he wasn't a champion. Could have been, I expect, if he wanted."

"You know how to do that kind of fighting?" Gilder asked.

"Pa taught my brother and me—both."

Able Rome flipped his spent cigarette into the surging flames. "I once saw a boxing match," he said, speaking for the first time since words had passed between him and Shawn at their arrival. "It was quite a show."

Starbuck turned to the man. "Was that somewhere around here?"

"No, it was during the war. At the camp where I was stationed."

Shawn settled back. "I thought maybe one of the boxers might've been my brother. He puts on exhibition matches now and then. . . . About the only way I ever turn up a line on him."

"Is he lost or something?" Gilder asked.

"Not lost," Brandon explained. "Starbuck just can't locate him. Been hunting him all over the country for years. He thinks maybe one of them outlaws could be him."

"It was your idea, not mine," Shawn said drily. "But I'm not saying you couldn't be right. It's been a long time since I last saw Ben. He could've changed. I doubt he'd turn to killing as a way of making a living, though."

There was silence after that, broken only by the noisy clacking of innumerable rain crickets filling the night with their prophecies. Able Rome began to roll a fresh cigarette.

"What's he look like? Could be I've run into him somewheres."

Shawn went into details, such as they were, of Ben, noting that he could be living under the name of Damon Friend. When he had finished the men all shook their heads. None could recall ever encountering anyone of either name or who fit the meager description he could supply.

"What's got you figuring he might be one of them killers?" Dave Gilder asked.

Shawn ducked his head at the lawman. "The marshal said one of them is named Ben and that he sort of fills the bill."

Brandon nodded. "If it's the Ben Snow I'm thinking

of," he said, tossing more wood into the fire," he does. You got to remember, howsomever, I ain't seen none of them killers. I only know what the guard told me."

Able Rome studied Starbuck with narrowed eyes. "You volunteer for this posse on the strength of that?"

"Partly. Sometimes I have to go on what I can get—even if it is a slim lead. Otherwise it could turn out someday that I spent a lot of time looking without really looking at all."

"I know what you mean," Dave Gilder murmured, staring into the flames. "A man can keep promising himself tomorrows—that he's going to do something, I mean, and then one day he wakes up and finds out all he's got is a lot of empty yesterdays laying behind him, and he ain't done nothing."

"Just the way it can turn out," Brandon said. Picking up a small clod of dirt, he tossed it at Walt Moody. "Ain't that what you say, greenhorn?"

Moody, in brooding silence through it all, roused himself. Hunched forward, shoulders slumped, he locked his hands together and stared off into the night.

"I don't think I'm an authority on much of anything," he said. "I figure that what's going to happen to a man is going to happen. God's will, I guess you'd call it—"

"God," Gilder broke in, stirring restlessly, "I don't know whether there's such a thing as God or not, but there sure is a hell! I've been in it from the day I was born, and I don't figure I'll be out of it until I'm dead—if then."

Walt Moody shifted his sick eyes to Dave. "I agree with that. The drawback is that a man gets born whether he wants to be or not. Has no say in it—just has to start living and making the best of what comes his way and whatever happens to him. Some make a go of it, others fail—even though they try."

Thunder rolled menacingly again, now somewhat louder and nearer. Brandon grinned across the flickering flames at Able.

"Ain't you got nothing to say about this, Mister Rome? I figured you'd be a genuine humdinger of a expert when it comes to this here moaning and groaning about living."

"I expect I am, Marshal," Rome replied coolly, and glanced at Starbuck. "That name of yours—Shawn. Are you part Indian?

"No. My mother once taught some Shawnee kids. I guess she liked the sound of the word, made it into a name for me."

The answer seemed to disappoint Able Rome. It was as if he had been hoping for a kindred soul in variance. He shrugged, and once again drew out his cigarette makings.

Brandon looked up into the blackness that was the sky, as a deep rumbling was again heard. "Aim to start early in the morning. Reckon we'd best be turning in. Boy—uh, Mister Rome, you sure them horses can't get loose?"

"They'll be there when we want them," Able said.

"Well, they sure better be or—"

Brandon's words were checked as the fire exploded suddenly into a shower of sparks and ashes and burning brands. A split second later, the hollow crack of a gunshot echoed through the night. For a long breath no one moved, and then Starbuck threw himself to one side, clear of the flames' pale glow.

"Get out of the light!" he yelled.

The outlaws had spotted them.

~~ 6 ~~

"That goddam fire—" Gilder muttered, plunging backwards into the brush. "Was too big—I knew it!"

Shawn, deep in the shadows, leaped to his feet. Drawing his pistol, he spun, started up the trail at a fast run. He heard the thud of boot heels close behind, looked around, expecting Harry Brandon. It was Able Rome.

Together they rushed on, holding to the edge of the path where brush and trees could mask their movements. Back in the direction of the camp Brandon's voice was booming into the night but the loud rasp of their own labored breathing, and the noise of their passage as they raced up the steep grade, made his words unintelligible.

The trail cut right, topped out a small ridge. Starbuck halted, eyes searching the blackness ahead, ears straining to pick up any sound that would reveal the location of the outlaws.

Rome moved up to his side. "Anything?"

Shawn wagged his head.

Able waited until a roll of thunder had died, then said, "Probably gone by now. Saw they'd missed the marshal, or whoever they were shooting at, and run for it."

"About the way of it, but we'll wait a bit," Shawn said, and moving to a log beside the trail, sat down. He sucked in a deep breath, exhaled. "That was a hard climb."

"For a fact," Rome said, finding himself a place on the fallen tree. "What happened to Brandon?"

"Don't know. I heard him yelling, but couldn't get what he was saying."

"Something about coming back."

Starbuck rubbed at his jaw. "I figured he'd be right with us."

"Same here, but I reckon he believes in playing it safe."

Shawn gave that brief thought. "Could be, but Brandon strikes me as a man who's not scared of anything much."

Able Rome was silent for a long moment. Then, "I expected you'd say that," he said in a stiff voice. "The flawless white man, as my pa used to put it."

"Not necessarily," Starbuck came back quickly. "Just stands to reason—and don't go blaming me because you're black and I'm white. I had nothing to do with it and sure as hell can't do anything about it, so, far as I'm concerned, either take that chip off your shoulder or head on back to camp."

Far to the west lightning winked across the sky, underscored its presence with a deep rumbling. Able Rome shifted on the log, toyed with the pistol in his hands.

"Is that the way it strikes you—that I'm blaming white men because I'm black?"

Starbuck shrugged. "It's pretty plain to me. Probably looks that way to others."

"That's not it at all," Rome said. "Leastwise, it's not how I feel. . . . I guess it could seem like it." He sighed, holstered his weapon. "All I'm hunting for is the chance to be the same as other men—their equal and not something separate that is to be treated different."

"You've had some education. You ought to realize that the day when that'll come to pass is probably a long time off despite what the war did for your people. This is a white man's country—it was founded by whites and has always been run by whites. It'll be quite a few years before you'll see any change from that, I think."

"That's nothing but prejudice and—"

"No prejudice to it, just a fact of life. But I won't argue with you about it because that's what you're looking for and arguing won't change anything."

"Maybe you won't because you know I'm right."

"Right—about what?"

"The unfairness of it all."

Starbuck sighed heavily. He'd been caught up in similar word exchanges before, and he knew such conversations accomplished no purpose.

"Nothing unfair to it far as I can see. Maybe the day will come when there'll be no difference in color noticed, but it'll be a while."

"There's no reason why it shouldn't be now. Mr. Lincoln made it plain that it was what he wanted—and why he was fighting a war."

"The purpose of the war was to keep the Union from breaking up. The slavery issue was only part of it."

Rome paused, nodded. "Anyway, he won the war and made it clear that he wanted folks to forget there was a difference in races and—"

"I wasn't in the war myself and maybe you know more about it than I, but the way I understood it was that he made it plain there was to be no more slavery. I think he figured time would take care of the rest."

"That's not the way I took it. I heard him talk once. He came to the camp where I was. He said every man was equal and that it had to be that way."

"I doubt if he meant it exactly like you took it. Sure, all men are born free and equal, but it's up to them from then on. They can do something with their lives or they can waste them."

"And if they never get a chance—"

"Most men do. Some get fewer and perhaps smaller chances than others but they get them. . . . And doing something with a small opportunity usually leads up to a bigger one."

"Not for the blacks."

"For everybody," Starbuck said patiently. "You're a good example—but you're so close to it you can't see it. I—"

Shawn came to his feet slowly. A faint noise up the trail had caught his attention. Hand resting on the butt of his pistol, he stood motionless in the darkness listening into the night. The sound did not come again, and after a bit he settled back on the log. Some small animal rustling about in the dry leaves, he supposed.

He was rested now from the hurried climb he had made and his breathing was again at normal flow. The thought of his blanket back at camp, and a few hours of sleep, brought him to his feet again.

"I expect we'd best be heading down-trail," he said.

Rome drew himself upright. "You said I was a good example. . . . Example of what?"

"What a man can do to pull himself up to a higher notch."

"I was luckier than most blacks. My father got some schooling."

"How?"

"Man who owned him gave it to him."

"Why?"

Able Rome's head came up. "Why? Because he wanted him to have it, I reckon."

"Exactly. He wanted him to have some education and helped him to get it. It wasn't because he was black or because he felt sorry for him. It was because he wanted him to have it. Chances are he would, or maybe did, do as much for some white man. There're plenty of them, too, you know, who can't read or write and have never been able to get anywhere in this life. . . . Colored people don't have a patent on being poor and having things hard."

Starbuck, warming slightly under the discussion, moved out onto the trail and started slowly down the grade. Rome, thoughtful for several moments, quickly caught up with him.

"I hadn't looked at it that way, and I expect it's true, but it's the white who always get help first. They're favored when it comes to jobs, things like that—and you can't tell me it's not so."

"I won't even try. I'll tell you this much, I've been to a lot of places, seen a lot of things, and there's plenty of men who hire on the strength of ability—not color. I won't say it happens every time, because it doesn't, but it's sure not as bad as you seem to think."

"Then why does it happen I'm the one that's let off a job first, and always find it hard to get back on?"

"Could be that chip on your shoulder," Starbuck said dryly. "It's a foot wide and a yard long. . . . You—yourself—forget about being colored. Don't even think about it and most everybody you come up against will forget it, too. Quit trying so hard to be a man—and just be one. The way you're going about it now the hate's sticking out all over you."

"It'd be a waste of time. Men like Brandon—"

"There'll always be his kind, and it's not only colored people they take their bigotry out on. Count in the Chinese, the Indians, Mexicans, Italians, Spaniards, all races that aren't the same as they are."

"I know that, but—"

"And we're not all that way. You'll find several rotten potatoes in a sackful. You believe that every colored man is good and honest and fair?"

"No, of course not."

"It works the same with white people. We've plenty of the kind we're not proud of and it's wrong to judge the whole by the few. Now, I expect you'd find most men would treat you all right if you'd give them a chance, but that cloud of hate you're wearing like a halo won't even let them get close."

Able Rome swore quietly, helplessly. "That's been the only defense I've had—only thing I could do. Other way got me nowhere."

"Maybe. You can't be sure. The big thing you've got to remember is that you're not going to change it all overnight. It'll take time—and that's another fact of life."

Rome's shoulders lifted, fell. "Maybe I'm beginning to see. . . . My pa once told me something I never did for sure understand. He said the weather won't wear a sharp rock smooth in just a day or even a year—that it sometimes took a lifetime. . . . I think now I know what he was driving at."

"He must have been a wise man."

"He was. I think about him in the same light as I

think about Mr. Lincoln. He had a deep-down way of looking at things and making sense of them. I wish they could have met and talked.

"I keep remembering things they both said, but I think I remember most what Mr. Lincoln told us once about ideas. He said that once a man had one and got it stuck in his mind, there was nothing anybody could do about taking it away from him. And if he told his idea to others and it was a good one, it'd stay in their minds, too, and keep on growing even though the man who started it was dead and gone.

"That's how I think about myself and other Negroes. We're free and we're good as anybody else. The same God lives in us that lives in white people and we're entitled to walk shoulder to shoulder with every other living person and not always be apologizing for what we are. . . . They killed Mr. Lincoln for thinking that—starting the idea."

"They?"

"Some say it was the people close to him, the politicians. Others claim it was a bunch of Confederates, crazy mad because they lost the war. I reckon nobody really knows for certain—but in the end it didn't make any difference. They couldn't kill and bury the idea he started and I expect that's what counts—the good things a man leaves behind after he's gone.

"Anyway, it's what I live by—that idea. All I want to do is prove I'm a man, not a Negro, or a nigger, or a black—but a man."

"Starbuck!" Harry Brandon's shout came from down the trail. "That you?"

"Right," Shawn yelled back.

Able Rome laughed in a quiet, desperate sort of way.

"You see? I'm not even here—don't exist. He knew we both went up that trail, but he called out your name—not mine. He didn't even yell for us both—only you. How do I prove that I'm alive?"

～ 7 ～

Only a few faintly glowing embers remained of the bullet-shattered fire as Shawn and Able Rome rounded the last clump of brush and stepped into the clearing. At once Harry Brandon, bristling with anger, strode toward them.

"What the hell you mean taking off like that?"

Starbuck pulled up in surprise. "I thought we were here to catch those outlaws."

"We are, but by God, we're doing it my way!"

Shawn stirred wearily. "What difference does it make whose way it is as long as we get them? Whoever fired that shot wasn't far up the trail. Could be, if we'd all gone after him, we might've finished this job tonight."

"And maybe we could've got ourselves filled full of lead, too, tearing around in the dark like that!" the lawman snapped.

Shawn wagged his head, glanced at Dave Gilder. The man's features were bleak, hungering, and his eyes were fixed on the bulge the bottle of whiskey made in Brandon's pocket. Moody, apparently half asleep, slumped against a stump and was taking no interest in any of it.

"I doubt if they could see any farther in the dark than we could."

"I ain't saying they could, but they sure'n hell knew you was coming up the trail. Likely just set there and watched. . . . Goddam lucky you're alive. Now, from here on, you wait for me to give you orders, understand?"

45

"Whatever you say, Marshal," Starbuck replied indifferently.

He looked at Able Rome, who had stood to one side listening quietly but was now moving off toward the horses. Brandon had ignored him throughout the tongue-lashing, and directed his anger at Shawn alone. It was as if he felt he could expect nothing different from Rome and thereby excused his actions, but Starbuck, being a white man, should have known better. More fuel for the smoldering fires of outrage that glowed in Able Rome's breast, Starbuck thought tiredly.

A bright streak of lightning flooded the clearing. Thunder rolled ominously. Brandon glanced about, said: "Going to get plenty wet before morning. Best you all get yourself set for it."

There was little they could do. None of them had brought a tarp, only blankets which were useless when it came to shedding rain. Shawn had his slicker, and recalled he'd seen like gear on the saddles of Brandon and Rome. If a downpour set in he could share his with Moody, using it as a canopy. It would be up to one of the others to do the same with Dave Gilder.

He gave that some thought as he set about collecting a supply of wood for the morning cookfire and storing it back under the brush where it could remain dry. If that came to pass it would be interesting to see which of the two made the offer—Brandon or Rome.

The night was once again filled with a blinding flash of palest blue. Almost immediately thunder set up its rolling echoes. Shawn paused, swung his attention to Dave Gilder spreading his blanket on the opposite side of the clearing.

"Close," he said.

Gilder only nodded, continuing to prepare his bed.

Starbuck, satisfied that he had sufficent wood cached, moved to where his saddle lay, and picking it up, carried it back to his blanket roll which had been placed next to Walt Moody's. Pulling his slicker free, he shook it out, laid it close by where it would be handy, and then settled down.

Harry Brandon stood at the edge of the camp staring off into the blackness of the slope. He could be

wondering if the outlaws posed a threat for the night,
Shawn guessed, and he could also be realizing that
it might have been better for the entire posse to have
gone in search of the rifleman who had scattered the
fire—and who probably wasn't alone.

But if that was his thought, the lawman would never
admit it. He was not the kind to acknowledge a
mistake—that had become apparent earlier.

"You see anything up there?" Moody asked as he
began to draw his blanket about him.

"No, we didn't," Starbuck replied, making a point
of the pronoun. There was some justification for
Rome's attitude.

"We wanted to follow. The marshal said no—was
too big a risk to take."

"Not much difference in staying here and maybe
getting picked off one by one."

"I suppose not," Moody said heavily. "I don't
think we're going to get much sleep—especially if it
starts raining."

"You can figure on it," Shawn said, "but it could
hold off until morning." He paused, looked more
closely at Moody's pale features, oddly lax in the shroud
of his blanket. "You all right?"

"All right, I guess."

Starbuck continued to study the man for a few
more moments, then shook his head. "No place for you
on a deal like this. How'd you happen to volunteer,
anyway? Sure can't be your line of work."

"Hardly. I was a bookkeeper—back in a town near
St. Louis before I came west."

"Good, comfortable way of making a living that
sure beats this. Why'd you change? Looking for something better?"

"No—oblivion."

Starbuck frowned. "What?"

Walt Moody turned upon his back, drew his blanket
tighter around his slight frame. "I wanted to lose myself, if I could."

"I see. . . . Trouble of some kind, I take it."

"The worst, far as I'm concerned." Moody's voice
faltered, fell silent.

Shawn lay back, watched the sky light up, silhouetting the tips of the swaying pines, listened to the subsequent deep-throated grumble. Brandon no longer stood at the edge of the clearing, but was now finding himself a place to sleep beneath an overhang of brush. Rome was already curled in his wool cover an arm's reach beyond Dave Gilder. Shawn yawned, felt an easiness steal over him, wondered idly what Moody had meant, but he wouldn't press the man for an explanation. If he wished to go further into it, it would be his choice.

"You think it's possible for a man to ever get away from himself?"

Starbuck stared up into the black sky and considered Walt Moody's question. "Be hard to do. A man can't get away from his own thoughts—and I expect it amounts to the same thing. That what you're trying to do?"

"Guess it is."

"Well, I doubt if you'll ever be able to do it just waiting around, looking for it. That just lets whatever it is eating at your mind have its way. You need to fill it with something else—crowd out all the old things."

"But if I can't do that—"

"Can't—or don't want to? Which is it? Maybe that's what you'd better figure out first."

Walt Moody made no reply. Shawn heard him moving about restlessly as if seeking greater comfort. He yawned again. His own eyes were getting heavy.

"I expect you're right. I'm not sure what the answer is, or that I can even find it. It's easy for a man to lie to himself."

Shawn brushed at his mouth. . . . First Able Rome, now Walt Moody. . . . "Just as easy to be truthful since nobody but himself knows what's in his head."

"But if a man's done something, been responsible for some terrible thing, how can he get it out of his mind?"

"I can't give you any answer to that, but I'm pretty sure the same problem's been faced by others and licked. I expect the big thing is that you've got to want to lick it, not let the guilt make a slave of you. That's always the easy way out. Self-pity is plenty cheap. It's the other way that's tough going."

The night came alive again with the awesome flare of electricity, shuddered with the tumbling of sound. Shawn closed his eyes.

"It's that—the guilt, that rides me so hard—"

Moody's voice seemed far away, a mere echo in a vast emptiness.

"I'd like to tell you about it—just what happened—"

The words slipped away from Starbuck, faded into silence without registering on his mind. . . . Later, he'd listen . . . later. . . .

~~~ 8 ~~~

The storm held off throughout the night, and then as Brandon's posse moved onto the trail that next morning under a sullen, gray sky, the first spatter of raindrops struck.

They came in a gusty blast, cold and stinging in their intensity. Immediately Starbuck halted the sorrel and drew on his slicker. A few paces away Able Rome also donned his rain gear as well as pulling on a pair of worn, leather chaps as further protection from the wet. Brandon, cursing steadily at the inconvenience, followed their example, but Moody and Gilder, not similarly equipped, were forced to choose between using their blankets or nothing. Both elected to drape themselves with the woolen covers.

Lightning, with its accompanying hammer of thunder, quiet during the early hours of the morning, again began to flood the slopes and canyons with its brilliance and rock the land with resounding echoes. There was a difference, however; where before there had been broad flashes succeeded after a pause by deep rumblings, there now were swift, jagged flashes, and the thunder, crackling and deafening, came almost in the same breath.

The trail, in only short minutes, became a narrow, muddy stream bed surging with water racing down-slope, washing topsoil, small rocks, loose brush and other litter before it. The horses, moving slow at best up the fairly steep grade, dropped to a yet more deliberate pace, their hides glistening in the wet, eyes showing white with each garish flare of light.

"That's the hell of this goddam country!" Brandon

shouted above the howl of the storm when they paused under the partly protective bulk of a pine that overshadowed their course. "Always too much of something. It's too hot or too cold, or maybe too dry and then we're getting flooded out by a damned cloudburst that takes half the land with it."

A vivid streak of lightning slashed through the murk. A hundred yards back up the slope a tree split with a thunderous crash, and became a flaming torch. The horses began to mince nervously, frightened by the fire, the sizzling sound of water dashing against it.

Again a jagged, blue line of light split the wet gloom. A ball of fire struck high on a ridge of rocks above them, rolled a short distance and exploded against the face of a glistening butte.

Starbuck, wiping the water from his eyes, glanced at the men huddled beside him under the pine. They were all staring at the hogback as if transfixed. Thunder crackled, seemingly right upon them. He reached out, touched Harry Brandon's arm.

"We stay here or go on?"

The lawman shook his head. "Won't get no wetter riding than standing."

Shawn mentally agreed. There was the possibility they were in the center of the downpour. Climbing higher could put them on its fringe, or perhaps entirely out of it.

A new sound began to fill the air, rising above the chatter of the drops. It was the deep, rushing roar of wild water, pent up by natural dams in the higher canyons, suddenly released and now pouring down the steep slopes for the flat land far below. Gouging and slashing, the torrents were following none of the prescribed channels cut by previous, more gentle storms, but were knifing new troughs in a turbulent, irresistible race to low ground.

The posse moved out from beneath the tree, horses reluctant, taking each step with hesitant care, fearful of the unstable footing and frightened by the persistent pushing of the swirling water around their hooves.

Shawn tried to look ahead, to determine if there were canyons coming in at right angles to the trail. If so they could expect to encounter a rushing wall of silt- and brush-laden floodwater, perhaps even come to a point where a gash had been cut in their path.

He could tell nothing about it. Rain was a gray sheet before his eyes and even when the almost continuous lightning spread its eerie, blue glow over the mountainside, his vision was limited to a dozen yards.

There was a good chance they would be spared the problem. The trail appeared to be following along a spine that lifted its way steadily toward a crest lying somewhere in the soaked distance. Very likely the canyons drained to either side of the ridge, and if so, they were in luck.

Another flaming torch appeared on the slope below them as they drew to a halt once more, this time under a shoulder of granite that extended over the trail. There was no room there for the horses, but the men, by crowding close, were able to get out of the driving drops, wipe their faces and breathe deeper.

He glanced at Dave Gilder. The man was shivering from the cold. His eyes were partly closed and water dripped steadily off the tip of his nose. Moody appeared more withdrawn than ever and there was resentment in the look he gave Shawn when his gaze met the tall rider's. Able Rome alone appeared unperturbed, his black skin shining with wet as he stared off beyond the rocks.

"Best we start leading the horses," Brandon said. "Trail gets narrower on up a ways."

Shawn agreed silently. The last quarter-mile had been dangerous. Dave Gilder, the glow of the burning tree upon him, shook his head.

"I'm figuring it'd be better to hold off, Marshal, wait for the storm to pass. This here's a pretty good place."

Dave was shouting to make himself heard above the drumming sound that filled the air. Brandon's wide shoulders shifted.

"It ain't passing—not for two, maybe three hours. And we can't wait. Them killers'll keep right on moving."

"There any caves, places like that where they could hole up?" Shawn asked.

Again the lawman stirred. "Nope, ain't none they can reach for a couple of days. Trail just runs straight on to the top of the mountains with nothing on either side but slopes, same as it's been since we left camp."

At least there was no need to worry about arroyos cutting the path out from under them, Starbuck thought, but now something else was becoming apparent. Both Moody and Gilder were showing signs of strain. The constant spurts of lightning striking nearby, the crackle of thunder and the sound of rushing water coupled to the never slackening drive of the rain, were unnerving them.

He glanced at Rome, caught the man looking at him. Able forced a smile, one designed to reassert his self-assurance as opposed to the apprehension being displayed by the two others. But the smile was only on the surface and there were tight lines around his eyes.

Their anxiety was warranted and Shawn could not blame them for their concern. Being trapped in the heart of a wild storm high on a mountain while lightning crackled and shattered mighty trees as though they were matchsticks and set the earth to trembling underfoot with thunderous accompaniment, was far from a tranquil experience.

For himself he tried not to dwell on possibilities too much. He avoided such circumstances whenever possible, feeling that any man was a fool to tempt fate by exposing himself, but once involved in a situation of danger, he accepted it, realizing that there was little he could do to avoid whatever was inevitable, and the less thought he gave it, the better. Long ago he had learned that all the worrying and stewing he did affected the end result not at all.

"Let's move out—"

At Harry Brandon's order, he looked up. The marshal stepped from beneath the slanting canopy of granite, and taking up the reins of his horse, nodded.

"Could be letting up a mite at that," the lawman said. "Don't seem to be stinging so hard."

Starbuck could note little difference. The raindrops were still coming down with slashing force, the lightning continued to rip the wet pall clothing the mountain, and thunder rolled and thudded ominously. It would be good if they could find shelter, wait for a time as Dave Gilder had suggested, but he could see Brandon's point, too.

The outlaws knew that a posse was at their heels hoping to close in; they would not risk a halt, but press on regardless of conditions. With the store of gold they had killed to obtain as well as their own lives at stake, they would throw caution aside in their hurry to escape.

Starbuck peered from under the cupped shelter of his hand. The footing was slippery as mud steadily deepened on the trail, narrower here as Harry Brandon had said it would be. The lawman was well ahead of Gilder, second in line, and moving slowly. Moody followed next, with Able Rome, from choice, again bringing up the rear.

A blinding flash of lightning, striking close by, filled the air with a pungent, scorched odor. The ground rocked with the concussion of thunder.

Starbuck, hanging tight to the sorrel's reins, saw Brandon's horse balk, go to his hind legs, paw at the hammering rain with his front hooves, as if doing battle with an invisible stallion.

In the next fragment of time Walt Moody's buckskin jerked back, attempted to wheel on the narrow, slippery surface of the trail. His hindquarters slapped hard against Moody, knocked him aside. For an instant the man tottered on the edge of the ridge, mouth blared in a soundless cry of fear, and then he was gone.

~~ 9 ~~

Shawn, clinging to the sorrel's leathers with one hand, wheeled to the rope hanging from his saddle and jerked it free with the other. Shaking out its coils, he started for the crumbling brink of the slope. Farther up the trail he could hear Gilder shouting at Brandon, informing him of the accident while he sought to control his horse and catch up the dragging reins of the buckskin.

Reaching the point where he had last seen Moody, Shawn threw his glance down the rock-studded incline. It was shining wet in the semidarkness, and a hundred feet below he could see the boiling water of a rushing arroyo where it emptied.

There was no sign of Moody. The thought crossed his mind that the man had plunged into the swollen torrent and had been swept away. And then through the rain dimmed murk his eyes picked up vague motion about halfway down. Relief coursed through him. Moody's fall had been broken by a jutting shaft of rock.

"See him?"

It was Able Rome. Starbuck nodded, and pointing in the direction of the rock, waited out a long moment for a flash of lightning. It came suddenly, filling the canyon with dazzling brilliance.

"There—just above that hump."

"I saw him," Rome said, and began to lay out his own rope. Picking up the end of Shawn's lariat, he joined them together. "It'll take them both to reach him."

Harry Brandon crowded in beside Starbuck and

55

peered through the driving rain into the canyon. "He gone?"

"Caught on a rock."

The lawman shook his head. "Tough break, cashing in like—"

"He's not dead—I'm pretty sure I saw him move," Shawn said, eyes on Rome now looping the rope around his chest and securing it with a hard knot.

"Body was just slipping, I expect. A fall like that'd kill a man for certain." He paused, his gaze on Able. "What the hell you doing?"

"Going after him."

Brandon straightened up. "Forget it—he's dead."

"I'm not sure of that," Starbuck said.

"Well, I am . . . . No big loss anyway. Way he's been acting, I'd say he was looking for something like this and found it—besides, we ain't got the time to waste fooling around here."

"We're taking time," Shawn said quietly and rising, looked about for something solid to which he could anchor the rope. He located a juniper on the opposite side of the trail. Gnarled and storm-tested, it had withstood the elements for years, and undoubtedly would serve the purpose well.

He crossed to it at once, threw a hitch about its rough trunk, knotted it close, turned to where Rome and Brandon waited.

The lawman, his features set, faced Shawn angrily as he hurried up. "I'm giving you orders, Starbuck, we ain't taking time now. We can stop on our way back for the body—"

Shawn nodded to Rome. "All set. . . . I'll ease you down slow."

"You hear me?" Brandon shouted through the pouring rain. "He's dead—and it won't hurt to leave him."

"Alive or dead, we're bringing him up," Starbuck shot back, and bracing himself, started Able Rome's descent of the slippery grade.

The footing was treacherous. Water had soaked into the soil, converting it to a slick paste that provided no purchase for Rome's boots. Rivulets of water were coursing downward in almost a solid sheet. Several times the man went down, slamming hard against the canyon's side. With the aid of the lightning, Starbuck maintained a close watch on him. He could himself become injured, in which event someone else would have to follow. He'd be the one to do it, Shawn decided. Dave Gilder would have to stay above and see to their getting back; he felt he couldn't trust Harry Brandon.

Brushing at the water clouding his eyes, he stared into the grayness of the canyon. The storm raged on, periodically filling the deep gap with blinding light and ear-splitting thunder while the rain continued to hammer at them relentlessly. The wet rope became slick between his gloved hands and he began to fight to keep his footing on the mushy soil of the trail. He turned to Gilder, hoping the man could come to his aid, but Dave was having his troubles with the nervous horses. Suddenly angered, he swung his eyes to Brandon.

"Give me some help here!" he snarled. "We're not moving on till we get him up!"

The marshal, jaw clamped shut, hesitated briefly, and then as if realizing the truth of Shawn's statement, stepped in behind him, and taking a grip on the lariat, threw his weight against the pull of Able Rome's body.

The strain on Shawn eased considerably with that and he turned his attention to the slope. In the next flash of lightning he saw Able reach the finger of rock against which Walt Moody had lodged and felt the drag on the rope slacken.

"He's reached him," he shouted over his shoulder, and going to hands and knees, stared down into the murky depths of the canyon, searching for a sign from Rome as to Moody's condition.

It was difficult to determine what was taking place. The rain was like a curtain and he could make out only blurred motion on Able's part. Then, faint through the howling storm, he heard a yell. There was a tug on the rope. Rome was signaling.

Shawn got to his feet hurriedly, braced himself. "Haul in!" he shouted to Brandon.

Together they began to draw in the rope. It would have been a simple task for one of the horses, but the narrowness of the trail and its condition plus the nervousness of the animals made that out of the question. But it was not too difficult.

Shortly the head and shoulders of the man appeared at the lip of the canyon. Starbuck dug his heels deep into the mud, set himself and barked at the lawman.

"Get him!"

Brandon stepped around Shawn, bent over the limp form of Moody and dragged him up onto the trail. Immediately Starbuck moved to him, began to remove the rope looped under his armpits. Moody stared up at him from his tired eyes.

"Ain't dead," Brandon muttered, hunching over him. "Banged up plenty, but he's alive."

Shawn returned to the edge of the slope. Locating Rome, he bunched the soaked rope and tossed it at the near-invisible shape crouched beside the shaft of rock. After a moment he felt a jerk on the line. Starbuck again braced himself, called to Brandon.

"Let's haul him up."

Rising from where he knelt beside Walt Moody, the lawman took his position behind Starbuck and once more they began to retrieve the rain-slicked line. It was easier. Where Moody had been unable to give any assistance and offered only dead weight, Able Rome helped by digging his feet into the slope and grabbing onto the rocks and few brush clumps that were available.

In a short time he was on the trail, plastered with mud that was slowly washing away under the driving raindrops. He grinned at Shawn as he began to loosen the coil about his body and in his eyes there was a look of satisfaction, as if he had demonstrated an ability others might not have suspected.

Shawn smiled back and turned to Moody. The dazed, worn stare was gone from his eyes and he had pulled himself to a sitting position. Pain distorted his features as he felt at his left arm.

"You hurt bad?" Starbuck asked, crouching beside him.

Dave Gilder was yelling again, this time wanting to

know about Moody's condition. Rome, coiling the ropes, moved toward him to give a report.

"Only—my arm," Moody replied.

"Lucky," Harry Brandon said gruffly. "Mighty goddam lucky, I'd say. Was the mud being soft that did it."

Walt started to rise, winced at the effort. Shawn, taking him by his uninjured arm, assisted him to his feet.

"Got to be getting on," the marshal continued, mopping at his streaming face. "You make it?"

Lips tight, Moody nodded and turned to start up the trail. Starbuck halted him.

"That arm's got to be set."

Again Walt moved his head. "I know that—but later on, when we stop."

"He's right," Brandon said. "Hard to do it here on this ridge. Farther up there'll be a place where we can pull off."

"How far?"

"Couple hours—maybe less."

Shawn peered closely at Moody through the grey curtain. "Can you stand it that long?"

"Guess so—"

"Then let's get started," Brandon said briskly, crossing to his horse. "We lost too damned much time already. Going to have to hurry things some."

Moody stared at the marshal woodenly and then faced Starbuck. "Walking's going to be a little hard—mind looking after my animal?"

"I'll see to him," Shawn answered. "Just hang tight until we can get to where that arm can get fixed."

Walt Moody smiled wearily. "Fixing it will be easy. It's what's inside me that I can't do anything about."

Starbuck watched him head on up the trail and then crossed to where Dave Gilder waited with the horses. The injured man's words trickled slowly through his mind. Whatever the trouble was that plagued Moody, it weighed heavily on him.

He recalled that Moody had been about to tell him, take him into his confidence the night before, but he had dropped off to sleep. Likely that had turned the man inward more than ever. He'd try and square it, explain that exhaustion had simply gotten the best of him, and that he'd like to hear about his problem—and perhaps be of help. Maybe Walt would listen to an apology and open up. That was what he needed to do—talk, unload, get whatever it was eating at him out into the open.

The rain had finally ceased, leaving behind a damp, chilled world of dripping trees and soggy ground. Walt Moody sat on a rotting log in a small clearing off the trail where they had halted for the night, and watched the other men moving about making camp. Starbuck and Rome had taken their slickers, hooked them together and suspended them, lean-to fashion, between four trees for a shelter under which they could spend the hours until morning.

Gilder, his eyes sunk deep in his head as the craving that everybody by now recognized, gripped him, was endeavoring to scare up dry wood for a fire and was not having much success. The marshal, irritated by the delay that the storm and the accident had occasioned, was a short distance up the trail, looking to the south as if hopeful of catching sight of the outlaws.

Walt Moody shifted, carefully holding his repaired arm with the right hand so that it would not move. Starbuck and the black man had done a good job setting it and pinning it firmly between the straight sticks they used as splints. It throbbed dully, like a bad toothache, but he guessed he'd live through it.

For what?

The question seeped its bitter way into his brain. Why the hell couldn't he have done the job up right and tumbled all the way down that damned slope into the floodwater—and ended it all once and for good? No—it was his luck to have a rock waiting there to catch him, keep him alive. . . . Nothing ever went his way.

Morose, he watched Starbuck and Able Rome now busy stretching a rope near where the fire was to be built so that the soaked blankets could be dried. The pair worked together smoothly and efficiently, talking little, each seemingly aware of the other's capabilities.

He had thanked Starbuck for his part in dragging him out of that canyon—had to remember to thank the colored man also. He'd been the one who did the climbing down with the rope. . . . He'd say what he should when they all gathered around the fire if Gilder ever got one going.

But the thanks would be for nothing as far as he was concerned. He'd a thousand times prefer to be dead and floating down that arroyo than sitting where he was, alive, able to think and a prisoner of all the tormenting recollections that were stuck fast to his mind, like bottom land chiggers, and never let him rest.

Yesterday—last night to be exact—when he and Starbuck had been talking, he had sensed a sympathetic and perhaps understanding heart on the part of the tall, hard-jawed rider, and something had come over him, a lift—a hope; and for the first time since it had all happened it seemed he could see a light at the end of the interminable tunnel of despair through which he had been groping for so long. . . . But it had turned out just as things always did for him.

He had told Starbuck of Rozella, of what they had meant to each other, and how she had died that terrible day when they had been boating on the lake. It had been his fault, cutting up, acting the fool the way he did, and then when the small craft overturned, he had clung to it, paralyzed, horrified and unnerved by her screams, powerless to save her.

He was no swimmer but he could have saved her. He could have gotten to her, managed somehow to drag her back to the boat where they both could have hung on until help arrived—but he hadn't. Instead he'd just stayed there, fingers locked to the bottom of the craft, listening to her piteous cries and watching while the dark water swallowed her. He knew then that he was a coward.

And later, when the full realization of the tragedy hit him, he knew also that Rozella was dead by his own hand as surely as if he'd held a pistol to her temple and pulled the trigger.

At that point in the narration he had paused. It came

to him that he was baring his soul to the wind; Starbuck had fallen asleep, had heard none of what had been said.

That had finished it for him. He had never before unburdened himself to another in his desperate search for understanding—now he would never do so again.

But it was done and he was back, mentally, where he started, still facing the accusing fingers that pointed at him from a hundred dark hiding places in his mind, still torn by doubt and the fear of fear that constantly reproved him.

No one was ever interested in another's troubles, anyway; he should have remembered that. . . . He'd find his own answers alone—unaided.

~~~ 10 ~~~

They held the fire to a small size, not just because dry wood was scarce and available only by seeking out the larger rocks and probing about beneath them, but also to avoid a repeat performance on the part of the outlaws; this time a rifle bullet could find a human target.

The evening meal over and the blankets hanging on the leeward side of the flames where a combination of smoke and heat was slowly accomplishing their drying, Starbuck seated himself within the limited fan of light and glanced to the sky. The overcast had broken to some extent and a few stars were visible, but the threat of more rain was still there.

He sighed heavily, hoped it would not come to pass; much more water pouring down upon the mountain would make the trail impassable and all their efforts to overtake the outlaws would go for nothing. Too, Walt Moody should be taken to a doctor as soon as possible; the medical attention he and Able Rome had provided was crude and only of an emergency nature at best.

He glanced at Walt Moody. He was hunched against a pine, head slung forward, arms cradled, apparently sleeping. He'd had a bad time of it, going over the cliff, walking for all that time with the injured arm uncared for and then withstanding the treatment necessary to accord it without uttering more than an occasional groan. He should be sent back to Wolf Crossing; he would be of little use to the posse, anyway. He'd talk to Brandon about it in the morning, Shawn decided.

Able Rome, his features reflecting the weariness that rode him, came up from where the horses had been picketed. Nodding to Shawn and Gilder, and glancing at the dozing Moody, he sat down, leaned forward to capture some of the fire's warmth.

"Where is he—the marshal?" he asked after a time.

Gilder, scrubbing agitatedly at the stubble of whiskers on his chin, said, "Up the trail. Trying to spot them killers, I reckon."

Rome grunted. "Surprised he didn't want to keep moving."

Only the exhausted condition of the horses had prevented the lawman from insisting on it, Starbuck guessed. Between the storm and Moody's accident they had made little progress that day. Probably the realization that the outlaws could have done no better was the major factor in persuading him to lay over for the night.

Gilder turned his strained features to Shawn. "You figure there's a chance we can catch up to them tomorrow and head back to town?"

"Could be. Don't think they're too far ahead."

"God—I'm hoping so." Dave Gilder muttered in an exhausted tone.

Rome picked up one of the empty cups setting nearby, filled it half full from the simmering pot of coffee and offered it to the trembling man.

"Ease off," he said quietly.

Gilder took the cup, held it to his lips and gulped its contents, shivering uncontrollably.

"Thanks," he murmured, and hunching forward, buried his face in cupped hands.

"Everybody's got a problem," Able observed quietly, shifting his eyes to Starbuck. "Comes with living, it seems."

Shawn shrugged, and glanced up as Harry Brandon came down the short slope from the trail and stepped into the ring of firelight.

"Any sign?"

The lawman shook his head. "Naw—nothing, but they ain't far. Can't be, not with all this rain and the trail being in the shape it is." He reached into his pocket, drew out the almost empty bottle of whiskey and took a long pull of it. "We'll nail 'em in the morning."

David Gilder stirred restlessly. A small sound escaped his throat. Shawn spoke up quickly.

"Be glad to go after them now—the two of us, if you figure it's the thing to do."

"No sense in it. Like I said before, they can't do nothing but stick to this trail. Tomorrow'll be soon enough." The lawman moved in closer to the fire. Bottle in hand, he hunched. "Be a fool risk, anyways, trying to get to them in the dark.

Starbuck watched Brandon take another swallow of liquor. He disagreed as to the merits of closing in on the outlaws under cover of night, but it was Brandon's posse and the lawman had made it clear he was running it.

"There's something I want to say," the marshal continued, wiping his mouth with the back of a hand. "We see them, I want every man jack of you to open up—shoot. Don't hold off."

Shawn drew himself up slowly. "You're not giving them a chance to throw down their guns?"

"Hell, no! Be a waste of breath. I know them birds—they won't give up—and they'll kill you if you don't kill them first."

"How about Starbuck's brother?" Rome asked. "Ain't he one of them?"

"Who knows—and I sure'n hell ain't waltzing up to them and asking!"

"Then I will," Shawn said, "or are you going to say now that it was all a lie to start with?"

Brandon wagged his head. "No, I wasn't lying to you. One of them is Ben Snow—just like I told you."

"Then I'm going to do some talking before there's any shooting—"

"The hell you will!" Brandon shouted, his face hardening. "You'll do what I tell you—all of you will! Now maybe one of them is your brother and maybe he ain't, it don't make no difference. They're all killers and I ain't taking no chances. I'm telling you again—and by God I'm heading up this posse—when we jump them, start shooting and shooting to kill. I make myself plain?"

Starbuck remained silent. There was still a strong

doubt in his mind that Ben would be found with the
outlaws, but the slim possibility that he could would
not permit him to obey the lawman's orders. . . . He'd
simply wait, somehow find a way to make sure before
it was too late.

"How's the cripple doing?" Brandon asked then,
jerking his thumb at Moody.

"Needs a doctor. Best you send him back to town in
the morning."

"He can wait," the lawman said bluntly. "He's got
one good arm he can use. Besides, I expect we'll all be
heading back before the day's over."

"You're mighty sure of them," Able Rome said,
studying the marshal closely.

Brandon tipped the bottle to his lips, swallowed,
smiled. "Sure enough," he replied, and lowering the
container, gauged its contents. Little more than one
drink remained. Still grinning, he turned to Dave
Gilder.

"And how're you doing, mister?"

Gilder stirred helplessly. "Not—so—good."

"That so? Well, maybe you could use this here last
swallow," Brandon said, and leaning forward, waved
the bottle in front of the man's nose.

Gilder jerked back, face contorted, eyes bright.
"No—well, I can't—"

"Slop it down! Sure won't hurt none."

"Trying not—been fighting it—"

"Ain't nothing better for a man on a cold, wet
night."

Dave squirmed, turned his head. His mouth was
working convulsively and there was a wildness to him.

"All yours—if you want it," Brandon said in a taunting voice. "And there ain't no more this side of the
Crossing!"

Starbuck, unable to endure the torture Brandon was
putting Gilder through any further, came to his feet. His
hand swept down, struck the bottle, knocked it from
the lawman's grasp, sent it shattering on the rocks.

Eyes flaring with anger, Brandon sprang upright.
"What the hell you think you're doing?" he demanded.

Shawn's cold gaze locked with the lawman's. "You want to play games, try *me*."

Brandon's hulking figure hung motionless against the darkness for a long moment, and then his thick shoulders came down. He forced a smile, brushed at his mustache, nodded.

"Just having a little fun with the sot. . . . Not meaning no harm."

"That kind of fun we can do without," Starbuck replied, and turned to the blankets, stirring in the fresh breeze.

The woolen covers had dried. Pulling them off the ropes, he tossed one to Rome, another to Dave Gilder, and then crossing to Moody, laid the third on the sleeping man's knees. Walt roused, stared about numbly, and then taking the blanket, drew it about himself.

Shawn retraced his steps to the line, collected the remaining covers, and draping one over his shoulder, handed the other to the lawman.

"We heading out early?" he asked, settling down.

"Sunrise," the marshal said and crossed to the opposite side of the fire where he could be to himself.

Dave Gilder hugged his blanket tighter to his body and shivered, but it was not from the night's cold; rather, it came from an inner chill. He shifted his feverish eyes to the bits of broken glass scattered around the stones he had arranged for the fire. The strong smell of whiskey still hung in the air, tantalizing, taunting him cruelly. God, how he had wanted that drink—and Brandon had known the depth of his need!

But Starbuck—damn him, too—had snatched it away from him just as he was about to give in, surrender to the raving, unholy thirst that was ravaging him from scalp to toe.

He'd wanted it in the worst way—and he hadn't wanted it, knowing that once that first drop had slid down his throat he would be off once more—lost again. But wasn't it better to be lost and alive—than dead?

He groaned, again clutched at the blanket as he

glanced about at the sleeping men around him. They didn't know what it was like, this whiskey fever that possessed him. They maybe thought they did, but no man could really know unless he'd been through it himself.

And that goddam Brandon, that stinking, lousy excuse for a lawman, teasing him the way he had! The smell of the whiskey when he'd held it under his nose had almost turned him inside out. He wished now he'd made a grab for it, gulped it down before Brandon could snatch it away—if that's what he intended to do—and likely it was.

What the hell was the use of fighting it? He'd never lick it, never win. No matter how hard and often he'd tried, he always found himself waking up one day with all the demons in hell running loose inside his head, gut-sick and more dead than alive.

The real answer, he guessed, lay not in waking up someday, just passing out in the back of some saloon and never coming out of it. . . . But that meant never seeing Felicity and the boys again and he'd not been able to get that hope out of his mind.

He supposed that was the one reason for the continual warfare that half of him waged with the other half—that solitary, shining hope that someday it would all be as it had once been; but was keeping alive that hope worth the price he was paying? Right now he doubted it and that disturbed him, for never before had any such uncertainty filtered into his mind.

Was he slipping farther down, going deeper into the black morass of alcoholic nothingness? Was he losing sight of the only things that meant something to him?

Exhausted beyond the point of needing sleep, Dave Gilder stirred, shakily reached for the cup Able Rome had handed him earlier. Maybe another swallow or two of Starbuck's black, bitter coffee would stifle the torment within him.

A tremor shook him. A small portion of the broken bottle lay near the blackened pot. In its curve a teaspoon or so of golden liquid winked up at him.

He let the cup fall, extended a forefinger toward the bit of glass. . . . Just a taste, that's all he wanted—all he needed. It would quiet his nerves, let him settle down. Yes, just a taste. . . . It wouldn't hurt. . . .

An anguished sound burst from his lips. His hand swept down, fingers scooping through the ashes and bits of charred twigs, sent it showering over the curve of glass and its tempting contents. And then folding his arms across his knees, Dave Gilder lowered his head and wept like a child.

～～ 11 ～～

The predawn hour was cold, and because of the shortage of dry wood, the fire was large enough only to boil coffee and fry bacon and grease bread. The meal was eaten and camp broken in the deep silence of men chilled to the bone and in ill humor.

But later the sun caught them moving up the trail in single file, and as its warmth spread subtly over the mountain and seeped into their bodies, they began to loosen up and some of the hostility faded from their manner.

Starbuck, intentionally choosing the second-in-line position behind Harry Brandon where he would be able to see the outlaws at the same moment the lawman located them, scoured his mind for some plan by which he could get to the three before the marshal could carry out his threat to shoot first and ask no questions.

He felt sure Ben would not be one of the killers; Brandon had voiced the possibility only as a means to enlist him in the posse, but he was not so convinced that he would blindly accept the conviction without making an effort to be certain. Ben *could* have changed—and he must know for certain, one way or the other, before any shooting was done.

Just how he could do so was the question. He might break away from the posse, circle ahead and put himself well out in front and thereby be able to spot the outlaws first. But that would be difficult. The trail still clung to the crest of a narrow hogback and the slopes dropping away on either side were both steep and exceedingly slippery from the rain. Footing for either man or horse was impossible.

Also, to determine definitely if one of the men was Ben, he would have to move in close to them. Even then it would be only a guess. Ben likely had changed much in ten years, and from a distance there would be only a hoped-for family resemblance to go by. To be absolutely certain, it would be necessary to draw near enough to talk and look for the small scar that could be found above his brother's left eye.

Starbuck shrugged in impatience. There seemed no way other than persuading Brandon to close in quietly on the men and capture them rather than to shoot them down when sighted.

Spurring the sorrel nearer to the lawman, he said, "Marshal, I'd like to make you a deal."

Brandon, the incident of the whiskey bottle plainly a galling recollection still in his mind, half turned on his saddle.

"On what?" he asked sourly.

"The outlaws. When we spot them, how about letting me go ahead, slip in close and see if I can recognize my brother. You keep them covered and I'll offer to let them throw down their guns while I'm having my look—"

"Forget it, Starbuck," the lawman snapped, his mouth a hard line. "You'd never be able to get that close."

"It would be me taking the chance."

"Buying yourself a grave'd be more like it."

"It's my neck."

"And getting them's my responsibility. Like as not your messing around would fix it so's they could make a run for it—get away."

"Not if you had them covered," Shawn persisted, stubbornly.

Brandon was silent for a brief time, then he shook his head. "No, I ain't risking losing them."

Anger welled through Starbuck. "You do some thinking about it, Marshal," he said in a level voice.

The lawman came fully around, gave Shawn's taut features a calculating appraisal. Reading the determination in the tall rider's eyes, he nodded slowly.

"All right, I'll think on it," he said curtly, and squared himself on his saddle.

Starbuck dropped back into his place in the slow-moving cavalcade, glancing at the others as he did. Dave Gilder, drawn and desolate, looking as if he'd had no sleep at all, was behind him. Moody, slumped to one side, nursing his arm, came next. Able Rome, as before, brought up the rear. His solemn eyes met Shawn's, held, expressing nothing.

The thought came into Starbuck's mind as he rocked gently with the motion of the sorrel and listened to the quiet *thunk* of his hooves on the mushy ground, that turning on Brandon, taking charge of the posse himself might be the solution. The marshal was handling the matter unlike any lawman he had ever known—planning to murder the men he pursued without giving them a chance to surrender—and that actually was ample reason to assume command.

It wouldn't matter to the townspeople who had expressed their dislike for their marshal, or to the Paradise Mine, which was interested only in recovering its stolen gold. All that mattered to either faction was the apprehension of the outlaws.

But he would need the support of the rest of the posse and that was something he could not be sure of. Moody was more or less out of it, although he could use a gun, if need be; the two others, unstable and unpredictable, were hard to measure.

Gilder, in his present state of mind, could fall apart completely or he might, in consideration of what he believed to be his best interests, stand by Brandon. That could also apply to Able Rome—a man bent on carving a niche for himself in an unfriendly world, regardless of opposition—or tradition.

But most important of all he would be breaking the law himself by deposing the marshal, and that he did not relish the thought of doing. No matter how he looked at it, Harry Brandon was a duly elected representative of the law, the merits of his judgment, good or bad, notwithstanding. To oppose him meant defiance of the law and that was something that ran counter to Shawn Starbuck's nature and beliefs. . . . Best he give the idea serious deliberation before making such a move.

Reaching up, he released the top button of his brush jacket. The day was warming rapidly and signs of the heavy rain were beginning to disappear. Pools of water yet lay on the trail and brush and trees on the slopes still glistened wetly in the bright sunlight, but such evidence would all have disappeared by sundown.

Overheard in the cloudless sky an eagle soared effortlessly on broad wings, and here and there on the upper slopes irregular patches of gold marked the location of aspen groves. They were in high country, Shawn realized, and still climbing. It would seem they should be topping out the range and dropping off onto its yonder side before too long. It was difficult to tell, however, just where that point would lie because the timber growth was dense and visibility limited to a short distance.

Near noon they reached a small clearing that lay off the trail to the left. More rock was in evidence now and the timber had thinned to some extent, indicating they were drawing near the summit.

"Get some coffee made," Brandon directed, swinging down onto the flat and dismounting. His mien had changed to one of cheerfulness and he seemed to have forgotten the cross-purpose words he'd had with Starbuck. "Hard climb coming up. Horses need a bit of rest."

Shawn and the others had followed suit, grunting a little as they came off their saddles. It had been a slow, tedious climb and leaving the leather was a welcome break.

Taking up the sack of grub and cooking gear, Starbuck motioned Walt Moody to a log where he could sit and be out of the way, and then moved to the center of the clearing. Brandon, rifle in hand, doubled back to the trail for his customary look at the country ahead. Rome led the horses off to one side and Dave Gilder began his quest for dry wood.

It was more plentiful among the rocks, and shortly he had a brisk fire going for Shawn to set his containers of water over. A piñon jay appeared and began to flit nervously about in the nearby trees. His noisy scolding quickly attracted others and soon a dozen or more of the slate blue birds were voicing their harsh disapproval of intruders, from the safety of the pines and spruces.

Shawn, hunched over the flames, frying bacon and chunks of potatoes he'd baked that previous night while they lazed around the campfire, glanced up as Rome paused before him.

"I heard you arguing with the marshal about your brother. He willing to let you go first?"

"Hasn't said so."

"Still aims to shoot first—then look?"

Starbuck nodded. "I don't much think my brother's with them, but I'd like to be sure."

Rome drew out his cigarette sack. "That's not the way the law's supposed to work, anyway. We ought to give them a chance to quit."

"That's the way I see it, too, but I figured, having a personal interest, I could be looking at it one-sided." Starbuck hesitated, then said: "If I was to take over from the marshal, handle this the way I think a lawman should, where would you stand?"

"With you," Rome said promptly. "Right's right, and Brandon's sure wrong—planning murder the way he is."

Shawn stirred the contents of the spider slowly. "I'm not one to buck the law. I always believed it was due respect regardless of who wore the star, and that's got me trying to convince myself that what I'm thinking of doing is for the sake of the law and not because of my brother."

Rome turned to Dave Gilder, coming back into the clearing with another armload of wood. "We'd like for you to hear this. We don't figure the marshal's acting like a marshal," he said. "The way we see it, he ought to give those outlaws a chance to give in—not shoot them down."

"It amounts to murder," Moody said from his place on the log.

Shawn glanced at the man. He had assumed him to be dozing and unaware of the conversation.

Gilder dropped the firewood, rubbed at his jaw nervously. "I—I don't know. They ain't nothing but killers. Not deserving of decent treatment."

"The law says every man's entitled to a fair trial," Rome pointed out. "Or don't you figure the law ought to apply to every man?"

Gilder stared at Able bleakly. "Sure I do, only when—"

The sudden smash of rifle shots echoed through the canyons and across the plateaus. Starbuck, features grim, leaped to his feet. Drawing his pistol, he ran toward the trail.

"No use talking about it," he shouted. "Brandon's spotted them!"

~~ 12 ~~

There had been no distant, answering gunshots, only those coming from Harry Brandon's rifle. Anger surged through Starbuck. The lawman had gone ahead with his plan, opened up on the outlaws without giving them a chance to surrender. If one of them was Ben—

He swore harshly, rushed on toward what appeared to be a rocky summit a hundred yards farther up the trail. The others were close behind him—Able Rome to his right, Gilder to the left and Walt Moody, holding his broken arm slightly forward to prevent it from striking against his body as he ran, in the center and to the rear. Despite his injury, Walt was doing his part.

Brandon appeared suddenly on the crest, stepping from behind a wagon-size boulder that stood at the end of a straggling pile of lesser rocks. The lawman waved vigorously, signaling them to him.

"Got them boxed in a coulee—bottom of the slope!" he shouted as they drew near.

Stiff with anger, Shawn strode by him to the edge of the formation and threw his glance down the grade. A man lay in a small clearing at its base not far below. His hat had come off to reveal a shock of corn yellow hair. Both arms were outstretched, his hands empty. There was no doubt that he was dead.

"Opened up on me when I showed myself."

At Brandon's words Starbuck spun. His jaw was set to a hard line and his eyes were narrowed.

"We heard only your shots," he said, accusation in his voice.

"You calling me a liar?" the lawman demanded.

Starbuck's shoulders stirred. He should ·have expected Brandon to do as he'd planned. But it was too late to do anything about it now.

"The rest of them still down there?"

Brandon, head thrust forward belligerently, said, "Hell yes, they're down there. You don't believe it, step out there into the open."

Shawn moved to the forward edge of the rocks, leveled his pistol and pressed off a shot. The bullet struck in the center of the coulee, showered twigs and dirt on the dead outlaw. Immediately two rifles laid their quick answers across the rolling echoes loosed by his weapon.

Brandon, mouth pulled into a sneer, nodded. "Reckon that ought to satisfy you."

"That they're there—not that they started the shooting," Starbuck said coldly and turned back to the rocks. "You men in the coulee—throw down your guns and step out where we can see you!" he called.

"Go to hell!" The reply floated lazily up the slope.

"You don't have a chance. Quit now and we'll see you get a fair trial."

There was no response. Shawn brushed at the sweat on his face. "Is one of you Ben Starbuck? I'm his brother—Shawn."

The rifles cracked again. Bullets caromed off the rocks with a weird, shrilling sound.

"You done?" Brandon asked in a low, scornful voice. "You ready for me to take over, Mister Starbuck?"

Shawn pulled back from the rocks into the little hollow in which they'd gathered. The lawman had voided any possibility of talking the outlaws into surrendering. As for Ben, he was still unsure—but he had done all he could.

"It's your posse," he said.

"I'll be obliged if you'll keep remembering that," the marshal replied, his tone heavy with sarcasm. He swung to Gilder and the others. "Now, I want you to spread out, start pouring lead into that coulee. Good chance we'll wing them two that's left."

Able Rome immediately moved off to the right. Gilder and Walt Moody cut to the opposite direction. Shawn returned to where he had first looked down the slope, a place near center. He could see little point in following out the lawman's plan; it would serve only to pin down the outlaws, eventually force them to abandon their positions, fall back into the surrounding brush and make a run for it.

But Brandon could have a plan in mind that he was not making known, and stationing himself, he rested his weapon on the flat, top surface of the boulder behind which he stood and began to fire. The others also opened up, as did the cornered outlaws, and for a time the mountains were filled with the thunder of guns.

"Hold up!" Brandon yelled, finally. "We ain't doing no good—just wasting ammunition."

The lawman drew back to where the massive pile of rocks gave him full protection from the men below. Pulling off his hat, he mopped at his forehead, glanced around.

"I figure they're forted up behind something that we ain't seeing. Got to get at them from the side." He paused, pointed to a lesser scatter of rocks at the far end of narrow plateau to their right. "Want one of you to get over there. Maybe we can get them in a sort of crossfire."

Shawn frowned. There was no way a man could reach the point indicated without fully exposing himself.

"It'd be suicide," he snapped. "Nobody could cross that flat without getting cut down. Be smarter for us to separate, work our way around in a circle, come in on that coulee from all sides."

"They'd pull out on us, if we was to try that, and it'd take too much time."

"It'll beat getting somebody killed—"

"Goddammit!" Brandon exploded. "You trying to run this outfit again?"

"Start showing sense and—"

"I can make it," Rome cut in abruptly. "Cover me."

Shawn whirled to the man. Able's eyes were bright and there was the look on his round face of a small boy about to take a dare.

"Don't be a fool—you won't get halfway—"

"Move out—you're covered!" Brandon shouted, and

hurrying to the rocks began to fire into the coulee.

Rome, flinging a quick smile at Starbuck, darted into the open. Bent low, he started across the rounded surface of the ridge-like flat, running erratically, dodging from side to side. The outlaws opened up at once. Bullets dug into the ground at his feet, spanged off into space as they glanced against rocks.

Brandon's shots, supported by those of the remaining posse members, did nothing to deter them. Evidently they were well protected, as the lawman had thought.

"He's hit!"

At Moody's yell, Shawn came about. Rome was down on one knee, was struggling to crawl, gain the protection of the rocks. Another slug smashed into him, knocked him flat. He stirred feebly, tried to rise.

"I'll get him," Walt Moody said quietly, and holstering his pistol, rushed out onto the flat.

"No!" Starbuck yelled. "Too late to help—"

But Moody, following Able Rome's example, was already beyond the rocks, running fast, swerving from side to side. Almost to Rome's unmoving shape, he hesitated in stride as a bullet caught him. His body jerked as half a dozen more drove into him, spun him around and sent him sprawling.

An abrupt hush fell across the slope. Harry Brandon cursed in a low voice. "Goddammit to hell."

Shawn stared at him. "What did you expect? They didn't stand a chance out there."

Brandon shook his head, spat. "The nigger might've made it—with a little luck."

He swung back to the rocks, looked down into the coulee. "Ain't but one thing to do," he murmured, as if thinking aloud. "That's slip up on them from the side."

Shawn stirred wearily. It was what he had wanted to do at the beginning but the marshal had waved off the suggestion. Now, after the lives of two men had been spent, he was willing to try it.

"Little late to think of that," he said coldly.

Brandon shrugged. "Nobody said this was going to be a picnic. They knew what they was liable to run into."

"Maybe, but I don't think they counted on dying for nothing."

Starbuck mulled his own words over in his mind. Able Rome had seemed uncommonly anxious to take the risk that had cost him his life. Had he, in those brief moments, visualized some goal he felt was worth an attempt to reach? To prove himself the equal or better than any white man had been an obsession with him; had this been the means of confirming that avowal?

And Walt Moody . . . whatever it was that had twisted and tormented him and made of him a morose, frustrated man had been washed away by his act of bravery. Shawn wished now that he had been able to talk more with him, that he had not failed him that night by falling asleep. Perhaps he could have helped— and he would have had a better understanding of the man.

"You two stay put here," Brandon said, leaning his empty rifle against the rocks. His voice was low, firm. "That's a order."

Starbuck turned his attention on the lawman. "You going down there after them?"

"I aim to circle, come in from behind. Every little bit you throw a few shots into that coulee, make them think we're still up here. Understand?"

Shawn nodded.

"I get things set, I'll yell for you—and the both of you come running down that slope fast as you can. That clear?"

"We'll be ready," Starbuck said, glancing at Gilder.

"Just don't waste no time when you hear me," the lawman said, and cutting back to the trail, turned off and disappeared into the brush and trees.

~~~ 13 ~~~

Starbuck made his way back into the rocks and looked toward the coulee. The dead outlaw still lay as he had fallen. There were no signs of the others. He turned as Dave Gilder moved in beside him.

"Think they're still down there?"

For a reply Shawn pressed off two quick shots into the clearing. Instantly the outlaws returned a barrage of bullets that whined and thudded as they struck the boulders.

Gilder grinned wryly. "Reckon that's as good a answer as a man could want." He lay back, eyes on the bodies of Moody and Able Rome. "I wish't we could drag them off there. Ain't right, letting them lay."

"Nothing we can do about it now."

"I know that. . . . Sure too bad. Like you said, died for nothing."

To our way of thinking, perhaps so, Shawn thought, but he was not so certain how Rome and Moody looked at it. But he didn't feel like going into it with Gilder.

"Sure hate that about your brother. Wasn't no reason why the marshal couldn't've let you find out for sure whether he was down there before he started shooting. You think he'd a answered you, if he was one of them that's left?"

"Hard to say," Starbuck replied. "Pretty sure he would." Well off to the west and high in the heavens, two dark shapes were wheeling lazily, drifting closer. . . . Buzzards.

"Well, if he is, reckon there ain't much chance of you ever seeing him alive again. Brandon'll kill them both when he gets to them."

Starbuck nodded. Ben would have answered his call, he was sure, unless he had turned his back irrevocably on the family. He reckoned he should have gone with Harry Brandon but if he had done so Gilder would be alone in the rocks and there was no assurance that he could be depended on.

Dave, however, seemed to have changed for the better. The coming to grips with the killers, the shooting, the deaths of Rome and Moody and the hard, thrusting tension that went with it all appeared to have had a salutary effect.

His features were not so haggard, the bleak desperation had left his eyes and a stability had come over him. Shawn glanced to the sky again. There were four buzzards now and they were much nearer. He jerked his thumb at the dark, broad-winged silhouettes.

"They're moving in."

Gilder swore, raised his pistol and fired several times at the scavengers. The birds seemed not to notice.

"Just got to get them two off there," Gilder said worriedly. "You think, if I was to get a rope, we might—"

"The way they're laying there's nothing we could throw a loop over."

Dave swore. "Must be something we can do."

Starbuck loosened his collar. Heat was beginning to build in the rocks and the evidence of rain, where the sun could get to it, was vanishing. In among the trees and brush it was a different story; soft mud would still be underfoot and the foliage of the growth would be wet with the moisture that had fallen.

"We keep shooting at those buzzards we'll hold them off for awhile," he said, and then turning to the rocks, fired three more bullets into the coulee. As before, the response from the outlaws was immediate.

"How long you figure it'll take Brandon to get down there?" Gilder asked.

"Be slow going, and he'll have to circle wide, come in from the side. Thirty minutes, I'd say."

"Ought to be about there, then."

Shawn made no reply. He glanced once more at the soaring vultures. They were staying high, not following their usual pattern of gradual descent. It could mean they had spotted movement—possibly Brandon or the outlaws—and were holding off. At once he turned to the coulee, emptied his pistol into the small brush-bound area. Gilder added three more bullets and then sank back to watch Starbuck reload and fill his own weapon while the outlaws hammered at the rocks with their rifles.

"I've been wanting to thank you for last night," he said after a time.

Shawn paused. "Forget it. Brandon was out of line."

"I cussed you some, too, for doing it—got to tell you that because I sure wanted that drink. Then I was glad you done it. . . . I reckon you know I've got trouble with—with—"

"Whiskey," Starbuck said flatly, bringing it out into the open where it belonged. "You're not alone. Plenty others with the same problem."

Gilder toyed with the empty brass cartridges he had removed from his pistol. "I reckon so. A man always feels like it's only him having a bad time of it, though. It's a regular sickness."

"Same with everybody else that's fighting it—and you're the only doctor who can cure it."

Dave shifted nervously, tossed the spent casings into the brush. "It's not the first time I've been told that."

"I know it's easy for me to say it, but it's the truth. You're the only man alive who can make you lay off a bottle."

Gilder swore, brushed at his lips as if the mere talking of it was arousing a thirst within him. "It ain't that I haven't tried—God knows that! Got off it a hundred times—more, but I always end up right back where I started. It cost me my wife, my boys—my home—and they meant plenty to me. You think I wouldn't leave it alone so's I could get them back, if I could?"

Starbuck considered the man quietly, knowing what he would say would be brutal and cut deep.

"Maybe, inside, you don't want them back as much as you claim."

Dave Gilder started visibly. "The devil—" he began and then fell silent. He rubbed at his mouth again, lowered his head. "I'd give anything if I could lick it, but it's got such a hold on me I can't do nothing. Man that ain't been through it just plain don't know what a hell it is."

"Every man's got some kind of a private hell. Whiskey's not the only one."

Starbuck half turned, threw two shots into the clearing. Rifles crackled as he came back around, swung his glance to the vultures. They were circling at a high level and there was an even dozen of them now. It must be Harry Brandon moving along the edge of the slope that was keeping them back. . . . The lawman should have reached the coulee by then, it seemed.

"What you said about me not wanting to quit drinking bad enough—I think I do, but maybe that's it. Maybe I could want to more only I don't realize it. How the hell's a man know when he's trying his best?"

"Something else that only a man can answer for himself. . . . Brandon ought to be close enough by now. Time we laid a barrage into that clearing, gave him some help. Do your aiming at what you can see—the marshal could be in that brush and we don't want to hit him."

Gilder checked the cylinder of his pistol and moved up beside Shawn in the rocks. They opened fire together, thoroughly lacing the small circle of ground with lead. Their shots were returned instantly and once more the canyons and slopes rocked' with continuing echoes.

"If Brandon was there, that should've fixed it so's he could move in," Gilder said, thumbing fresh shells into his weapon.

Shawn agreed. "I expect we'll be hearing him sing out pretty quick."

"Drove them goddam buzzards off a mite, too."

His own pistol again ready, Starbuck looked skyward. The vultures had withdrawn a considerable distance. That worry should end soon now. Brandon would signal and the outlaws would either be his captives or his victims and no longer a threat. Either way they could soon remove Rome and Moody from the plateau.

The minutes dragged on and the signal did not come. A quarter-hour passed. Starbuck and Gilder, holding their fire for fear of hitting the lawman, waited restlessly among the rocks. Once again the buzzards began to drift in. The quarter-hour became a full half.

Abruptly Shawn came to his feet. "Something's gone wrong," he said in a tight voice. "You keep watching—I'm going down there."

~~ 14 ~~

When Harry Brandon stepped into the brush fringing the rocky plateau, he paused and looked back. Starbuck and the drunk were moving up to where they could see the coulee where Ollie Kastman and Snow were waiting. They had a moment's conversation and then Starbuck fired his pistol, drawing reply from the rifles below.

Brandon grinned, bobbed his head in satisfaction. So far his plan had worked perfectly except for that one little error—his putting a bullet in Charlie Cole and killing him. That hadn't been just exactly the way he'd set it up, but he guessed it didn't matter; it all worked out to the same end.

Moving on, he began to pick his route down the steep slope. Within a dozen strides he was soaking wet from the waterlogged brush and the still dripping trees, but he gave it no thought. Soon it would all be behind him. He'd be a rich man, taking it easy, enjoying life.

Abruptly his feet went out from under him as he trod upon an unusually slippery patch of soil. He went down hard, jarring a curse from his lips, but he was unhurt, only thoroughly muddied, and he quickly resumed the descent.

He'd fooled them all—the town, the mining company, the posse, and he was about to top it off by outsmarting his own partners. No one would ever know what really had happened there in the rocks and the coulee they overlooked, and while the search party that would eventually come upon the scene was trying to puzzle it out, he'd be somewhere deep in Mexico soaking up sunshine, rolling in luxury and living the sort of life he'd often dreamed of but had entertained small hope of ever achieving.

Halting to catch his breath, he steadied himself

against a juniper. Gunshots racketed again across the slope. The sound revived the smile on his lips and, pleased, he spent a few moments smoothing his heavy mustache. Starbuck and Gilder were following his orders to the letter, and Kastman and Ben Snow were shooting back just as he'd instructed them to do.

He continued on, mind turning now to the past. He'd had plans then, too, big plans to make something of his life, of stepping up from a lowly town marshal in a place such as Wolf Crossing to a position of wearing the badge in a larger settlement.

From there he would go on to take over the star in an even larger town, become a sheriff with power reaching throughout an entire county. And then it would be a U. S. marshal's job and he'd be a federal officer.

But it hadn't worked out that way, and piece by piece, he'd lost the dream. He could never seem to rise above the little one-horse dumps like Wolf Crossing and take that first, long step up to a bigger, more important position.

Then one day he realized it was too late. He'd become too old and deep inside him was a voice saying that he wasn't good enough anymore to do the job that even a small town expected.

Harry Brandon had made up his mind at that point; he couldn't reach the goal he'd set for himself, no matter how hard he tried, by doing it one way, so he'd turn his efforts toward attaining it in another. The opportunity presented itself not too long after he had come to that decision.

Word had come to him privately from the Paradise Mine authorities of a special shipment of gold being transported secretly to Dodge City by four men who would be posing as engineers; he, as a lawman, was asked to see to any needs they might develop.

He'd seen to needs, all right—his own. He'd sent word to Dodge, where he knew Ollie Kastman was dealing faro in one of the saloons, instructed him to recruit two or three dependable partners and meet him at a deserted cabin not far out of Wolf Crossing. Ollie had been a shotgun rider for one of the stage-coach lines and more or less understood the problems and drawbacks of packing a star, only he'd been smart enough to chuck it all and take up a more lucrative way of making a living.

Kastman had shown up with two friends, as directed, and he'd outlined his plan, it being that they were to ambush the four supposed engineers, relieve them of the gold and flee southward on the trail that cut through the mountains. To make it look good and to circumvent the entry of any outside law forces, he would follow with a small posse, lead them into a second ambush, after which the four of them would split the gold and go their separate ways.

They would have plenty of time to make an escape because it would likely be a week, perhaps even two, before someone finally decided to organize a search party and go looking for the posse.

Everything worked out just as he'd planned, even to the posse. The town had played right into his hands; he'd asked for help, and feeling as they did about him and the Paradise Mine people, they'd turned their backs on him and there'd been no volunteers except the black man, the greenhorn and Dave Gilder, who'd do anything for the price of a drink.

At that point he'd acted on a hunch. The three who had agreed to ride with him weren't impressive enough; he needed someone in the party with a little higher standing. Starbuck, who had the look of a gunslinger and the manner of a straight-down-the-line sort of U.S. marshal he'd once hoped to be, came drifting into town at that moment and he'd persuaded him to join up.

But now he was thinking that could be his one mistake. Starbuck was pretty much living up to the impression he gave. He was no ordinary saddlebum and he wasn't going to be fooled easily, but so far he'd posed no big problem. There'd been some opposition on his part, none of which was serious—and in a few more minutes it wouldn't make any difference. He'd be dead just like all the others.

Two down and two to go—insofar as the posse was concerned. The nigger had been cut down by Kastman and Snow when he'd tried to cross the ridge—no thanks to Starbuck. And too bad it hadn't been him, but he was too smart to fall for that order. It would have been comforting to get the tall rider out of the way.

And that damned fool greenhorn, as loco as they get for some reason, had obliged by trying to reach the black and drag him off the ridge—thus there were only Gilder and Starbuck to account for. Gilder would be a cinch, but Starbuck—

Brandon halted again, once more listened to a rattling exchange of gunshots. He was fairly near the coulee now, judging from the sound of the outlaws' rifles. . . . Outlaws. . . . He sleeved away the water dashed onto his face by swinging branches and reckoned he belonged in that category. But what the hell, better to be a rich, fat outlaw than an old, worn-out lawman that nobody cared a rap about.

He pushed on, moving with greater care, endeavoring to make his approach as quiet as possible. Kastman and Snow were expecting him, after which the idea was for him to signal down whatever remained of the posse—in this case Starbuck and Gilder—with the word that he had captured the outlaws and they were his prisoners.

They would all wait quietly there in the coulee until Starbuck and Dave Gilder, coming down the slope, got in range and then he and his partners would open up on them. That would mark the end of the posse.

Days—or maybe weeks—later when the search party came upon their dead bodies, it would appear to have been a showdown fight in which the forces of the law had come out second best. The fact that Charlie Cole now would be found there also would lend credence to the affair.

As for himself, the fact that his body was missing would lead to the conclusion that he had attempted to pursue the fleeing outlaws farther and was probably killed somewhere in the vast wilderness that stretched around them. They would decide it was useless to look for his body.

That was the general plan—the one concocted by him and Kastman and the two others. But Harry Brandon had a scheme of his own.

~~ 15 ~~

The course Brandon had taken down the treacherous slope was not hard to follow; the difficulty lay in staying upright. Shawn made his way carefully—this was no time for a broken leg or arm—bracing himself whenever possible by catching onto an extending branch or a hand on a boulder.

The route was apparently a familiar one to the lawman, for not once had he ended up in any of the numerous, small, dead-end draws or been forced to backtrack after running into a butte or similar formation. It was as if he had made the descent before but that was not likely, Starbuck was sure. The area was far removed from Wolf Crossing, and while Brandon did profess to be familiar with the country, his knowledge would be confined to the trail itself.

Brandon's tracks began to veer right, taking a circular course about midway of the slope. Shawn paused, to catch up with his labored breathing. He could not be far from the coulee and it was best he proceed henceforth with caution. He was certain now that the marshal had walked into a trap, was either in bad trouble or dead. Far too much time had elapsed since he left the crowning rocks of the slope and started down the grade for the hiding outlaws.

Breath recovered, Starbuck moved on, placing each booted foot carefully, choosing his own path now while his eyes searched the brush ahead for signs of the clearing where the outlaws were making their stand, and his ears strained for any sounds that would warn him.

He reached a roll in the land, again halted. Wet

90

to the skin, he was cold there in the shadows of the
trees where the sun could not find its way. Rubbing his
hands together, he looked back up the slope. He could
see the ledge-like pile of rocks where Dave Gilder
waited and a section of the slope directly below it.
Like the plateau where Able Rome and Walt Moody
had died, it was open ground with only a few small
rocks and stringy clumps of brush to break its steep
surface.

He was no more than halfway to the coulee, he
realized, gauging the probable location from its remembered position below the summit. At once he
resumed the descent, pushed now by a strong sense
of urgency to reach the clearing, convinced that something was wrong.

At quickened pace he hurried down the slope, taking
longer strides, slipping, sliding, catching himself time
after time. Twice he went to his knees, saved himself
from falling completely by clutching at the brush.

"Starbuck—Gilder!"

The shout brought him to a quick stop. Brandon's
voice came from a considerably lower level on the
slope and well to his right.

"Come on down here and help me. . . . I got 'em
cold!"

Shawn heaved a deep sigh. The marshal was all
right. Apparently he had managed to close in on the
two outlaws and capture them without firing a shot.
Glancing to the crest of the slope, he saw Dave Gilder
silhouette briefly against the skyline and then move
forward to start the descent to the coulee.

Pulling out his handkerchief, Starbuck dried his
face and moved on. There was no great hurry now to
reach the clearing. Brandon had everything under
control.

Abruptly a half-dozen gunshots shattered the stillness of the mountainside. Starbuck wheeled, looked
toward the rocks. Dave Gilder was down, rolling
frantically to reach the safety of a mound of weedy
earth. Bullets were digging into the soil around him,
sending up small spurts of sand.

It could mean only one thing; the outlaws had

somehow overcome Brandon, had opened up on Gilder with their rifles when he started toward them in obedience to the lawman's summons. They had overlooked one thing—him.

Grim, he drew his pistol and headed off along the slope at a run. The location of the coulee was established in his mind now, thanks to Brandon's yell and the gunshots, and he need waste no time searching for it; he had only to bear straight on the slanting course he was taking and be led to it.

In that next instant Shawn felt his feet shoot out from under him. For a fraction of time he seemed suspended in midair, and then he struck hard. Breath gushed from his lips as he slid into the unyielding trunk of a deep-rooted pine. Lights popped before his eyes as his head thudded into a half-buried ledge of granite. . . . And then all was in darkness.

Harry Brandon hunched low in the brush that skirted the coulee. He could hear Ben Snow and Kastman talking but their voices were low, guarded, and he could not make out the words.

He drew his pistol, examined it, making sure no mud had become jammed in its muzzle during his passage down the slope. It was clean, and shoving it back into its holster, he stood upright.

"Ollie," he called softly.

"Here."

The reply came at once. Brandon stepped forward, taking no pains to conceal his approach, and entered the clearing.

"Keep your head down!" Kastman warned hastily. "Them friends of your's've done killed old Charlie. Shoot at everything that moves."

Brandon moved in behind the two men, took up a position between and slightly to the rear.

"Was wondering which one of you it was. Deputy jumped the gun on me, started shooting before I could stop him. Sure hate it."

"So does Charlie," Ben Snow said laconically. "We was expecting you sooner."

"It was that damned storm—and then one of them

fool posse members fell down the side of the mountain.
Had to waste time dragging him back up. . . . Everything all set?"

"Just waiting on you to give the word," Kastman
replied. "Horses and mules are right down the trail
a piece."

"What're we doing about Charlie?" Snow, a scarred,
dark-faced man with a week's growth of beard on his
jaws, asked.

"Leaving him lay," Brandon said promptly. "Makes
it look like there was a real, stem-winder of a hoedown
between the posse and you—us. Two dead men up
there on the ridge, be two more on the slope and him
down here. Works out good."

"That all of the posse that's left—two?"

Brandon nodded. "Was only me and four of them
to start with."

Ben Snow chuckled. "Nailing them two was like
picking off them little ducks in a shooting gallery,
way they was running across there."

Brandon glanced at the sun. "Reckon we'd best get
things going. I'll sing out, like I told them I would, and
they'll start coming down the slope. That's when you
open up."

"You just get on with your signaling," Snow said.
"Me'n Ollie'll do the rest."

Brandon pulled back a step to where the brush
would conceal him, and drawing his pistol with his right
hand, cupped the left to his mouth.

"Starbuck—Gilder! Come on down here and help
me. . . . I got 'em cold!"

He remained motionless until he saw the first
figure step into view at the edge of the rocks and start
down the slope. Gilder, he thought. Starbuck would
probably show up at the opposite end of the pile.

Abruptly Ben Snow began to fire. Kastman also
opened up. He saw Gilder stumble and fall, then scram-
ble on all fours to reach cover. Starbuck—where the
hell was that goddam Starbuck?

There was no time to wait, to wonder where he
was or curse his two partners for not holding off until
both men were in view. Starbuck could have taken it

upon himself to follow him down the east side of the mountain. It would be like the sonofabitch to cross him that way. Regardless—there was no time to lose.

Crouching, he brought his weapon to bear on Ollie Kastman's broad back. He pressed off a shot. The impact of the bullet at such close range drove the man forward, knocked him sprawling into the clearing beside Charlie Cole.

Snow, still levering shots at Gilder, paused, half turned. His features were blanked with surprise and fear.

"Hey—" he said in a high pitched voice. "What the hell—"

Brandon's second bullet caught him in the right breast, slammed him into the stump next to which he was sitting.

His mouth pulled into a hard, tight line, Harry Brandon drew back farther into the brush, ears straining to pick up any noise that would tell him of Starbuck's location, if he was nearby. There was only silence.

He swore feelingly. Starbuck had screwed up his plans but good! He was supposed to be laying dead there on the slope with Gilder—dead as the two whose job it was to kill them. Why the hell hadn't he stayed put like he was told, and then come down the slope with that lousy drunk of a Gilder the way it had been planned? All that careful scheming blown to hell. . . .

Brandon shook his head. There was no use getting all spooked over it. It wasn't that serious. He'd simply wait for Starbuck to show up, then put a bullet in him same as he had Ollie and Ben Snow.

He frowned, giving that thought. Maybe that wasn't the best thing to do; maybe it would be smarter to get the horses and the pack mules and move on. That way he could settle with Starbuck, who was sure to follow, in his own time and on his own terms. Waiting there at the clearing could be risky. He'd have to watch all sides, never being sure just which way Starbuck, a tricky bastard if ever he saw one, would move in from.

No, best to move out, grab whichever of the horses looked good, and with the pack animals, head south with the gold—the whole hundred thousand dollars worth. . . . My God, a man could hardly realize just how much money that really was! A hundred thousand dollars—and it was all his just like he'd planned it would be.

Stepping forward, he snatched up the rifle that had fallen from Ben Snow's hands. A long gun would be better to use on Starbuck; it would give him distance as well as greater accuracy. He wheeled, started down the trail at a run. A good headstart on Starbuck would help, too, afford him time to pick a spot where he could pull in, set up an ambush.

~~~ 16 ~~~

Starbuck picked himself up slowly. Dazed, he looked about, shook his head in an effort to dispel the mist shrouding it. He had been unconscious for only a few minutes, he guessed, and he seemed unhurt except for a tenderness along his left temple. Lucky. . . . He could have collected a broken bone or two as reward for his haste.

He looked down at the pistol, still held tight in his hand. It was smeared with mud. Taking out his spare bandana, he wiped it clean, made sure the barrel was not clogged. He frowned, again shook his head. . . . The forty-five—why was he holding it? In that next moment it all came rushing back to him.

Mind functioning properly again, he swung his eyes to the slope below the rocks. Dave Gilder was no longer in sight, had evidently made his way to the side of the grade where more brush was available for cover. Whether he was alive or not was a question.

And Brandon. . . . At once he moved off, taking slow, careful steps. The muscles of his legs were trembling but he pushed on, the feeling that he was needed in the clearing a driving force that pushed aside the uncertainty gripping his body.

He reached the point near which he thought the coulee lay, halted, listened intently. Off to the right he heard a faint rasping sound. Dropping low, he made his way forward until he gained the brush that encircled the area of open ground. There, pistol once more in hand, he stopped short. Three bodies lay in the coulee. Harry Brandon's was not one of them.

Giving that a moment's consideration, he called softly: "Marshal?"

There was no response. He repeated the summons in a louder voice.

"Starbuck—that you?"

It was Dave Gilder. Shawn wheeled to the slope. "Here," he said, and hurried through the undergrowth to the upper edge of the clearing.

Gilder, his neckerchief knotted about his left leg at a point just above the knee, struggled to an upright position as Shawn approached. His eyes were bright and there was a grimness to his mouth.

"What the hell's happened down there?"

"Three dead men," Starbuck replied. "Brandon's not among them. You hit bad?"

"Bullet went clean through, missed the bone," Gilder said, pulling at the makeshift bandage. "I can manage."

Shawn glanced up the slope. "You crawl all the way to here?"

Dave nodded. "Figured the marshal was in trouble and I'd best get here to help fast as I could. Just made it when I heard you calling him. Where you reckon he is?"

Starbuck shifted his gaze to the clearing. "Something I'd like to know," he said thoughtfully.

"Could be dead—laying off in the brush somewheres."

"Just what I was thinking. I'll have a look around. Wait here—best you stay off that leg."

Gilder shrugged. "No, I reckon I can get about all right."

Shawn studied the man for a moment. It came to him again that this was a different Dave Gilder from the one he'd ridden out of Wolf Crossing with.

"Suit yourself," he said. "Best we do it quiet, however. I'm beginning to wonder about something."

Gilder pulled off his hat, ran a hand through his shock of red hair. "What's that?"

"I'd as soon not say until I'm sure. I don't like having to eat my own words if I'm wrong—which I'm hoping I am."

They separated, Dave, hobbling painfully, going to

the right, Starbuck to the left. They probed the coulee's brushy perimeter, turned up no sign of the lawman. Rejoining, the two men moved then into the clearing.

Tight-lipped, Starbuck crossed to the side of the nearest outlaw, rolled him to his back. It wasn't Ben, but to make doubly certain, he knelt, looked close at the eyebrows. There was no scar. He glanced at the two other bodies, neither of which remotely resembled his brother, breathed a sigh of relief. Brandon had just suckered him into joining up—

"This one's still alive!"

Starbuck came about. Gilder, on his knees, was supporting the outlaw's head and shoulders and reaching for a half-empty bottle of whiskey standing against a nearby stump. Shawn picked up the liquor, and dropping to a crouch, forced a drink between the man's lips. The outlaw gagged, shuddered. His eyes opened.

He stared up at Starbuck and Gilder. The slackness in his features hardened, became angry planes. "That goddam . . . Brandon. . . ."

Shawn leaned nearer to catch the faltering words. "Where is he?"

"Run . . . for it. . . . Double-crossed me . . . and Ben. . . . Took . . . the gold."

"Double-crossed?" Gilder echoed. "You telling us that Harry Brandon was in on the holdup and killings?"

The outlaw coughed. Blood dribbled from one corner of his mouth. "Was him . . . setting . . . it up. Sent for me . . . letter . . . in my . . . pocket."

Shawn reached into the man's shirt pocket, withdrew a soiled, folded envelope. It was addressed to Ollie Kastman, Great Western Saloon, Dodge City, Kansas. Unfolding the sheet of paper that was inside, he read it quickly and passed it to Gilder.

"Can . . . use another . . . drink."

Shawn took up the bottle and helped the outlaw down a second portion of the liquor. Kastman's eyes were glazing but he managed a weak smile.

"Obliged . . . to you."

Starbuck bent over the man. "This ambush Brandon's idea, too?"

Kastman moved his head with effort. "Was . . . to wipe out . . . the posse. Wanted to make . . . it look like . . . a big shoot-out. Aimed . . . to swap duds with one of . . . you so's nobody'd know . . . he was in . . . on it."

Gilder had finished the letter, was returning it to its envelope. Starbuck shook Kastman gently.

"Where were you going then?"

"South . . . Mexico."

"You figure that's where Brandon's headed?" Dave asked, thrusting the letter into his own pocket.

"Sure. . . . No place else . . . to go."

Undoubtedly Ollie Kastman was right, Shawn thought, except for one thing; Brandon would not be lining out straight for Mexico just yet. He had rid himself of his partners and the necessity to share the gold, but not all of the posse members were dead, as he'd planned. He would have noticed that only Dave Gilder appeared on the slope to face the bullets of the outlaw rifles and that would have stirred up a strong worry within him.

Only with everyone involved dead could he feel safe, and he would set about to repair the hitch that had developed in his scheme. Somewhere close by, Harry Brandon was waiting to finish what he had started.

Starbuck turned his attention back to Kastman. The outlaw was sucking for breath, his features again slack.

"Your horses and the pack mules—where'd you leave them?"

"On the trail . . . below a ways. . . . A drink . . . like to have . . . one more."

Gilder took up the bottle quickly, held it to Kastman's mouth, watched him gulp the fiery liquid. When he had taken sufficient, he shook his head.

"Obliged again. . . . You going . . . after Harry?"

Shawn said, "No choice."

"Good. . . . The sonofabitch's got it . . . coming to him. . . . Man can't . . . play both sides . . . of the . . . table."

The outlaw's words faded into silence. Dave Gilder hunched low over him, drew back.

"Dead," he said. "Wonder he lived long as he did. Brandon must've been standing right behind him when he put that bullet in his back."

Starbuck drew himself upright. In the sky above the rocky plateau the buzzards were circling low, bolder now that there was no more shooting and they no longer saw movement along the slope. He faced Gilder.

"There'll be two horses around here somewhere, if Brandon didn't drive them off. I'll take one, go after him—he'll be ahead of us on the trail, I figure. You take the other, go up and get Rome and Moody, and our own animals, make camp here."

Gilder nodded, pointed at the outlaws. "What about them?"

"Wrap them in their blankets and we'll tote them back to town, same as we'll be doing Rome and Moody."

Gilder smiled grimly. "Be quite a sight, us riding down the street, packing all them bodies—"

"I'm hoping you're right—that it'll be the two of us and not just you."

"Same here," Gilder said, sobering. "How long you want me to wait?"

"If I've got Brandon figured, he'll be holed up somewhere along the trail, watching for me to show—he's looking for me because he thinks everybody else is dead. And he won't go far before he sets his ambush. With luck I ought to be back by sundown."

Gilder bobbed his head. "I'll be here," he said, throwing a glance at the buzzards. "Let's find them horses. Want to get up to the rocks before them carrion eaters take a notion to light."

～ 17 ～

The tracks left by Brandon's horse and the two pack mules carrying the gold were clear in the soft mud of the trail, and Starbuck had no difficulty in following.

But the need for caution was apparent and he held the pursuit to a slow walk. Brandon would be expecting him, thus every bend in the path, every clump of dense brush and pile of rocks along its twisting course could prove to be the point where the lawman turned outlaw could be lying in ambush for him.

Several times Shawn halted to listen, hoping to pick up the sound of the moving animals, but on each occasion there were only the usual, everyday noises of the high hills. Brandon had gotten a good start on him and it quickly became apparent that he was pushing on steadily to maintain that lead.

Late in the afternoon he drew to a halt at the foot of a long grade, The black he had appropriated was tired and he wished now he had taken the time to get the sorrel, but at that moment he had expected to overtake Harry Brandon much sooner.

Dismounting, he stepped ahead on the trail, examined it briefly, reassuring himself that he was still on the right track, and then crossed to a mound of earth and rock covering the partly exposed roots of a wind-capsized fir. Climbing to its top, he looked out over the land, now beginning to shadow as the day lengthened.

To his left the slope dropped sharply into a deep canyon; to the right it lifted up in an almost perpendicu-

101

lar wall thinly populated by scrubby junipers, mountain mahogany, pines and spruce.

Starbuck nodded grimly. Brandon's escape route was also his trap; the trail he followed was like an eyebrow on the face of the massive hill, and there was no turning off; he could do nothing but continue on its narrow width and hope to reach a suitable place where a stand could be made.

That could take days, Shawn realized. He swore wearily; another sidetrack, another delay in his search for Ben. It seemed he was forever becoming involved in the problems of others while seeking only to fulfill his own obligations. . . . But this had been a little different from usual. There had been the possibility of one of the outlaws being his missing brother. He had doubted it from the beginning, but he had felt, nevertheless, that he should be certain.

He supposed he could have pulled out back at the coulee when he had seen with his own eyes that Ben Snow was not Ben Starbuck. His personal interest and reason for being a member of Brandon's posse had ended at that moment.

But the thought had not occurred to him. His mind had been crowded with the memory of Able Rome and Walt Moody lying dead on a plateau while vultures circled patiently overhead, and the knowledge that they were there because a man who wore a star had used his good offices and the prestige of the law to flaunt his trust to satisfy personal greed.

No man could turn his back on that. Others were dead, the law had been broken by one entrusted with its upholding; it was imperative, therefore, that he be caught, returned and brought to justice. Otherwise the sacred tablet of principles by which all lived would be damaged and thereby lessened.

But why was he always the one to find himself jockeyed into a position of assuming such responsibilities? Starbuck had often pondered that question when he found himself deeply involved. Why could he never find it in himself to ride on, look to his own problem?

Shawn Starbuck had never found an answer—nor

did he lose any sleep over it. Perhaps it was his up-bringing at the hands of iron-willed old Hiram Starbuck to whom there were only two factors deserving consideration in this life—right and wrong. A thing was either white or it was black and there were no shadings of gray; and while that somewhat uncharitable philosophy had been tempered in Shawn by circumstance from time to time, the basic honesty of it still burned within him and adherence to it was second nature.

He moved off the mound, slipping and sliding a bit on the mud, and returned to his horse. The short rest had helped the black some, but he was in poor condition at best and Starbuck knew he could expect little from the animal. There was but one consolation; the horse Brandon was riding, also one of the outlaw's string, would be in no better shape and thus, in that respect, they were on equal footing.

It ended with that, Starbuck thought as he swung back onto the saddle and continued up the trail. Harry Brandon had all the advantages. He was somewhere ahead and on a higher elevation that permitted him to look back—and down, simplifying the task of keeping an eye out for anyone following.

Thus he could exercise judgment, either finding eventually a suitable place to halt, set up an ambush or simply continue on, mile after mile, maintaining his distance, and hope to wear down anyone pursuing him and finally lose them.

It was difficult to predict which course Brandon would choose. Probably he would elect to kill—to stop once and for all time anyone seeking to track him down and bring him to justice. Using his gun as a means for accomplishment meant nothing to him, as the murders of his partners proved, and he doubtless would feel more secure in the knowledge that no one who had witnessed his sanguinary acts still lived.

The timber was thinning. They were again moving into high country where there was less brush growth and more firs and spruces interspersed with groves of white-trunked, golden-leafed aspens.

He realized he could no longer rely on the protection of trees that before had more or less obscured the trail, and he began to ride nearer the inside edge of the rough pathway, seeking to make himself a less visible target.

The day was growing late and darkness would be of help, but there was little he could do to take advantage of it. With the sorrel under him he could have kept moving, climbing, certain that Brandon had been forced to halt for the night; the poor condition of the black ruled out the possibility of his use. Head low, laboring with each step, he would have to rest soon or cave in.

Shawn brushed his hat to the back of his head and stared up-trail. He could see short stretches of open ground now through the scattered trees, but there was no sign of Harry Brandon.

Twice Brandon had caught a glimpse of the man so relentlessly dogging his tracks. It was Starbuck, he knew. It could be no one else. Able Rome and the greenhorn, Moody, were dead. He'd seen Gilder go down when Snow and Kastman opened up on him with their rifles. He, too, was dead or badly wounded. Therefore it had to be the big drifter. He swore harshly. Why the hell couldn't his luck have held and Starbuck headed down that slope with Gilder like he was told to do instead of going off on some idea of his own! Then it would have worked out just as he'd planned.

But he reckoned he should be satisfied that only one slip had developed in his carefully plotted scheme—and a minor one at that. He was still holding all the high cards despite Starbuck, and when the proper time came, that moment when he could be absolutely sure, he'd play the ace that would end the game and set him free to enjoy the new life he longed for.

He threw a glance at the pack mules. They were barely moving, making their displeasure evident, as mules would do, at being forced to continue when they were tired and believed they had done enough for one day. He'd make them keep moving until dark, then pull in. The horse he was riding was in a hell of a shape, too.

He gauged the sun. Still another hour or so until

it set—and that much time, more or less, would put
him pretty well up on the summit at that flat place
that was a good spot for camp as well as offering a
position from which a man, so desiring, could make
mighty good use of a rifle.

Harry grinned, rubbed at the side of his head
in a satisfied way. . . . He'd never forget the look on
Ben Snow's face back there in the coulee when he
turned and saw that six gun pointing at him! Surprised
just wasn't a good enough word for it.

He supposed he ought to feel a little guilty about
double-crossing him and Ollie and Charlie Cole. They
had pitched right in with him on the scheme and not
only done a good job of grabbing the gold and taking
it to the agreed-upon rendezvous, but had followed out
all his instructions—even to firing a bullet into the
fire that first night to let him know they were just
ahead and on schedule—just as he had directed.

But a man couldn't afford to get soft-hearted when
it came to staking his claim on a fortune. He had to
think only of himself and make plans accordingly. Hell,
there wasn't any big loss, anyway! All three of them
were living on borrowed time. Sooner or later they
were bound to get themselves killed off.

He reckoned he was entitled to a pat on the back;
everything had worked out fine when you considered
it, except for Starbuck. If he was to fault himself on
any one thing, he guessed it was for misjudging him
and talking him into riding with the posse. But he did
need one man a cut better than the three who'd volunteered, and he was the only available prospect. How
was he to know Starbuck wasn't just another saddle-
tramp, anyway?

Harry Brandon shrugged, spat. The hell with hash-
ing over Starbuck. He'd take care of him, come dark,
and that would be the end of it. What if he had made a
little mistake and was being pushed a bit when he'd
planned on being able to take his time, just fade out,
vanish? It would all work out to the same end in the
long run.

There was one thing that would pose a bit of a
problem, once Starbuck was taken care of; he had no

grub. Moving out in a hurry the way he'd been forced to do in the coulee, he'd had no time to grab the supplies Kastman and the others had been carrying. He didn't know whose horse he'd taken, but it wasn't the one packing the grub. He'd get by, however. He'd kill himself a rabbit or one of the numerous tassle-eared squirrels he'd noticed running around under the trees. That would keep him going until he reached one of the Mexican settlements he knew he'd find once the ridge was topped out and he dropped into the valley country on the other side. What the hell—for a hundred thousand dollars in gold a man could afford to go hungry for a couple of days!

The mules began to hold back. He halted, again looked to the sun. He could stop anytime now, he decided, swinging his gaze about. A hundred yards farther, a small flat, covered with thin grass and bordered on two sides with boulders, caught his attention. It was exactly what he had been looking for.

Goading the horses and yanking impatiently on the mules' lead rope, he moved into the clearing and stopped. Immediately the smaller mule lay down, ears slung forward, eyes half shut in a stubborn declaration of no further work.

Brandon, ignoring the brute, led the horse to a nearby stump, picketed him and the two pack animals. Wheeling, he jerked Ben Snow's rifle from the saddle boot and doubled back across the small flat to the ledge of rocks at its lower end. Pulling himself up onto the highest point, he looked down onto the trail.

For a time he saw nothing and the thought came to him that Starbuck had given up after all and was returning to Wolf Crossing. That set up a disturbance within him at once; he didn't want it that way; the final success of his plan depended on there being no survivors of the ambush. That damned Starbuck—a man couldn't figure—

A grunt of satisfaction slipped through his lips. A solitary rider had come into view, rounding a bulge of rock on the trail far below. It took only a few moments' steady observation to verify the identity; it was Starbuck, as he had been sure it would be.

Flattening himself, he rested the rifle on a slight hump in the storm-scoured surface of the ledge and sighted in on the next open area in the trail that Starbuck would shortly be entering. . . . A long shot but an easy one.

Settled and waiting, Brandon glanced back to the clearing. The smaller mule, apparently concluding that his day's labor was finally over, had gotten to his feet and was now grazing contentedly alongside his associate. It would be a good idea to pull off the pack saddles for the night, give the contrary bastards a good night's rest, Harry Brandon thought. Like as not their loads hadn't been off their backs since they left the Paradise Mine. . . . Besides, he wanted a look at that gold and run his fingers over its smooth softness—and, by God, he just might eat a little of it! Yes sir, he'd shave a bit off one of the bars and swallow it so's he could tell around that he'd eaten gold. . . . That would open some eyes.

He shifted his attention back to the trail. Starbuck was still hidden from view by an outward swing of the slope. . . . That was something else he would do, actually must do—go down to where Starbuck would be lying and get rid of the body. It wouldn't do to have him found by a search party, so it would be into the canyon for him, where the buzzards and the coyotes could take care of the remains. The horse he'd keep. Between it and the jughead he was riding he might have the makings of one good animal.

There he was—Starbuck. Brandon levered the rifle, checked to be certain a live cartridge was in the chamber. He wished he'd brought his own weapon. This one of Snow's was an old Henry whereas the one he packed and was accustomed to was a later model Winchester. But it didn't matter; a rifle was a rifle and one make would kill a man as dead as another. Drawing a bead on the approaching rider, he caught his breath and squeezed off a shot.

~~~ 13 ~~~

Starbuck, hunched forward on the plodding black, stared moodily at the steep rise in the trail ahead. He had expected Brandon to make his stand before this; could he be wrong about what the man had in mind? Was he going to just keep running, hope to wear out any pursuit?

It didn't seem logical. For him to believe he could push on without a break made little sense. Slowed by the two pack mules, he would know that he could not outdistance another rider not so encumbered.

A puff of smoke blossomed from the rim of a rock ledge near what appeared to be a crest. In that same particle of time the black faltered. Realization hit Shawn as the animal started to fall. *Brandon! Ambush!* He reacted instinctively. Kicking his feet free of the stirrups, he threw himself from the saddle as the flat, cracking sound of the rifle floated hollowly through the canyon.

Dirt spurted from the wall of the low embankment beside him as a second bullet dug into it. But Starbuck was already plunging into the thin brush and racing for the protection of a pine a dozen strides up the slope. He gained the thick-trunked tree, and gasping for wind, hunched behind it.

Jerking off his hat, he looked to the top of the trail. He could see Brandon, a vague shape in the darkening day, barely visible on a ledge of rocks that overlooked the land below. Evidently he was uncertain whether he had scored with his two bullets or not, since there had been no third. The long shadows undoubtedly were hindering his vision.

Starbuck swore harshly. That first bullet had been close. Only the fact that Brandon had slightly miscalculated in his aiming, and the black's bobbing head coming up at the exact moment it did, had saved his life.

But it was over now——all the tense watching and waiting for him to stop and make a fight of it. He was there, sprawled high in the rocks. The chase was finished.

Shawn's left hand dropped to the pistol on his hip. Drawing it, he checked its loads, found the cylinder ready except for the one chamber reserved for the hammer. Thumbing a cartridge from his belt, he filled it. It could come down to the point where his life depended on that one extra bullet.

Again he looked to the ledge. Brandon had not stirred, was still watching the trail. He held the upper hand and knew it. Up higher where he could see well, and with a far-ranging rifle, he was in control.

Starbuck sank to a crouch, made a studied survey of the hillside beyond the pine, the trail and the slope falling away from it. Trying to approach Brandon by the narrow path was out of the question; to attempt to reach him by working his way up through the scanty growth of the lower slope might be possible, but the odds were against it.

He shifted his attention back to the lifting hillside where the pine had given him safety. Its rise was steep and here cover was also scarce——but it was possible to climb. By holding to an almost direct, straight-up course he could gain a rocky outcrop that paralleled the trail. He looked close, traced the ragged line of granite with his eyes. It curved away from the crest where Harry Brandon had forted himself, but it would be possible to drop from it when he drew more or less abreast that point, cross a narrow saddle and come in behind the man.

The problem would be getting up to the ledge. There was much open ground lying between his position behind the pine and the rocks. Chances that Brandon would spot him while making the climb were better

than good, but once he reached the higher level it
would be easy to keep out of sight. . . . And he just
couldn't stay there behind the pine.

There wasn't much daylight left. What he would do
must be done soon, for once night closed in, Brandon's
advantage would increase. He could be sure the man
would find a safe hiding place from which to protect
himself on all sides—or he could even change his
location completely, move on for a distance. Then it
would all have to be done over again—the search, the
pursuit during which he would never know when
Brandon would halt, turn his rifle upon him and perhaps, this time, not miss.

Jaw set, Starbuck came to decision. He glanced
once more to the summit of the trail. Brandon had
pulled himself to hands and knees striving for a better
view. Shawn wished briefly for a rifle of his own and
then, dismissing that obviously impossible hope, bent
low and pulled away from the protection of the pine. If
Brandon would only keep his eyes on the trail, not
permit them to stray to probe the adjacent land, all
would go well. . . .

He came to a stop behind a clump of scrub oak as a
thought came to him. Keeping the man's attention
elsewhere was the answer. Glancing about, he located a
cup-sized rock. Picking it up, he moved a few steps
farther until the pine no longer blocked his way to the
trail. Then, putting all his strength into it, he threw the
stone as hard as he could.

It fell on the slope on the far side of the trail, set up
a hollow clatter. Harry Brandon pivoted on his heels.
Rifle poised, he stared down into the canyon, certain
now that his second bullet had not scored and that his
pursuer was working his way up the steep grade below him.

Shawn waited no longer. Brandon was quartered
away from him and would not shift his attention for
several minutes, at least, and so the time to make
the climb to the ledge with all possible speed was at
hand. There was that possibility that Brandon would
turn back for some reason, spot him and open up with
his rifle—but it was a risk he had to take.

Bent forward, he started up the grade, keeping as low as movement permitted, assisting himself whenever opportunity presented itself by grabbing onto a bush, a rock jutting out of the dark soil, or one of the few trees that were present.

Within only a short distance he began to labor for breath as the near vertical climb took its toll of him. Once he fell, the still slippery soil giving way under him and sending him sprawling full length while a trickle of small stones rattled down the slope.

He lay motionless, certain that the racket would be heard by Brandon, but when no rifle shots came, he twisted his head, and without rising, looked to the crest of the trail. A sigh escaped him. Harry Brandon still hunched at the far end of the ledge. The falling pebbles had gone unnoticed.

Resuming his partly upright stance, Starbuck continued. The grade immediately below the rocks had become steeper and now, at closer range, he saw that what he hoped to gain was the top of a butte formation that extended shelf-like from the breast of the mountain.

The face of the escarpment was much higher than it had appeared from below and he again halted, this time from choice as he scanned the frowning, ragged wall for a break that would permit him to climb to its top.

A darkness-filled wedge lay a hundred paces to his right. It would be a wash, a spillway through which storm waters draining from upper levels poured off the shelf in their rage to reach lower ground. . . . It meant doubling back, losing precious minutes of daylight, but there was nothing else he could do.

He flung another glance at Brandon, now barely visible, and hurried on toward the gash. Cutting across the slope on a fairly level course enabled him to regain his robbed breath to some extent, and when he finally reached the break in the bluff, he was not heaving so hard and the paining of his leg muscles had lessened considerably.

The opening in the rocky wall was only a little less steep than the slope itself, but by wedging his feet against the water-smoothed rocks protruding from either side and clinging to others, he was able to draw himself, panting, sweating and aching from the strain, to the flat surface of the shelf.

Starbuck lay there for a full minute, recovering his wind, allowing the trembling to fade from his body. Then, rolling over, he got to hands and knees and once again looked to the rocks at the top of the trail. He swore exhaustedly. Brandon was no longer there.

~~~ 19 ~~~

Starbuck crawled to a higher point on the ledge and, flat on his belly, scoured the darkening rocks for a sign of Brandon. He was not to be seen and the possibility that he had moved on again came to mind.

It seemed unlikely. That he had started down the trail with the thought of getting a shot at the man he believed was climbing the slope, or had simply pulled back from the shelf to a more advantageous position, made better sense.

Regardless, Shawn knew he must continue although he would again be going up against the man and his rifle blindly, not knowing where or when to expect him—and this time with the further handicap of darkness. He shrugged, swore quietly; nothing was ever easy, it seemed—and the job had to be done. Glancing again to the rocks, now almost wholly dark, he got to his feet, and remembering to keep well back from the edge of the ledge along which he moved, hurried on.

He came to the swale that separated the butte from the summit of the trail. There was no break in the wall, and reluctant to spend any time searching for one, he crossed to the edge, chose what appeared to be a fairly level section on the ground below, one devoid of rocks, and jumped.

It was a good fifteen-foot drop. He struck on the balls of his feet and, off balance because of the slanting grade, plunged forward and went to his knees. But he was up instantly, unhurt, and hurried on.

He went down the near side of the saddle, taking pains only to be as quiet as possible, and started up the opposite slope. Shortly the rocks crowning the crest became more distinct and he slowed his pace. Harry Brandon could have returned; it would be wise to approach with care until he was sure of just where the man might be.

He paused, gave that consideration. It would also be smart to come in from the back side of the plateau. At once he cut to the right, made a circle of the crest, halting when he reached a patch of junipers and oak brush at its lower end. Gauging the distance to the rocks, he dropped low and worked toward the opposite edge of the springy growth, listening intently as he slowly progressed.

A horse stamped wearily, blew. Starbuck halted instantly. Brandon had not moved camp, had only changed his position on the rocks. He was somewhere nearby. Pistol in hand, Shawn resumed the tedious approach. The horse was off to his right, probably picketed in a clearing where there was grass to be had. On beyond that would be the slope; therefore it was reasonable to assume Brandon was to his left.

Scarcely breathing and taking each step with utmost care, Starbuck pushed on until he reached the end of the brush. Low to the ground, he peered through the filagree screen of leaves and branches. A small flat, beginning to brighten with the night's first stars, lay before him. The two mules and the horse Brandon was riding were in a small pocket of rocks and undergrowth to one side. Elsewhere there was no sign of life.

Shawn settled back on his haunches, easing the strain on his leg muscles. He could cut back, circle to where the animals were grazing, but his appearance could frighten them and cause a racket. Brandon, he thought, would be on the other side of the rocky formation that capped the forward edge of the plateau like a dull, gray tiara, still keeping watch on the trail and the slope. But there was no real assurance of that; the man could be hiding nearby, actually aware of his presence, Shawn realized, and waiting to open fire when he appeared.

Two could play the game. . . . Starbuck shifted to a more comfortable position and, weapon ready, stared out over the flat. Coyotes barked into the brightening night from somewhere high in the ridges. A pumpkin-yellow edge of the moon appeared on the eastern horizon, began to grow, and the sudden, quiet swish of wings overhead marked the swift passage of an owl. A chill, born of sunset, was moving in, settling over the land and Shawn pulled at the edges of his jacket, drew it tighter around his body.

Dave Gilder would be wondering about the delay. He had expected him to return by the end of the day, would now have assumed that something had gone wrong and could even be contemplating taking the trail himself. It would be a mistake; with Harry Brandon lying in wait with his rifle, Dave would ride straight into a bullet.

Starbuck drew himself up sharply. A dark figure separated itself from the end of the rocks, coming from a shadow-filled hollow along the fringe. Shawn understood then; Brandon had simply exchanged his position on the top of the formation to a more convenient one where he figured he'd be less likely seen but could still cover the slope and the trail.

Tense, Starbuck held himself motionless, watched the man walk slowly into the open. Apparently he had decided there was no point in further surveillance and was likely considering the wisdom of moving his camp. Muscles taut, Shawn waited, allowed the man to reach the center of the plateau where he was in full starlight.

"Brandon—"

At the sound of Starbuck's voice, Harry Brandon lurched to one side instinctively. His rifle rapped through the stillness as he fired fast from the hip. Shawn triggered a shot at the man as a bullet clipped through the oak leaves crowding about him. He saw that he had missed, and pressed off a second shot at Brandon throwing himself into the brush at the end of the rocks.

Starbuck, not about to let himself be trapped, leaped to his feet, and snapping another at the point where Harry Brandon had disappeared, raced for the massive pile of boulders. The mules and the horse were milling around anxiously, frightened by the gunshots, but they were making no effort to break loose. They were either picketed securely or hobbled.

Shawn reached the rocks, reloaded his weapon as he began to circle the formation. Brandon could only be at the opposite end or else retreating down the trail, which was not likely. He halted suddenly, ears picking up the faint scrape of boot leather against stone.

Pulling in tight against the cool granite, he hunched in the shadows, listened, striving to pin down the location of the sound. It came again—from somewhere above. Brandon was climbing to the top of the pile, hoping to catch him below.

Shawn rode out the breathless moments. There was silence again, and then once more that scraping noise. It was closer. A change came into the starlight—as if something had moved through it. He pulled back from the boulders, eyes sweeping the arcing level of the pile.

Harry Brandon, crouched, was silhouetted against the night ten paces away. Head cocked, he held his pistol ready, having given up the rifle for a more quickly managed six gun.

"Last chance, Brandon," Starbuck murmured. "Don't—"

Brandon spun, went to one knee. The weapon in his hand burnt a small orange hole in the night in the same instant that Shawn fired. Starbuck felt a bullet whip past his arm, and fired again.

Brandon slumped forward. His gun slipped from his fingers, clattered noisily upon the rocks. He twisted half about, fought to regain his feet, fell heavily instead and rolled limply back into the clearing.

Starbuck, motionless in the pale glow, sucked in a deep breath. He had hoped to take the man to Wolf Crossing alive, but Brandon had not seen it that way. Holding his pistol in his right hand, Shawn rodded out the spent cartridges, and while tension ebbed slowly from his tall frame, reloaded.

Afterwards he circled the rocks to where Brandon lay. For a time he stared at the slack face and then, bending down, unpinned the star from the man's pocket. Dropping it into a pocket, he turned away.

* * *

The night had been long and cold and a deep thoughtfulness had weighed heavily on Shawn Starbuck. He had tried to avoid a shoot-out—twice—but Harry Brandon, aware no doubt that he had closed all gates behind him, had made his own desperate choice.

At sunup, Shawn roused from his place beside the fire he had built, and crossing to the horse Brandon had been riding, dug around in the saddlebags for food. He found none. A search of the packs the mules carried also failed to turn up anything. Brandon had departed the coulee in such haste he had neglected to take any grub—only gold.

Low in spirit and hungry, Shawn returned to the fire. He could, he supposed, take Brandon's rifle and do a bit of hunting in the grassy saddle beyond the plateau. He'd find rabbits there, he was sure, and one broiled over flames would take the edge off his need and keep him going until he could get back to camp where Dave Gilder waited.

But the idea didn't appeal to him for some reason obscure even to himself, and after a bit, he kicked out the fire, and leading the horse to where Brandon lay, he loaded the body on behind the saddle and secured it.

He turned then to the mules, made certain their loads were riding properly, and linking the string ropes, brought them into the center of the clearing. There he mounted to the saddle. The horse grunted a little under the additional weight and Starbuck knew he was in for some walking before the return trip was over, but it didn't matter. All he wanted now was to get back to Wolf Crossing, rid himself of the unwanted responsibility that had fallen on him, and be on his way.

Moving off the flat, he swung onto the trail and started down the steep grade. A short time later he passed the horse he had been riding when Brandon's bullet had come reaching for him and found, instead, a different target, and then around noon he came into sight of the high, rock ridge where Able Rome and Walt Moody had died.

A thin curl of smoke twisting up from the base of the slope below it told him that Gilder was still there, likely had coffee and a meal on the fire. The thought induced him to put spurs to the lagging horse and jerk impatiently at the rope leading the stolid mules.

Dave was standing at the back edge of the clearing when he rode in. Face expressionless, he made brief acknowledgment of Starbuck's greeting, touched the lifeless shape of Harry Brandon with a glance, and brought his attention again to bear upon Shawn, now swinging off the saddle.

"I'm hating to do this," he said in a tight voice.

Starbuck pivoted slowly. "What's that?"

"You heard," Dave Gilder replied coolly. "I'm taking that gold."

～ 20 ～

Starbuck settled gently on his heels, eyes on the pistol in Gilder's white knuckled hand. The hard, crushing pressure of what he was undertaking had caused him to neglect cocking the weapon. Shawn knew the odds for him to draw his own gun and fire before Dave could correct the error were better than good. There had been enough killing—far too much, in fact.

"What the hell's this all about?"

Sweat covered Gilder's face with a wet shine. "Told you. Gold's mine. I'm taking it—clearing out."

Starbuck shook his head slowly. "Forget it. Be the biggest mistake you ever made."

"No—I made that one a long time ago—when I took my first drink. That gold's the only way I can make up for all I've done. I can square myself, get a new start."

"It's not that easy. You think it'll end here? That mining company won't ever stop hunting you."

"Won't know who to hunt for. Brandon, the posse, and them outlaws—all dead."

"I'm not."

"That there part's up to you. Drop your gun, kick it over to me."

Shawn did not move, continued to study the man. There was a sullen determination in his eyes but beneath it all he detected a current of uncertainty. Dave Gilder was walking a path he never before had trod, and the tenseness of the experience was getting to him. Shrugging, Starbuck lifted his forty-five from its holster, let it fall to the ground. Gilder was still worth gambling on.

119

"Kick it over here."

Shawn complied, folded his arms across his chest. "What's next?"

Dave, squatting slowly, never removing his gaze from Starbuck, recovered the pistol. Straightening, he thrust it under the waistband of his faded denims.

"Up to you—I don't want to leave you laying here dead like all them others," he said, jerking a thumb at the blanket-wrapped bodies of Rome, Moody and the three outlaws lined up on the grass at the edge of the coulee. "Expect it's what I'll have to do if you ain't agreeable."

"To what?"

"Giving me your word."

The strain that gripped Gilder appeared to be tapering off as he talked. Shawn breathed a little easier.

"What's that got to do with it?"

"Everything. I want you to say you'll keep riding, not head back to Wolf Crossing and tell what happened here—and about me taking the gold."

Starbuck said, "No deal, Dave."

Gilder frowned, swallowed nervously. "Not even if I was to give you a part of the gold?"

"It'd make no difference."

Gilder forced a short laugh. "You meaning you ain't got no use for gold?"

"Sure I have—but not that kind. The blood of ten men has been spilled all over it, and that's something I'd not be able to forget. Be the same for you, too, if you go through with this."

"I've got to do it!" Gilder said in a high, desperate tone. "Only way I can fix up what I've done and make it right with my wife and boys!"

"You think that going to them with your pockets full of money's going to wipe out the past? Gold's not what they want from you—it's something else and you damn well know it!"

"But with the gold I can—"

"You can't do anything with it but buy more trouble, make things worse."

Dave Gilder mulled over Shawn's words in a morose

silence. One of the mules stirred restlessly, began to crop at the grass in the coulee.

"No!" Gilder said abruptly. "You ain't changing my mind. I done thought it all out. Got it figured the same as Brandon—and it'll work for me same as it would for him."

Starbuck lifted his hands, allowed them to fall in a gesture of resignation. "It means you'll have to kill me, too."

"I don't want to. You're the only man I've run up against that treated me decent. I owe you for that, but I can't let nothing stand in the way of my wife and boys. They're going to have all the things they've always wanted for and couldn't have."

"You think they'd take any of it knowing what you did to get it?"

"Won't know—"

"They will, Dave, don't fool yourself. You'll show it. You'll keep remembering those dead men laying there and you'll always be wondering if somebody's about to catch up with you and claim the gold—even kill you to get it back."

"It's my only chance—hope," Gilder said doggedly.

"Wrong. You've got a different kind of a chance facing you, one that'll make your family proud of you and let you live the right kind of a life."

Gilder brushed at the sweat on his face with his free hand. "What's that mean?"

"Just this—we're the last of Brandon's posse, the only ones left. We've done what we set out to do, get back the gold that was stolen—and we've got the outlaws who did it. Going to be a big feather in your cap."

Dave laughed scornfully. "Yours—won't be in mine."

"I'm only a part of it, and a stranger to boot. You're the man they know and folks in Wolf Crossing will be looking at you different from now on."

"With all that gold I can—"

"You don't need it. You're licking your whiskey problem and won't need it for a crutch anymore, and you've proved you're as good as any man and due the respect you're bound to get now—"

"Sure'n hell can't raise a family on respect!"

"No, but you can make that respect work for you, provide you with a job that will."

Gilder wagged his head hopelessly. "Job! What kind of a job could I get—a swamper in Ed Christian's saloon?"

"That's the kind the old Dave Gilder could get but not the new one. I'm talking about the man you can be now—not the one you were."

"Still don't mean nothing to me."

"It can. Wolf Crossing needs a marshal now. You can ask to fill in till election time, then run for the job."

Gilder's jaw sagged. "Me? Get elected marshal? Hell, folks'd laugh themselves sick."

"Maybe a little—at first. You've got to expect that. They only remember what you were and it's up to you to prove that things have changed—that you're different now."

"You're talking loco. They'd never let me pin on that star—even if it was just till election."

"I figure they will after I tell them how you dragged yourself down that slope, shot in the leg, to help Brandon when you thought he was in trouble and needed you. That kind of proof they'll understand."

Dave Gilder's expression slowly changed. The strain faded from his features and a flicker of hope touched his eyes. "You really meaning that? You ain't just talking, saying it because I'm holding a gun on you?"

Starbuck smiled. "One that's not even cocked? Not much. I'm only saying what's the truth." He raised his hand, pointed to the blackened pot balanced over the low fire. "It's been a long night. All right if I help myself to some coffee?"

Gilder was staring at the pistol he was holding. He nodded woodenly, a strange look on his face.

Shawn stepped to the circle of stones, picked up a cup. Dumping its cold dregs, he filled it with simmering black liquid. Taking a long drink, he sighed gratefully. "Needed that. Brandon forgot to take grub with him." Reaching into the spider sitting nearby he helped himself to several strips of fried meat and began to eat.

"It just wouldn't work out—not for me," Gilder

said finally, his tone forlorn. "I know how it'd be. Nothing'll ever change."

"Nobody's saying it'll be easy. You've got a long hill to climb, but you can do it if you set your mind to it."

"And if folks let me—"

"They'll throw in with you, work with you."

"I ain't sure," Dave Gilder murmured. "And about this here marshal's job—I can see you getting elected, but me—"

"I'm out of it. I'll be gone, which leaves you the only member of the posse still in Wolf Crossing—the one man left there that got the job done. That's a big recommendation—and people won't be overlooking it."

"Seems kind of funny—me—talking about being the marshal."

"It's the chance you've been waiting for but couldn't find because you were looking for it through the bottom of a bottle. You've got rid of that bottle now, so there's nothing standing in your way."

"I ain't so sure I have—"

"You have, if you keep on believing it."

Hunkered on his heels, Starbuck stole a glance at Gilder. Dave had lowered the pistol, was staring at the ground.

"What's it to be?" he asked quietly. "Put a bullet in me, run with the gold—and spend the rest of your life waiting for a lawman or a Pinkerton detective to step out of the dark with a gun in his hand? Or do we go back to Wolf Crossing and start building a new life for you and your family?"

Gilder stirred helplessly. "I don't know. . . . I just ain't for sure about anything."

"No problem deciding which is right and which is wrong."

"No, it ain't that. It's not for sure I can do all the things you figure I can. I tried before and couldn't make it."

"That's not hard to understand. You hadn't convinced yourself that you could—didn't believe in yourself. And a bottle was the wrong kind of courage. It's not that way now. You've already proved yourself and you've got yourself the chance to grab onto something good—a lawman's star."

Dave Gilder slid his weapon back into the holster. Taking Shawn's pistol from his waistband, he stepped up to the fire, passed it over, butt first His eyes were solemn and there was a resoluteness to his features.

"I'll sure as hell try—"

Shawn came to his feet. "That's all any man can do," he said, and reached into his shirt pocket. Taking the star he had removed from Harry Brandon's body, he pinned it on Gilder's shirt. "You might as well get used to wearing this. I expect it's going to be yours for a long time."

Dave Gilder looked down at the emblem. His hand rose slowly. His fingers touched the cool metal, traced the lettering hesitantly. He swallowed hard.

"I—I don't know—" he mumbled. "Maybe I ought to wait—see—"

"No need. We're the only ones left of Brandon's posse, and I'm just riding through. Only right that you take charge."

Gilder gave that consideration. After a moment he nodded, smiling faintly. And then once again his features clouded.

"Only thing—what about me throwing down on you, planning to take the gold—"

Starbuck shrugged. "It's between you and me, and best forgot. Let's get these bodies loaded up and head out. . . . It's a long way back to Wolf Crossing, Marshal."

～ 21 ～

They rode into the settlement around noon, and by the time they had led their pack train of yellow gold and lifeless bodies to a halt at the livery stable's rack, most of the town was gathered about them, peeking at the shrouded shapes in quiet awe and voicing questions in subdued voices.

Starbuck and Dave Gilder, trail-worn and stiff, dismounted and faced the stunned crowd. A man in the front, his ruddy features reflecting shock and disbelief, stared at them.

"You two the only ones left alive?"

Shawn nodded, started a reply, withheld his words as Ed Christian and four other men shouldered their way briskly through the gathering. The one to Christian's left, small, sharp-faced, with snapping dark eyes, swept the pack train with his glance, whipped it back to Starbuck and Gilder.

"I hear right—there only two of you left?"

"That's it, Mr. Stratton," Dave replied. "Just us."

"My God," Stratton breathed. "Even Brandon—"

"Even him," Gilder said, "only wasn't the way you maybe are thinking. He tried to take the gold himself. He was hooked up with them outlaws—had it all framed up. I got a letter of his proving that. He would've got away with it, too, if it hadn't been for Starbuck. He went after him, brought him and the gold both back."

A mutter of surprise ran through the crowd. Dave waited for it to die, then, looking about apprehensively, said: "I'll make a report on what happened."

Stratton bobbed his head. "Good. We'll be needing it for the town records." He broke off, eyes fixed on the badge pinned to Gilder's shirt pocket. "That Brandon's star you're wearing?"

"Yes, sir. I figured the town'd need a lawman, least-wise until election. Seeing as how I've already been deputized, I'm volunteering to hold down the job—it's all right with you and the rest of the town council."

Someone in the crowd laughed. Several others took it up. Shawn threw a hasty look at Gilder, saw the lines of his face tighten, his skin grow a shade lighter. It was a critical moment, he realized.

"I'm recommending it, if what I say's worth anything to you," Starbuck said, speaking in a loud and clear voice. "If it wasn't for Dave this could've all turned out different."

Stratton shifted his attention to Ed Christian and the three men flanking him closely; evidently they were the council. All nodded.

"All right," Stratton said, coming back to Gilder. "You're the acting marshal, temporary until election time. You sure you can handle it?"

"Yes, sir, I know I can—and I'll prove it to you, to the whole town."

"You're getting your chance," Stratton said. "Now if—"

"Something else," Gilder cut in. "I'd like to say now I'll be running for the job, permanent, when it comes up for voting."

Starbuck smiled. Dave Gilder had gotten the worst part of it over—the declaring of himself—and had discovered he was still alive and breathing and none the worse for it. It would be easier for him now.

Ed Christian pushed forward, extended his hand to Gilder. "I'll tell you this, Dave, I'm for you. Call on me if you need any help."

Gilder grinned broadly. "Obliged. I expect I'll be needing a lot of it—all I can get." He lifted his gaze to cover the crowd. "I hope I can figure on you all voting for me—"

"They get the gold?"

Shawn turned to face two men moving in from the side. Both were dressed in the customary corduroy suits, lace boots and narrow-brimmed hats associated with the mining companies.

"They did," Stratton said coldly, motioning toward the pack train. As the pair hurried to reach the mules, he nodded to Shawn and Gilder. "They're from the Paradise. Been hanging around here since the day after you left. Tall one's named Blaylock—he's the superintendent. The other's Otto Bond, office manager or something like that."

He turned away then, faced the crowd. "Some of you men unload those bodies, get them over to the undertaker's. Being there in the sun ain't helping them any. Tell Amos that Doc Marberry'll be along presently and do his coroner duties. Can bury them later."

"Mr. Mayor—" Blaylock said, moving back into the center of the gathering with his partner. "I want to thank you. The gold's all there. Putting your lawmen on it quick like you did and making the recovery won't be forgotten by the Paradise Mining Company."

"There are the men to thank," Stratton replied, jerking his thumb at Starbuck and Gilder, "them and the ones that died doing it."

"Sorry about them, and like I said, we won't forget it. We aim to transfer a part of our business here as a show of appreciation—"

A cheer went up from the crowd. Blaylock raised his arms for silence.

"That's not all. There'll be a generous reward for these two men—a generous one."

Dave Gilder smiled, evidently seeing the possibilities of sending for his family growing brighter. Shawn caught at Blaylock's arm.

"I'd appreciate it if you'll just turn my part over to the marshal."

The mine superintendent frowned, puzzled. "Sure, Mr.—"

"Starbuck."

"Mr. Starbuck. Whatever you say."

Dave Gilder frowned. "No, it ain't right. I won't let—"

"It's what I want. Sooner you get your wife and boys here, the better it'll be."

Gilder looked down, murmured: "Hell, Starbuck, I don't know how to thank you."

"You know all right. We talked it all out back there in the coulee."

"I guess we did," Dave said slowly. He raised his

head, nodded. "And don't worry none. I'll make it."

"I know you will," Shawn answered, and taking the sorrel's reins, started for the stable.

"Now wait, seems we ought to owe you something," Ed Christian said, halting him with an outstretched hand.

Starbuck turned to him. "Just one thing—a favor. Get folks behind Dave Gilder and elect him marshal. He'll make you a damned good one."

"We'll do it," Christian said promptly. "But what about yourself?"

Shawn brushed at the stubble on his chin. "All I want is to get cleaned up, do a bit of eating and sleeping and then I'm riding on. I got a brother somewhere. I figure he could be in Santa Fe so I'm going to have a look."

Otto Bond, standing on the porch of the Grand Central that next morning with mine superintendent Joe Blaylock, watched Starbuck ride slowly down the street and disappear around the corner of the last building.

"Sure cool customer," he said. "I wish't we could get somebody like him to take over the bullion wagons."

Blaylock hawked, spat into the already dry dust. "The right kind, all right, only they never stick. Always move on—like that one we had working for a spell. Damon his name was."

"Damon," Bond repeated, frowning. "Oh, sure, I remember him now. Come to think of it, they even look something alike. You reckon they're related?"

"Names ain't the same. Don't seem likely."

"Still, he could be a relative—cousin or something."

"Yeh, suppose so. We could've asked if we'd thought."

"Just never come to me. Maybe it won't make any difference."

"Why's that?"

"I recollect Damon saying he was going on to Santa Fe when he quit. They'll probably be bumping into each other if he's still there. Santa Fe's no big town."

"No, it sure ain't. . . . What do you say we eat?"

"I'm ready," Otto Bond said, and stepped down into the street.

THE
HELL
MERCHANT

1 ~

It was a land of majestic beauty, of stirring grandeur, Starbuck thought, easing forward on his saddle as the sorrel loped tirelessly on.

To the west the mighty Sangre de Cristo Mountains, like a towering wall dividing the universe, lifted into a hazy, afternoon sky. Pine, fir, golden-clad aspen and triangular-shaped spruce studded slopes peppered with nodding blue asters, and in the higher levels snow already banked the layered ledges and rugged peaks with glistening white. Here and there a worn face of granite bared its storm-swept surface to the winds as it lay steeped in the secrets of the past, content with memories while it defied time and man.

He'd heard wolves challenging the stars that previous night when he camped, and in the early morning as he moved out, he had twice seen herds of deer, the does with their huge ears cocked forward, the bucks sporting rocking chair racks of antlers as they bounded through the piñon and cedar groves on the lower flats.

Settling back he looked over his shoulder. Behind him lay the rolling hill and grass land that stretched on to the east—to Kansas and farther. Bathed now in the amber glow of the lowering sun, it appeared soft, gentle —and brought to his mind the realization that night was near, that he should be looking for a suitable campsite. He was yet three days out of Santa Fe and had expected to be closer to the mountains by that sundown, but it was evident that he would fall short. He shrugged; it had happened before, this misjudging of distance in the startlingly clear atmosphere.

He disliked camping on open ground and so swung his attention ahead to a not too-distant mass of rock and timber thrusting upward from the surrounding land. That would be Cold Water Mountain, he supposed. There would be a creek and places that enabled him to escape the early morning wind that always came just before sunrise. He'd ride on, make his night stop there.

Touching the gelding with spurs, Starbuck moved on, the sharp, crisp promise of winter in the air definite in his nostrils. It wouldn't be long until icy storms would roar in from the lofty peaks of the Colorados to the north, and the vast country would fall silent under a numbing blanket of white, become a danger to all those who did not respect or know its subtle ways.

The old Santa Fe Trail was behind him, the cutoff favored by some, on farther east. He had crossed the main route earlier, had been surprised to find no one pursuing its deeply rutted course. But it was October—late—and he guessed it was only normal. His own plans called for getting out of the high country before winter set in; he'd go on to Arizona immediately if he failed to find Ben in Santa Fe.

Ben . . . Shawn Starbuck's square-cut features grew thoughtful. A tall, lean man, not long out of boyhood, he sat in his saddle in an easy, offhand manner. His eyes, gray-blue in the slimming light, were overhung by a shelf of thick brows and the dark hair, inclined to curl about his neck when he neglected to trim it, as it was now, had a deep, glossy sheen.

He appeared much older than his years. The change that had come upon him when he was turned from an Ohio farm boy into a trail rider in quest of a brother had quickly weathered him, laid its mark upon him to the point where age was indeterminate and there was no calculation in time. Trouble, danger, bitter disappointment and experience had interfused to turn boy into man, convert youth to age without the building of days.

But if he were aware of the rapid transition, Shawn did not regret it, and the life of constant motion he led never palled, perhaps because it had all begun in his early years and he knew no other.

There was no denying, however, there were times when he felt a tug at his heart and the pointed pangs of loneliness did catch up and fill him with a dark thoughtfulness. He would dwell then upon what might have been, on a life purely his own with no hampering strings attached; he would remember his dream of a home, a ranch, a woman such as Rhoda Hagerman whom he'd met in faraway south Texas, or the quiet-faced girl in Hebren Valley.

They, and others, had much to offer and he'd felt the stirring need to halt, to settle down, take a wife and fulfill his own needs, but in the end he had faced up to the duty that, like an unbending bar of steel, dictated his way of life. All such must be denied him until he found Ben and the matter of Hiram Starbuck's estate was settled. . . . But—someday—

Shawn brushed his hat to the back of his head, stared at the gradually approaching mountain where he intended to make camp. Day's-end hush had fallen over the land and the purple heads of the bunch grass that carpeted the flats and slopes were nodding slowly from side to side in the faint breeze. . . . It would be good to stop, to climb down from the sorrel's back; he'd been in the saddle since sunup and the muscles of his legs were beginning to take note of the fact.

Somewhere off to the right a quail called into the quiet—the sound plaintive and lost. The small, blue-scaled birds would have their nesting done by now and be gathering into coveys. A brace would make a tasty evening meal if he had some means of getting them. Back on the farm he and Ben had often trapped them, brought them in to their mother, Clare, as a special table treat. . . . But that was another day, another time —another world.

He shrugged off his thoughts. He was in no mood to remember, to think of how it had been once. His mind now wanted only to consider the present; bed down for the night, then on to Santa Fe with the sun. If Ben wasn't there, move on. Ben could be anywhere in that broad expanse known as the frontier.

It was a task best taken as it came. *All journeys begin with the first step,* he had heard his schoolteacher mother say many times. *Each thing done must have a beginning.* So it was with him, so it had been—and so it would be until, at last, he found Ben and the quest would end.

He drew the sorrel to a slow walk, eyes now on the dark green of the mountain just ahead. A short distance within it he caught the faint sparkle of silver; a creek. That was where he would halt. Veering the gelding around a rocky, brush-cluttered mound, he angled for that point.

He pulled to a stop in a small couleé bordered on one side by the murmuring stream, the other by low bushes and by rocks that had in times past come tumbling down the steep slopes during the wild storms that periodically lashed the area.

The last of the sun's rays were fanning up in the west, filling the sky with a riotous blend of gold, yellow, and orange across which an arrowhead of geese knifed its way. He watched the migrating flock briefly and then turned aside, aware that he had little time left in which to prepare his camp before darkness set in. But that realization did not move him to undue haste.

He remained in the saddle while the sorrel stretched its neck and bobbed its head impatiently toward the stream, allowing its eyes to probe the brush and the deep shadows behind the rocks intently. He could neither hear nor see anything, man or beast, yet Shawn was conscious of an uneasiness.

The quail called again into the stillness, and far up on the mountain a coyote barked a reply. Starbuck's wide shoulders twitched, and swinging off the sorrel, he led it to the water. He waited a few moments, permitting the big horse only a few swallows, and then drew him away; he could take his fill later after the heat was gone from his body.

Shawn glanced again to the western sky, judged he'd best collect his firewood while there was still some light, tend the sorrel later. Picketing the animal, he began to rustle up dry limbs, branches, and other bits of litter that would burn, moving about slowly, quietly, the strong feeling that he was not alone, that he was being watched, yet plaguing his mind.

He piled what he considered a sufficient quantity of fuel in the center of the clearing and crossed back to the gelding. Tripping the tongue of the cinch buckle, he pulled off the hull, draped it over a log in a fashion designed to keep the stirrup flaps and skirt straight, and then spread the padded blanket over it to shed the night's moisture. That done, he carried his bedroll and saddlebags to the coulee and dropped them near a fair-sized rock and, squatting, began to assemble some of the wood for a fire.

Starbuck came up fast, hearing a quick step behind him. His left hand swept down instinctively for the low-slung pistol on his hip, dropped away as an iron hard fist crashed into the side of his head.

Dazed, he went over sideways, and again from instinct, rolled fast as a towering shape surged toward him through a thin, gray haze. He gained his feet, and slightly off balance, met the oncoming figure with a stiff left and a wide, swinging right.

The man grunted as the blows drove home, but he did not falter. Shawn fell back before the crowding hulk, the flailing arms. He took a sharp rap to the head, another to the ribs. He was having difficulty getting set, planting his feet squarely under him on the uneven ground. A skilled fighter, well trained by old Hiram, he could hold his own ordinarily in any sort of combat— catch as catch can, or scientific—but he had been taken off guard, and, dazed at the outset, his reflexes were dull and not functioning efficiently.

He sought to back away, allow his brain to clear, his legs to steady, but the powerful stranger was giving him no chance; he continued to bore in, hammering furiously, relentlessly with big, hamlike fists, and Shawn could find time only to ward off the sledging blows.

The mist was fading slowly from his eyes. He was beginning to shake off the effects of the initial onslaught. His breathing had evened and he felt strength coming back into his legs. . . . A few moments more and he would be in condition to reply to the attack in kind. . . . *If you get in bad trouble,* Hiram had once told him, *back off, and keep backing 'til you get your head again. Then your chance will come.*

Starbuck, arms now raised in a rigid, protective stance, continued to move, to feint from side to side as he deflected the blows directed at him. . . . A big man, one with a thick, black beard, hard, glittering eyes, and broad, strong teeth. Anger flared through Shawn. What the hell was this all about? Who was the stranger—and why did he jump him? As far as he could recall they'd never crossed trails before. The anger cooled as quickly as it had come, leveled off into grimness. Those were questions he'd get the answer to shortly.

Eyes narrowed, watchful, Shawn fell back a long step, dodged as the man lunged forward in his wake. He snapped a punishing left to the side of the dark face, followed with a right that cracked as it landed. An ordinary man would have dropped to his knees from the blow, but the bearded giant only grunted, paused, and then came on.

Shawn struck again quickly, staggered him with another hard swing, capped it off with a stinging left to the eyes, and took a step away, once more laying a trap.

His motion was checked abruptly as a spur caught against an exposed root or some other obstacle on the ground. He rocked forward, tried to save himself from going over backwards. The bearded, distorted face was suddenly before him. A solid ball of knuckles rushed toward him through the dim light, connected squarely with the point of his chin, and he was lost in a fog of blackness.

2 ~

Starbuck opened his eyes slowly. His head ached and pain throbbed in his legs and arms. Without moving he stared about. It was full dark. The bearded man was hunched by the fire in the center of the coulee methodically stirring a concoction of some sort in a sooted spider with the blade of a skinning knife. A tin of coffee simmered at the edge of the flames.

The pain seeping through him was being caused by bonds drawn too tightly about his ankles and wrists, he realized, and he shifted slightly to ease the pressure of the buckskin thongs. The change did not draw the attention of his captor and Shawn continued to study him. . . . A big man, as he had noted at the start of the fight, well over two hundred pounds and probably an inch or two more than six feet in height. Burly and powerfully built, he was wide across the chest and his hairy arms were thick and muscular like those of men who followed the trade of blacksmith.

He had washed his face and combed the heavy shock of black hair that capped his head as well as brushing out the wedge of beard that jutted from the lower part of his features. Shawn could not see his eyes but he recalled them from before—hard and flashing, matching exactly the brutal set of the mouth.

Starbuck frowned as questions again pushed into his mind. What did the fellow want with him? That it was no holdup was apparent; he wouldn't be lying there trussed up like a sacrificial goat if that was the case— and the bearded man would have long since taken his leave. The same applied if, afoot for some reason, he had wanted the sorrel.

Considering his thoughts, Shawn swore silently, cursing the vagaries that somehow seemed to conspire in throwing problems onto the trails he followed. At times it seemed to him that luck or fate, or whatever it was that guided men's destiny, was determined that he should never find Ben.

The odor of cooking food began to hang in the coulee. It smelled good, stirred the hunger within Shawn; he hadn't eaten since daybreak, but the anger and resentment within him pushed the need aside. He pulled himself to a sitting position.

"Like to know what the hell this is all about," he said in a taut voice.

The bearded man paused in his stirring, looked up through bushy brows. "I ain't needing none of your lip."

"You're getting it anyway."

The man by the fire rose slowly, knife blade dripping. His eyes squeezed down into slots in which the glow of the flames reflected dully, and for a moment he seemed about to step across the narrow space that separated him from Starbuck and strike with the blade he was holding. And then he shrugged as if having second thoughts.

"You're my prisoner, that's what it's all about."

"Know that," Shawn said dryly. "Why?"

"Catching outlaws—that's my business," the big man said, squatting again and reaching for a tin plate. "You want some grub? I ain't caring one way or another whether you do or not."

Shawn nodded, continued to study the man at the fire. "I'm no outlaw," he said after a time. "Whoever you think I am, you're mistaken. I never saw you before—don't even know you——"

"Name's Hillister. Luke Hillister."

"Still makes you a stranger, and I doubt if you ever heard of me either—Starbuck."

"Names don't mean nothing. Can be changed easy," Hillister said. Taking up a second plate he filled it with the stew he had thrown together, again straightened to his full height, and circling the fire, placed the plate at Shawn's side.

"Ain't trusting you with something to eat with. Have to use your fingers," he said, looking down at Starbuck. "Now, I'm aiming to untie your wrists. You make a move to jump me and I'll kill you. Understand? Don't make a damn whether I hand you over to the law dead or alive. That plain?"

"It's plain," Starbuck said, leaning forward so Hillister could get to the leather linking his wrists. It was also clear what the problem was; Hillister, evidently some kind of a lawman, took him to be a wanted outlaw and was planning to turn him over to the nearest sheriff or marshal.

His hands came free suddenly and he dropped his arms, easing the pain in his shoulders, but not trusting Hillister, he remained motionless, waited until the man had returned to the fire. Then, picking up his own plate, he began to eat.

It was good stew—meat-chunked potatoes, onions, and some sort of greens apparently gathered along the creek. Shawn only barely noticed, and after a few bites, paused.

"You a lawman?"

Hillister's large head came up. "Kind of a special one. I take hold where them others leave off."

Shawn considered that, finally devised its meaning. "Bounty hunter," he murmured.

"There's some who call me that."

"Seems it fits."

Hillister wiped at his mouth with the back of a hand. "Ain't just the way you're a-figuring. Law's not what it ought to be. Soft, too easy on killers and the like. And them badge-toters, they ain't anxious to go out after the real outlaws. Make it my job."

"Well, you're wrong where I'm concerned. Not an outlaw. Never was."

"Sure wearing that gun like one."

Shawn stared. "That why you jumped me? That what you're going by?"

Hillister spat. "Good a sign as any."

"You're loco," Starbuck said flatly.

The bearded bounty hunter paused in his eating, eyes narrowing again. "That there lip of your'n is going to get——"

"Happens my first name was taken from an Indian word," Starbuck continued. "Looking at it the way you do that makes me an Indian. . . . Same kind of fool reasoning."

Luke Hillister relaxed, lifted the tin plate to his thick lips, and drained it of the last bits of stew. Setting it aside, he reached for the coffee.

"What're you doing in this part of the country?" he asked, conversationally.

"Riding through. On my way to Santa Fe. . . . I'll ask you the same question."

"Hunting two brothers, that's what——"

"And you saw me instead—grabbed me."

Hillister seemed not to be listening. Placing the can of coffee on the ground, he reached into an inside pocket, produced a small card. For several moments he was lost in the contemplation of it, and then returning it to his brush jacket, he once again took up the tin.

"You wanting a swallow of coffee?" he asked, thrusting it at Shawn.

Starbuck accepted, downed a mouthful of the black, bitter liquid. "That's the way of it, wasn't it?" he pressed, handing back the can.

"Like I said, catching outlaws is my job."

"Well, you've made a hell of a mistake this time," Shawn snapped in disgust.

"Maybe, but I'm misdoubting that. Ain't never been wrong before, so I ain't worrying none now." Hillister began to toy with the skinning knife, turning it over and over between his thick fingers while he cupped the tin of coffee with his free hand. "What're you heading to Santa Fe for? You meeting some of your friends there?"

"Looking for my brother. Chance he'll be there."

"Meaning you ain't sure?"

Shawn nodded. Perhaps if he told Luke Hillister of his purpose he might convince the man that he was no outlaw.

"Just don't know. He ran off from home—Ohio—

ten years ago. Been trying to find him, settle some family business. Name's Ben—or he could be calling himself Damon Friend."

The bounty hunter's eyes sharpened. "The law after him, too?"

Starbuck hesitated. There was a charge against Ben pending in southern New Mexico Territory. Nothing serious, the sheriff had assured him, but a matter that required his brother's presence to clear it up. He doubted Hillister would understand that, however; best he skirt the truth.

"Not an outlaw, if that's what you're driving at."

"Then why's he running and hiding?"

"Don't know that he is. Thing is we lost track of each other—and this is a big country to find a man in."

"Ain't so hard if a man's of a real mind. Been riding it plenty and I always find who I'm looking for. What's your brother look like?"

"Not sure. Expect we sort of look alike."

Hillister tipped the coffee can to his mouth, emptied it, dropped it to the ground. Far up on the mountain a coyote yipped into the night. The bounty hunter listened to the discordant sound for a time, finally shook his head.

"You think I'm believing a yarn like that? You ain't sure of his name and you don't know what he looks like—and you're traipsing all over the country hunting him! Mighty farfetched, was you to ask me."

"No more farfetched than your grabbing every man you run across that looks like an outlaw to you," Shawn replied quietly.

"Him changing his name——"

"Did that after he had a ruckus with our pa. Said he didn't want any connection with the family. And how he looks—been ten years—we were just kids when I saw him last. Man changes plenty when he grows out of being a boy."

Hillister, lightly rubbing the swelling under his left eye where Shawn's fist had left its mark, grunted, shrugged his shoulders. Reaching into his jacket again, he produced the card he'd viewed earlier, once more fell to considering it. It could be a picture, a tintype,

Starbuck decided. Evidently it meant much to the bounty hunter.

"Riding like you say you do, you ever run across a man you think might be him?"

Luke Hillister pocketed the picture, and leaning forward, began to collect the utensils scattered near the fire.

"Don't recollect nobody like that," he said without stopping. "Name sure ain't familiar. There's a bite or two of this sonofabitch left. You want it?"

Shawn glanced at the spider Hillister held out to him. The remainder of the stew, cold now, was little more than caked grease.

"Had enough," he said. "What're you aiming to do next?"

The bounty hunter came to his feet, the frying pan, plates, coffee tin, and spoons, together with his skinning knife, all clutched in his big hands.

"We're sleeping right here tonight," he replied. "Then, comes tomorrow, I'm doing you a favor. I figure you're a goddamn, no-account outlaw—you're claiming you ain't—so I'm trotting you back to Cimarron and letting Bart Trueman—he's the sheriff—look you up. When he gets the wanted dodger out on you, you'll see I know what I'm doing."

"He won't find one," Starbuck said, and let it drop. The sheriff would settle it—but Cimarron was north, in the opposite direction of Santa Fe. It meant losing a day or more.

"You'll be wasting your time and mine," he said, sighing. "But if that's what it'll take to convince you, I'm for it. . . . Like it better if we headed south, however."

"No sheriff that way—not until we get clean to Santa Fe—and I ain't aiming to be bothered with you that long. Got other cats to skin."

"Those two brothers?"

Hillister bobbed his head, moved toward the creek with his collection of pans. "Live around here somewheres and Santa Fe's three days' riding. Cost me a whole week was I to take you there. Can get to Cimarron tomorrow."

"Still means you'll lose two days and those brothers could get away. Turning me loose now——"

"You ain't doing nothing but blowing your breath," the bounty hunter said without pausing. "We're camping here and going to Cimarron tomorrow. . . . Now, set quiet while I wash up these here things. You make a move to get away and I'll put a bullet in your head. Easier to haul your kind in across a saddle, anyway. Less bother."

"Expect it is, only when you're wrong you've got murder on your hands."

"Ain't ever been wrong yet—and I don't figure I am with you."

"Comes a first time for everything," Starbuck said and lay back.

His hands were free and he could get to the knife he carried inside his left boot, slice through the buckskin binding his ankles. But it would be a mistake; Hillister was watching him closely, would shoot him down the instant he made a try to escape. Best to wait for a better opportunity—the bounty hunter could forget to tie his wrists or possibly get careless and, at close quarters, turn his back. Then would be the time to act.

3 ~

Luke Hillister did not forget. After completing his cleaning chore, he had crossed to where Shawn lay, roughly pulled the tall rider's arms behind his back, and tied them firmly at the wrists with the same strip of rawhide. In that position Starbuck spent an uncomfortable night. Although he tried for an hour or more after the bounty hunter had fallen asleep to work his fingers into the boot where he carried his knife, he found it impossible and eventually gave it up.

Silent, an early morning sourness claiming him, Hillister prepared a quick breakfast of fried meat, warmed bread, and coffee, and not long before sunrise they were mounted and striking north for Cimarron. The bounty hunter took no chances; he again restored the bonds to Starbuck's wrists, removed only those that linked his ankles, thus permitting him to bestride the sorrel. As an additional precaution, he attached a lead rope to the gelding's bit ring and fastened it to his own saddle in pack-horse fashion.

Shawn had given Hillister a great deal of thought during the long, cold night. That the man was no ordinary manhunter had become evident to him. With Hillister it was a passion bordering on a mania and unquestionably ranged far beyond the matter of cash reward. He appeared to be a man more on a crusade of vengeance, one driven by a determination to track down and kill or capture any and all malefactors regardless of situation or circumstances.

There was something chewing on the big, dark bearded man, Starbuck finally concluded, something

18

out of the past that possessed him, turned him into a ruthless, single-minded killer at large.

"This business of yours," Shawn said after a lapse of several miles had occurred; "you work out of some town—some lawman's office?"

Hillister shook his head. "Ain't got no use for badge-toters. Done told you that."

"Then how do you collect your rewards?"

"Only time I ever have something to do with them."

"You called the sheriff at Cimarron by name. Guess you've done business with him before."

Hillister was looking up, his gaze following the graceful dipping and gliding of an eagle high above a line of palisades to their left.

"Been a couple of times," he replied. "But we ain't friends. Ain't never no friend of a lawman."

Starbuck shifted on his saddle. It would be pleasant riding through the broad, green country had it been under different conditions. The air was cool and fresh and the miles-distant peaks around them appeared to be within easy reach.

It brought to his mind the words an old Arizona prospector had uttered once when they were standing on the edge of a bluff and looking out over a vast panorama of country: *so clear a man could see all the way to the Pearly Gates,* had been his observation. So it was there in far northern New Mexico, but Shawn was getting little enjoyment from it.

The buckskin was cutting into his wrists and the forced position of his shoulders was causing the muscles of his back to throb. He thought again of the knife in his boot, estimated his chances of getting it. It would require leaning far over, working it out of its sheath with the tips of his fingers, and then, after reversing the bone-handled blade, manipulating it in a manner that would cut through the tough thongs.

It would be risky; Hillister glanced back periodically—and the process would require time. Like as not they would reach Cimarron long before he could complete the task. Best he just swallow his pride and indignation and hope the sheriff—Bart Trueman the bounty hunter had called him—would be in his office when they arrived and could clear things up to Hillister's satisfaction.

He settled his eyes on the bounty hunter's thick shoulders, moved his arms again to ease the dull pain. "You making much money doing this?"

Luke Hillister stirred. "Can't see as that's any of your business!"

"Maybe not. Was only wondering. Long as you've been at it, seems you ought to have a pile by now."

"Well, I ain't. Living—what I've got to pay for— takes most of it. Been saving some for the day when I—"

The big man's voice trailed off into silence. Shawn realized he had struck a chord deep within Hillister, one that could lead to an understanding of the darkness that filled him.

"Guess everybody's got something in mind he's working and hoping for."

"Reckon so. Ain't always easy to come by, however."

"Nothing good ever is."

"For a fact, but I'm getting it someday. Place of my own, place where I can take Ellie, make her happy and comfortable."

Luke's low voice faded into nothing again. Shawn said, "Ellie—she your wife?"

Hillister spat impatiently. "No need for you knowing that."

"Guess not, but if it's her you're working to get money for, this is one time you'll fail her."

Hillister muttered something, brushed at his face. The day was beginning to warm as the horses plodded steadily on. Starbuck, twisting his arms, managed to loosen the buttons of his brush jacket and pull at the collar of his shirt, relieving the heat to some extent.

Another hour passed slowly by. They entered a long valley, crossed, climbed to the opposite rim. The horses were sweating freely and Hillister curved off the trail and halted in the shadow of a broadly spreading tree.

"Aiming to rest the animals a mite," he said. "Just you stay in the saddle."

Starbuck only shrugged. Dismounting, stretching his legs and moving about would have eased the cramp in his muscles, but he knew it would be useless to argue about it. Slumped forward, he watched the bounty hunter dig into his inner pocket again. Spurring the sorrel ahead carefully, he glanced over Hillister's shoulder. It was a tintype, one bearing the likeness of a woman and two young boys not yet in their teens. The woman was small and pretty.

"That your wife and sons?"

At the question Luke Hillister started violently. Jerking away, he thrust the photograph into his jacket and whirled. His broad face was angry and his dark eyes sparked.

"Keep your goddamn lip to yourself! I won't have the likes of you ever talking about them—hear?"

Shawn smiled. "Suit yourself. . . . No sense in a man being touchy about his family, though. Fine looking, all of them."

"Shut up—ain't telling you again! Don't want you even a-thinking about them! You keep on and I'll take you on into Cimarron a-laying across your saddle. Now, get back—get back!"

Starbuck eased the gelding away. Hillister, his face glistening with sweat, eyes still bright, abruptly hauled up on the reins of his grazing horse, and, yanking at the lead rope, moved on.

Shawn urged the sorrel forward, breaking the sudden tautness of the line and permitting his mount to lower its head to the usual angle. He was convinced now that Luke Hillister was not quite sane. He had seen violence and death in the big man's eyes in those brief moments and he was glad now he had made no effort to escape. With the odds the way they were he most probably would have ended up, as the bounty hunter had threatened, across his saddle. He'd hold his peace until they reached Cimarron.

Strangely, it was Hillister who broke the silence several miles later. He had calmed and his voice was low and conversational, and he was evidently speaking thoughts that were running through his oddly twisted mind.

"This here working for something you want—a dream maybe some folks calls it—there ain't nothing wrong with a man doing that. . . . Sort of keeps him going when things get real tough. Ain't no reason why I can't have me a dream, same as other people."

Starbuck shook his head. "None at all."

"And getting it the way I do—sort of selling killers and renegades into hell—there ain't nothing wrong with that either."

"Not when they have it coming to them."

"Just what I mean. Man earns what he gets. There's something in the Bible saying that a man living by the sword's going to be dying by it."

"Expect most outlaws know that's how it'll be for them. Part of the bargain they make with themselves."

"Getting caught and hung—that what you mean?"

"Sure. They know what's right and what's wrong, and they're willing to gamble on their chances of beating it out. Some do."

"And that's where I come in," Hillister said promptly. "I don't let them beat it. Just can't see why some folks look at me the way they do—like I was dead wrong—and treat me worse'n they do a dog because I'm doing it. . . . Not that I give a goddamn!"

"Probably because you hunt a man down for money——"

"That don't make no sense! Sheriffs and them other lawmen, they get paid for doing it."

"Part of their job—what they're hired to do."

"No difference that I can see. A outlaw is a outlaw, and who it is that brings him in oughtn't to bother nobody."

Starbuck's shoulders twitched. "Could be that regular lawmen usually try to keep a prisoner alive so's he can stand a trial, have a fair hearing in court. Bounty hunters aren't so particular—seem to prefer, in fact, to bring whoever they've caught in dead. Easier that way—you made that plain to me yourself."

"Can't see where that cuts any butter either. They're being hauled in to hang, and they're going to be dead, if the law does what it's supposed to, anyway—so what's the holler?"

"If you don't know," Shawn replied quietly, "there's not much chance of me making you see it."

"Maybe so, but right's right, and they earned what they've got coming, no matter how."

"And if a man's innocent—like me? What about him? What if you go ahead and do the executing yourself? That makes it murder and you're no better than any other killer."

"Always sure of what I'm doing. Just plain don't make no mistakes like that."

"You're making one now."

"And you're setting on that saddle, not hung across it——"

"But what if I made a run for it, tried to escape?"

"Reckon I'd have to kill you," Hillister said blandly.

"Which would make you a murderer in the same class as the killers you say you're after. How'd you explain it?"

The bounty hunter brushed his hat to the front of his head, scratched at the thick thatch covering it. "Why, I'd just say I had to do it, that's all. Was bringing you in and you tried to escape. Had to shoot."

"You think the law would let it go at that?"

"Sure. One man, more or less, don't mean nothing to them badge-toters. They'd figure you was guilty of something anyway, else you wouldn't have tried to run.

"You just don't understand how things is, Starbuck. It's mighty important that I keep hunting and bringing in killers and outlaws. Country's got to be shed of them so's decent folks'll be safe. You ought to understand that!"

Shawn fell silent. Being around Luke Hillister was like sitting on a powder keg while somebody played with lighted matches. The harsh, almost wild pitch of his voice, the fanatical gleam in his eyes made it clear that the slightest thing could set him off. He'd not argue

with the man anymore; he'd wait, let Sheriff Trueman
straighten him out.

Starbuck raised his head, looked beyond Hillister
as they topped a low rise. A sigh slipped from his lips.
The scatter of buildings in the hollow below would be
Cimarron.

4 ~

Lambert's Saloon . . . DeBaca's Livery Stable . . .
The St. James Hotel . . . Cimarron News & Press . . .
Brick House Bar . . . N. Solomon, General Merchandise . . . Starbuck's glance idly ran down the street, as
he ignored the interested stares of several persons moving along the sidewalks and of a group of blue-uniformed soldiers lounging in the shade of a cottonwood
near the hotel. They'd be from Fort Union, he supposed.

He knew a man from Cimarron—or at least, had
known. Allison his name was, a slim, limping gunhawk
who handled a weapon with amazing speed and deadly
accuracy. They had met, united forces briefly in some
trouble, and then parted. Allison had been sort of a
leader in a range war that had raged in that part of
New Mexico—something to do with a foreign-owned
syndicate, the local ranchers, and a cattle king who
had possessed at the time almost two million acres
of prime land. Shawn wondered, as they drew up before the sheriff's office, if Allison was still around.

The soldiers and two or three other men began to
drift toward the jail. Hillister, ignoring them, swung
from his saddle, looped the reins around the hitchrack
crossbar, and, hand resting on his pistol, turned to
watch Starbuck, hampered by bound wrists, come off
the sorrel.

As Shawn dropped to the ground, the bounty hunter
caught him by the shoulder, shoved him roughly toward
the open doorway of the lawman's quarters. Starbuck
swore as anger flared through him, but he said nothing

25

to Hillister, simply righted himself and entered the squat, adobe brick building.

Bart Trueman, a thin, gray man with a trailing mustache and small, beadlike eyes, was standing in the rear of the room, arms folded across his chest, legs apart. Leaning against the opposite wall was a short, skull-faced individual in rumpled business suit. A discussion had apparently been taking place between them, one interrupted by the bounty hunter and his prisoner.

Trueman waited until they had halted in front of the scarred table that served as a desk, and then nodded curtly to Hillister.

"Who's this?"

The bearded bounty hunter flicked a glance at the small crowd collected outside the doorway and said, "Claims his name's Starbuck. I figure him for a liar. . . . Want you to look him up," he added, dropping Shawn's pistol onto the table.

Starbuck felt the lawman's cold eyes rake him from head to toe. "That your real name, mister?"

"Same one I've had since I was born."

"You prove it?"

"If I have to," Shawn said.

Trueman was silent for a long moment and then moved up to the table. Reaching into a basket he took up a stack of printed reward posters, and sinking into a chair, began to go through them.

"Name don't ring no bell," he murmured.

"I'm betting it ain't his real one," Hillister said.

The sheriff paused, leveled his gaze at the bounty hunter. Anger was stirring him. "Then why the hell'd you bring him in if you don't know for sure who he is?"

Luke Hillister drew himself up stiffly. "Can see from looking at him that he's a bad one—wearing that gun low and tied down like he was—and it sure ain't brand new!" Raising his arm he pointed a thick finger at the weapon on the desk. "See for yourself, can't you?"

The man in the business suit pulled away from the wall, a look of amazement on his features. "You mean that's the reason you brought him in?" he asked in an incredulous tone.

The bounty hunter's eyes brightened. He clawed impatiently at his beard. Trueman glanced at the speaker, shook his head. "I'll handle this, Cameron," he said and continued to leaf through the stack of dodgers.

"That's him!" Hillister yelled suddenly, lunging forward and stabbing one of the posters with a forefinger. "Him, sure'n hell!"

The sheriff devoted a moment's study to the printed photograph on the sheet, shook his head, and leaned back. "Ain't him. This here's Buck Ward—and I know Buck."

"I'm telling you it's him!" Hillister shouted. "You just ain't wanting to jail him—and pay me my reward!"

Trueman raised his eyes to the crowd outside his office. The murmuring that had risen silenced immediately.

"Different man," he said and continued to go through the remainder of the posters. Finished, he stacked them between his fingers and dropped them back into the wire basket. "I got nothing on you, Starbuck."

"Knew that," Shawn said and extended his bound wrists. "Be obliged if you'll cut me loose."

"No—you ain't going to do that!" Hillister yelled, hand dropping to his pistol.

Bart Trueman's features froze as his eyes narrowed. He came to his feet slowly. "Don't give me any trouble, Hillister," he said in an icy voice. "You made a fool mistake this time. Admit it—and ride on out."

"You're just crooking me——"

"Get moving, Hillister—unless you want me to lock you up!"

The bounty hunter whirled angrily, eyes burning. "I'm going," he snarled, "but I ain't forgetting this! I ain't forgetting nothing!"

Shawn turned, watched the bounty hunter stamp heavily out of the room and cross to where his horse waited. A moment later he felt his wrists separate as the lawman cut the thongs binding him.

"Tried to tell him I was no outlaw," he said, facing Trueman. "Can give you the names of a few men who'll

vouch for me if you're not sure. Nearest'll be Wyatt
Earp in Dodge City."

The sheriff's eyes flickered. "Not necessary . . . You
riding through or did something special bring you to
Cimarron?"

"Was on my way to Santa Fe," Starbuck said, chafing
his wrists to restore circlulation.

"And Hillister jumped you?"

"While I was making camp. At Cold Water Mountain. Tried to tell him——"

"Pretty hard to tell that jasper anything," Trueman
said. "About half crazy. Pretty lucky for you he brought
you in alive."

Shawn picked up his gun, dropped it into its holster.
The crowd had dissipated, but the man called Cameron
still leaned against the wall.

"How's it happen you let somebody like him run
loose? Seems pretty dangerous."

"Reckon he is but there ain't nothing I can do about
it," the lawman said stiffly. "He ain't done nothing
wrong—yet. If he does, and it happens in my county,
I'll grab him quick."

"That'll be too late for the man he makes a mistake on. . . . He hang around here regularly?"

"Nope, just drifts back and forth all through the
country—Colorado, Texas, Arizona—even far as Cali-
fornia, I've heard. These parts mostly, however. Got
a wife in a sanitarium somewhere around Denver."

"Sanitarium? Saw him looking at a picture of her
and two boys. Was real touchy about it."

"Boys are dead—and she might as well be," Bart
Trueman said, settling back in his chair. "That's what
set old Luke Hillister off."

Starbuck frowned. "Figured there was something
wrong with him. Met a few bounty hunters in my time
but none of them like him. Seems to have a special
hate on for all outlaws—more than's ordinary."

"Natural. Was because a bunch raided his farm
one day—was back a few years ago. Caught his wife
and boys. Killed them and done some mighty bad
things to her. She lost her mind because of it.

"Reckon Luke sort of lost his, too, when he found

them. Ended up with him putting her in that place near Denver and him starting out to catch—or kill—every outlaw he could get tabs on. Does it all legal. Hands them over to the nearest lawman he can find, collects his reward, and moves on. Found out from the sheriff up in Canyon City that he uses the money he gets to pay for his wife's keep."

"Told me he was saving to buy a place. Aims to make a home for her, I guess."

Trueman shrugged. "Ain't never heard about that. Just no figuring a man like him. He say where this place he's getting is?"

Starbuck shook his head. "Never mentioned it."

"Well, I'm hoping it ain't around here. Place is just healing up from the war we had. Can do without trouble for a spell—a long spell."

"Don't think you'll see the last of him—at least not right away. He's looking for two brothers. Was after them when he jumped me."

The lawman frowned, stroked his mustache. Cameron once again drew away from the wall.

"He say what their names were?"

"No——"

"It'll be the Kings," Cameron said, facing Trueman. "Can't be anybody else."

"Expect you're right, but they don't live in my county. Be up to somebody else to look after them."

"But you can't——"

Bart Trueman came to his feet, extended his hand to Shawn. "Right sorry Hillister put you through what he did. Sort of gives us a bad name."

"No fault of yours," Starbuck replied. "And speaking of names, I used to know a man from here. Was called Allison. He still around?"

The lawman's manner changed swiftly. He withdrew his hand, considered Shawn coldly.

"Clay Allison?"

"That's him. Like to pass the time of day——"

"Moved on—to Colorado," Trueman said flatly. "He a close friend of yours?"

"Guess you could say that. We swapped favors once."

"Well, he ain't here no more. . . . Expect you'll be moving on."

It was more a statement of fact than a question, and its implication was clear. Evidently friends of Clay Allison were unwelcome.

"Seems I am," Starbuck said dryly, and turned for the door. "Obliged to you for pulling that bounty hunter off my back."

Bart Trueman grunted indifferently. "Reckon it comes under the heading of being my job."

5 ～

Shawn stepped out into the sunlight, moved up to the sorrel at the hitchrack. He heard a sound behind him, turned. It was the man called Cameron.

"Like to have a word with you."

Starbuck smiled tightly, jerked his head at the sheriff's office. "Don't think the law wants me around any longer it takes me to mount up and ride."

Cameron frowned and then nodded as understanding came to him. "Oh, Clay Allison. Don't hold that against Bart. Truth is, Clay's a friend of his, but he's a man trouble just naturally dogs along with, and after all the hell that roared in and out of here during the range war, Bart'd as soon not have him or any of his kind in the county. This place was an armed camp for quite a while."

"Not sure I'm being complimented by being put in the same class as Allison or not, but from what I know of the man, I'd say I am. What did you want to talk about?"

"That crazy bastard of a Hillister and the Kings. Can we do it over a drink? I'm a mite dry."

Starbuck shrugged, said, "Why not?" and, freeing the sorrel's leathers, led him toward the rack at Lambert's Saloon. Anchoring the big horse there, he followed Cameron into the low-ceilinged, dark structure and sat down at a table in the corner.

The bartender stepped up, bringing a half-empty bottle, apparently Cameron's private stock, and two glasses, and turned away. Two men standing at the

31

counter paused to watch and then also resumed their original positions.

Cameron poured drinks, lifted his, said *"Salud"* and tossed it off. Then, "Like to know what all it was Hillister said about the Kings."

"Don't know that it was the Kings he was talking about," Shawn replied, downing the liquor. "Only mentioned it was two brothers he was after."

Cameron nodded thoughtfully. "It's them, all right."

"They outlaws?"

"Guess you can say they were. Straight now far as I know."

Shawn considered the man quietly. "What's your interest in them? They some kin to you?"

The lean-faced man smiled, bobbed his head. "Guess Bart never did get around to introducing us, did he? I'm John Cameron. Came here from the east. Spot of lung trouble. Do a little newspaper writing for the press back there. Got interested in the Kings when they were having their trouble. Felt kind of sorry for them."

"They get it straightened out?"

"Far as the law was concerned. The two of them were sent to the pen a couple of years ago for a bank robbery in Colorado. Claimed they were innocent but the judge put them in anyway—ten years each. Then about a year ago they were turned loose—pardoned."

"Came out that they weren't guilty, that it?"

"Something like that, was never made exactly clear. It could've been there was no point keeping them locked up any longer. The younger of the two—Ollie—got worked over by a gang of other convicts one day. Ended up he'd been better off if they had killed him —shape they left him in. And I don't think the judge was ever dead sure in his own mind that Aaron, he's the other brother, was guilty in the first place. Anyhow, they were both pardoned."

"Then Hillister's making a mistake again——"

"Is as far as the law is concerned. What's worrying me is that Hillister being the kind of a crazy killer he is, he's liable to stir up some bad trouble."

Starbuck frowned. "Thing to do is catch up with

him, make him understand the Kings aren't wanted by the law."

"Too late for that. He's gone—and you heard what Bart Trueman said about it. The Kings don't live in this county, so it's not his problem. . . . Doubt if you could get Hillister to listen, anyway. The fact that the law pardoned them wouldn't mean a thing to him. He'd claim Ollie and Aaron were still outlaws and shouldn't have been turned loose—and he'll find a way to do his own executing."

"I can believe that. His mind runs in one groove. Why tell me about it?"

"I think the Kings ought to be warned—told to lay low until he moves on."

Shawn shook his head. "Don't think he's apt to do that."

Cameron swore wearily. "No, expect he won't. He's got his nose pointed at them and he won't back off until he's done something about what he thinks is a failure of the law to do what it should."

"Take it into his own hands, you mean?"

"Exactly, and I think the Kings ought to at least be warned so they can be ready."

A slow smile pulled at Starbuck's lips. "And you want me to be the one who warns them."

Cameron nodded. "You're headed that way, and with a little hard riding you could get in front of Hillister, beat him to the King place."

"Or maybe run smack into him doing it——"

"Good chance of that without going to the Kings. Expect you realize he's not through with you. He didn't believe what Bart Trueman told him, still figures you for a wanted outlaw. My guess is he'll be laying for you."

"Sort of got that idea myself."

"Well, if he does," John Cameron said, pouring himself another drink, "you'd better drop him before he can you because that's what he'll have in mind this time. He's got a hate bigger'n the whole Territory on for outlaws over this thing where he lost his boys, and he's out to avenge them whether the law's interested or not. Just happens that so far he's either killed or captured ones the law was after, so he's still in the clear."

"Appreciate the warning," Starbuck said. "Sort of had it figured that way—and I don't much like the idea of having to duck and dodge."

"Can't blame you there. Man's entitled to ride across country without fearing for his life. But there's one thing sure, if you meet up with him again, you'll have to kill him or he'll kill you."

Starbuck digested that quietly. After a time he brushed his hat back, said, "Could be what it'll come to, but it's something that'll have to be handled when I come to it."

"What about the Kings?"

"Don't like to get mixed up in things like this, but I guess something ought to be done. Hillister's a looney, or near to it, and I'd have trouble sleeping nights if I thought I'd let him walk in on them when I could've stopped it."

"Then you'll do it?"

Shawn nodded. "How do I get there?"

Cameron rubbed at his jaw. "Well, I don't exactly know. About a day's ride southeast is all I can tell you. Just have to ask when you get down in that part of the country."

Starbuck sighed, got to his feet. "That being the way of it, I reckon I'd best get started," he said and extended his hand. "Pleasure meeting you."

"Same here," Cameron replied, taking Shawn's fingers into his own. "It's a mighty fine thing you're doing for those folks."

Starbuck bobbed his head and turned for the door. It seemed he was forever getting caught up in someone else's trouble, so much so in fact that at times he almost lost sight of his own purpose—that of finding Ben.

6 ~

A wry grin twisted Shawn Starbuck's lips as he rode south out of Cimarron. In all the days and months he'd spent and the miles of trail he'd covered in search of his brother, he'd never been taken for an outlaw and hauled in before a sheriff.

There had been a couple of times when something akin to that had occurred, but being tied up, planted on his horse, and led in at the end of a rope was a new experience. He'd have a few things to tell Ben about what he'd gone through during the quest, once he found him.

If ever he did.

Shawn's weather-tempered features sobered as that amending thought came to him. It was true—there seemed to be no end to the search. He had cut back and forth across the frontier innumerable times, all to no avail. Ben was not to be found. Often he had come close, or seemed to, and that likely was the spur that kept him going—the prospect that his brother was nearby, could very possibly be in the next town he rode into.

But disappointment was always his reward and there came moments when he thought such was fated to be the case forever, and a pressing urge to forget it, to forsake all hope of locating Ben and settling old Hiram's estate would enter his mind.

He could spend his lifetime at the task; he could fritter away all opportunity for a home, the ranch he planned one day to own, the wife and family he'd like to have—and still come out loser. All too often this occurred to him, nagged at his consciousness; but in the end he doggedly moved on, continued the search, driven by some inner voice that told him it was right, that it must be done—an obligation he could not shirk.

Now, shading his eyes with a cupped hand, he stared across the gently rolling land that stretched before him. It was far removed from the farm along the Muskingum River, yet there was something about the scene that evoked memories of his distant home. The grass, turning now with the approach of the cold months, looked much the same as it carpeted the slopes and small valleys; and the trees, perhaps it was the trees, cottonwoods and not tall sycamores to be sure, but great, spreading friends nevertheless.

The Starbuck farm had been a fine one and growing up there had been good, a time of many pleasures and joys despite the unbending strictness of their father. He and Ben, seven years his senior, had whiled away countless hours playing in the fields, fishing for punkinseed perch in a nearby pond, or simply lying in the shade along the river dreaming aloud of the day when they would be men and go out into the world and do the things that fired their imaginations. . . . There had always been time for dreams although the chores that awaited them often seemed endless.

Chores—that was what had caused the break between Ben and their parent. Since he was the older of the two sons, Ben naturally assumed a larger share of the labor around the place than Shawn, and punishment visited upon him one day for a job neglected was what broke the dam of resentment.

It likely would have never occurred had Clare, their mother, still been alive. An understanding, educated woman, she was the reasoning and leveling force between her husband and their sons. When she died from a midwinter siege of lung fever, the prelude to the end of the family was signaled.

Hiram, a squat bull of a man skilled in the arts of both scientific boxing and practical farming, turned inward. His bitterness at losing the quiet, gray-eyed woman he worshiped settled upon his older son, who endured it for a time, and then in a frenzy of anger, renounced all kinship with his father and took his leave.

Shawn stayed on, living with his father in a relationship that heretofore he had not known, bearing the man's moods silently, applying himself to the teachings of old Hiram, and generally making the best of it all.

When his father died, leaving the farm and a sizable amount of cash as an estate, he accepted the terms of the will—that he first find Ben and return him to Muskingum before it would be settled—without question or rancor. Equipping himself as best he could on a small loan advanced by the administrator of the estate, he set out on what he had assumed at the start would be a simple task. Ben had often said he would like to go to Texas, join with a family there that had earlier made the move.

It had been Shawn's first stopping point, and initial disappointment. Ben had been there, tarried for a time, and ridden on.

Thus the search began, an endless trek punctuated by jobs taken periodically to obtain cash that would enable him to press on further to the next town—the next ranch—to anywhere where a man answering the meager description of his brother might be.

But Ben, if it were Ben, was never there; only the disheartening possibility that it could have been, and once more he would take to the saddle, move on while the transition from farm boy to cool-eyed, efficient trail rider, capable in all the skills of holding his own and staying alive in a world of violence steadily made itself more apparent.

The vast, sprawling land slumbering in the shadow of the Sangre de Cristo Mountains was empty. If Luke Hillister was somewhere ahead, he was taking pains to remain well hidden. Starbuck rubbed at the stubble on his cheeks, reached back into his mind to recall what he could about the country he had earlier crossed with the bounty hunter.

If Hillister planned an ambush, and it seemed logical, he most likely would set it in the rough, broken butte country still some distance ahead. Shawn glanced to the west; two hours or more of daylight left. Luke was timing it about right for him. He would be drawing near the bluffs around dark.

He hoped he could avoid the man, not come to a showdown with him. He had no real reason to shoot it out, to kill him, but he was fully aware that he could be faced with no choice. Hillister was bordering on total madness, wholly dangerous, and Starbuck knew he could not afford to let himself be taken captive again.

Again he swept the country with eyes half closed to cut down the glare; nothing in sight except a few larks dipping and curving as they skimmed above the grass. Easing back on the saddle, he allowed the sorrel to continue its steady lope.

A time later he came to the edge of the ragged, deeper-lying land. It was an area of short palisades, arroyos, and rocks tumbled recklessly to all quarters. He slowed the gelding, proceeded quietly.

Abruptly he came to a full stop. A trailing clump of brush growing at the end of a low butte caught his attention. He had seen no motion, no shadow, but instinct had stirred him, set up a hurried warning. He studied the rough-faced shoulder intently for several minutes and then glancing to the slope on his right, he cut the sorrel about and began to ascend it.

7 ~

There was no trail up the steep grade but Starbuck kept the sorrel climbing and after a bit, reached a fairly level bench that paralleled the road below. Dismounting to lower the silhouette, he took up the gelding's reins and stepped out in front of him, moving quietly and carefully.

He drew abreast the back of the low bluff with its beard of brush, halted. Leaving the sorrel ground reined, Shawn dropped to hands and knees and worked his way to the rim of the ledge. Brushing off his hat, he peered down into the arroyo.

Hillister was there. The bounty hunter had stationed himself in the center of the undergrowth after first concealing his horse farther back, and now stood, gun in hand, awaiting the arrival of his intended prisoner.

That he had been seen coming was evident to Starbuck as he lay motionless on the rocky shelf and studied the man. Hillister was set, ready to strike; and it was equally obvious his intentions were not to bother with taking his victim in alive this time.

A tight grin tugged at Starbuck's mouth. If he hadn't spotted the brush clump at the edge of the bluff when he did and obeyed the subconscious warning it had stirred to life within him, he would, in all likelihood at that moment be slung head down across his saddle and on his way to some lawman different from Bart Trueman who Hillister felt would be more receptive.

He pulled back, retraced his steps to the sorrel, his glance raking the slope on ahead as he crossed over. The ledge flattened into the grade and disappeared entirely a short distance on. The point was well below Luke Hillister but whether he could remain unseen during the final span and the subsequent descent to the road below, as well as go unheard, was problematical.

No other course was open to him. Doubling back would be risky and he would be facing the same danger of being seen and heard. Nor was waiting for full darkness an answer; it would be difficult enough negotiating the steep slope without the added problem of night obscuring his way.

He swore softly, irked at being forced to take such precautions to avoid the man—any man. It rubbed him wrong and he rebelled at the need, but he pushed his pride into the background; it was either that or run head-on into Luke Hillister and a gunfight in which he would either kill the man or himself be killed—all for no good purpose.

Gathering up the sorrel's reins, he continued along the narrowing ledge. Several times the horse's iron-shod hooves clicked against rock, caused him to halt abruptly, wait out a long, tense minute until he was certain he had not roused the bounty hunter's suspicions. Even then he was not completely sure; he could no longer see the man, could only listen, and, hearing nothing, believe his movements had gone unnoticed.

The shelf began to fade, dissolve into a slight, rolling hump and finally disappear into the hillside entirely. Starbuck paused there, debating the advisability of pursuing his present course of action or of simply mounting the sorrel, giving him his head and making a rapid, and undoubtedly noisy descent.

It would put Hillister on his trail instantly, and he had no liking for that thought. He faced a tedious job of locating the King place and passing the warning to them as it was without having the very person he would caution them about dogging his heels.

Best stick with his present plan, take the horse down slow, walking ahead of him, crowding him back hard to prevent him from breaking into a series of stiff-legged jumps that would set up a sure-to-be-heard racket. He'd need to be careful, however; the big gelding could get off balance, and, unable to stop, come down upon him.

Taking the sorrel's cheek strap in his hand, Starbuck started down the slope, moving in small steps, following a long tangent in an effort to cut down on the steepness. At once small cascades of dirt and gravel began to pour from under the sorrel's hooves, rattling hollowly over the rocks. Starbuck did not pause; there was no time to wait, only hope he was far enough beyond Luke Hillister for it to go unheard.

He reached the foot of the slope, halted, breathing hard from the effort of steadying the trembling sorrel. Mounting at once, he moved out of the small cluster of cedars at the base of the grade, and, keeping to the soft ground to deaden the sorrel's hoofbeats, angled for the road.

Movement to his left brought him up sharp. The towering shape of Luke Hillister, gun in hand, stepped from behind the thickly branched trees. Starbuck threw himself forward on the saddle, drove his spurs brutally into the flanks of the gelding, sent him lunging straight at the bounty hunter—it was too late for anything else.

The pistol in Hillister's grasp blasted echoes into the late afternoon hush. Starbuck felt the breath of a bullet as the shoulder of his shying horse grazed the man, knocked him backwards into the cedars. Veering sharp right, he raced on, glancing over his shoulder as the sorrel gained the road, began to pound along its hard, worn surface. There was no sign of Luke Hillister. He apparently still lay unconscious in the scrubby growth.

Shawn did not slacken the gelding's pace until full dark and then pulled off into a wide arroyo that came into the trail from the left. Choosing a spot high on the lower side that would enable him to see anyone entering the wash and also permit him to move on if the need arose, without being noticed, he made dry camp. He had shaken Hillister, he felt certain, but he took no chances and passed up his need for coffee since it would require a fire, and made a meal of cold biscuits, dried beef, canned peaches, and water from his canteen.

His needs and those of the sorrel satisfied, he climbed
to the top of a nearby hill for a look at his back trail.
By following the now dark rim of the bluffs along
which he had made his way he was able to ascertain the
approximate point where Luke Hillister had laid his
ambush.

He studied the area for some time but for all his
careful probing he could not detect a campfire; either
the bounty hunter was being as cautious as he or else,
once recovered from the hard blow he had taken, had
mounted his horse and followed. Understanding Hillister's devious mind, the latter appeared the most likely
to Starbuck, but he shrugged off the possibility as of no
consequence.

The graveled floor of the arroyo would show no
indication of his turning off and he was well hidden
far back from the road. The sorrel had weathered a
hard day and he was equally tired. Grim, he returned
to camp, rolled up in his blanket, and dropped off to
sleep. He would run no farther.

Daylight, crisp and bone chilling, roused him. Again
passing up the genuine need for a fire and the warmth
it would provide as well as the hot breakfast it would
make possible, he rode out immediately, slanting the
sorrel due southeast into the area where John Cameron
had told him the Kings lived.

By midmorning the sun had broken the chill, and as
periodic glances behind him failed to note a following
horseman, he pulled into a deep wash to prepare and
eat the breakfast he had passed up earlier.

Finished, he again went to the saddle, feeling much
better and certain now he had thrown Hillister off his
trail. He could ease off, look for someone who could
direct him to the King ranch, or homestead, whichever
it was; likely he was drawing near to it.

It was full noon, however, when he finally came
upon a rider hazing a jag of steers along the bed of a
sandy wash. Shawn swung up to the man at once, a
squat, slack-jowled individual in worn range clothing
and run-down boots who viewed him with cold suspi-
cion.

Starbuck passed the usual salutations, then asked: "Know a family around here named King?"

The puncher stared at him woodenly. "Maybe."

"You a friend of theirs?"

The cowhand shifted on the misshapen saddle he was forking. The horn had been broken off and the whole thing appeared to be held together with rawhide cord and baling wire.

"Reckon there ain't nobody can claim to be real friendly with them," he drawled and spat into the sand.

"But I guess you know them——"

"Ain't saying I don't."

"I've got an important message for them," Starbuck said. "Mind telling me how to find their place?"

"You a stranger around here?"

Shawn nodded, the point seeming to be self-evident to him.

"Well, I don't know," the puncher said, wagging his head. "You sure that's why you're wanting to see them?"

"The only reason. . . . Their ranch on to the south, or the east?"

The cowhand shifted on his creaky hull, lifting himself slightly in an evident precaution against getting himself pinched, and pointed to a long line of dark-shadowed hills.

"Can't say as it's a ranch, but the Kings've got a place 'round the end of them bluffs. You just keep heading the way you are and you'll run smack dab into it."

"Obliged to you," Starbuck said, nodding. "One thing more—if you come across a big, black-bearded man asking you the same question, you'll be doing the Kings a favor if you tell him you don't know."

The puncher considered Shawn with expressionless eyes, his slack mouth half open. After a few moments he shrugged. "I'll study on it," he said laconically, and slapping heels against the old gray he was riding, moved on.

8 ～

Starbuck drew up at the end point of the palisades and let his gaze run the scatter of buildings in the small valley below. . . . The King place. He shook his head.

It was a scene of near desolation. The main house, of logs, was gray and sagged from time and weather. Beyond it stood a barn, its bulk canted slightly to one side as if braving the wind. Nearby was a wagon shed, the roof of which drooped to the ground at its lower end, three or four crumbling minor structures, and a rotting, pole corral reinforced along its base to contain a flock of chickens. There was a small shack, a bit apart, where someone had planted morning glories along the walls in a pitiful attempt to soften the bleakness.

The area fronting the buildings had been cleared for a considerable distance, leaving the soil barren and baked hard by the sun, but in the rear, besides clumps of brush, Shawn could see the green oblong of a garden in which grew corn and other vegetables.

After a time Starbuck touched the sorrel with his rowels and rode down the slope toward the structures. He proceeded at slow pace and kept as much in the open as possible, not in the least interested in drawing a bullet intended for an intruder.

When he reached the edge of the brush that fringed the yard, he again halted. He hoped that some one in the house would have seen him by that moment and stepped into the open to challenge his arrival; it would have given him a more comfortable feeling. But there were no signs of life and the thought came to him that the place was deserted, that the Kings had moved on. . . . Still, there were chickens in their improvised pen, and the garden looked to be well tended.

Staying within the encroaching brush, Starbuck began to work in nearer, following the circle of rank growth to where he could attain a position close to the main house. He halted abruptly. There had been movement behind one of the windows. There was definitely someone inside—and that they had seen him was also certain.

Shawn felt the hair on the back of his neck crawl. There was no welcome here for him—not for anyone, he guessed. The Kings, having had their troubles with the outside world, had become hostile and wary of all strangers.

He was as near as it was prudent, he decided, and cupping his hand to his mouth, shouted: "Hello—the house!"

There was no response. He waited out a long minute, repeated the call. Again there was fleeting movement beyond the dusty, streaked glass of the window next to the door. Starbuck swore impatiently. He'd have to simply ride in, hope for the best. . . . At least it would be no surprise to them; they knew he was there.

"Climb down off that horse!"

Shawn stiffened at the sharp command. He started to turn, froze as the harsh, high-pitched voice struck at him once more.

"You hear? Climb down—and don't go reaching for no gun, or by God, I'll blow your head off!"

Raising one hand and grasping the saddle horn with the other, Starbuck swung from the sorrel. Feet on the ground, both arms now up, he wheeled slowly. Surprise rolled through him.

He faced a woman. Stringy, red hair streaked with gray, leathery face set, pale blue eyes snapping, she considered him with unmistakable hatred. Somewhere in her late fifties, she was dressed in a man's faded and patched shirt, baggy pants that were too large, and heavy, thick-soled sodbuster shoes.

She had tied an apron around her waist, had gathered

the two lower corners to form a basket in which she had placed several ears of corn, a few tomatoes, and onion. Likely she was the woman of the King clan and he had interrupted her while she gathered vegetables for the table.

But there was no motherliness in the manner in which she held an old Navy Colt. The hammer was drawn back and she held it leveled steadily at Starbuck's belly. That she had used it before and would do so again was apparent.

"Mean you no harm," he said, shaking his head.

"You're a goddam liar—and a spy, that's what," the woman snapped. "One of Harper's bunch, come here to try and trick us. Well, you ain't fooling me none!"

"Never heard of Harper——"

"Don't try lying to me! I've been watching you, sneaking through the brush. We know the whole lot of you're setting back there in the hills, waiting and hoping for the time when you could catch us not looking."

"Not with anybody," Starbuck said patiently. "I'm alone."

"Sure you are—same as I'm the queen of England! Move on ahead of me—and keep your hands up."

"Where——"

"To the house—where the hell else you think I'd take you? I'm keeping you a prisoner—a hostage. Maybe I can make that Chet Harper come to terms, does he find out I got one of his bunch hogtied and ready for slaughtering."

"You're all wrong, Mrs. King—if that's who you are——"

"You know goddamn well I'm Ma King! Move—start for the house—straight! You try something cute and you'll be deader'n a stuffed owl!"

Starbuck pushed forward through the waist-high brush, taking slow, careful steps and broke out onto the cleared ground. Halfway to the house Ma King jabbed him savagely in the spine with her pistol.

"Hold up right there," she barked, and pointing her

weapon at the sky, triggered a shot that roused a rolling chain of echoes.

"Want Harper for sure to see I've got you," she said, her brittle blue eyes looking beyond Shawn to the low hills several hundred yards to the west.

He followed her gaze. A half a dozen riders were gathered on the crest of the highest, were facing the yard, watching.

"Reckon that'll do it," Ma King said, and shifted her attention to the house. "Aaron, open the door!"

The hewn plank panel swung inward. The woman again jabbed Starbuck with her pistol. "All right, get inside—and no foolishness if you're of a mind to keep on living! . . . Get his gun, Aaron."

As Shawn stepped through the doorway into the dim, cluttered structure, a man, also redheaded and blue-eyed, closed in behind him, deftly lifted his weapon from its holster, and pulled back.

"Who's he?"

"One of Harper's bunch sent down here to spy on us," the woman replied, kicking the door shut with her heel. "Expecting they're getting ready for another try."

"You're all wrong," Starbuck began. "I'm——"

"Keep your gun pointing at him while I dump these vittles," the woman directed, circling toward a crude table built against the wall near the cookstove. "Then we'll tie him up. Maybe Harper'll hold off now that we've got one of his'n."

"Doubt it," Aaron replied, motioning Shawn toward a cowhide chair with the muzzle of the pistol he held.

Starbuck sat down, wondering as he did where the other brother might be. Apparently Ma King was a widow, had been forced to take over as head of the family years ago, and in the process had become as hard-minded and iron-fisted as her husband had probably been.

He watched her lay the old Navy Colt on the table and unload her apron. That done, she jerked at the strings tied about her middle, released the ankle-length square of calico, and hung it on a wall peg. Turning, she then rummaged about in a box under the table and produced a short length of rope.

"This here'll hold him," she said, and, crossing to where Starbuck sat, pulled his wrists behind him and lashed them securely together. As an added precaution she used the trailing end of the cord to bind his ankles.

"Want you to listen to me," Shawn said as she straightened up. "I came here to do you a favor——"

"You come here to spy on us," Ma King broke in, striding to the window near the door. "Harper sent you to watch, see if there was a way he could get inside, once we holed up, without getting his danged hide blasted!"

"No, you're wrong. I——"

"Well, we're a jump ahead of him now! He tries anything, we got you to dicker with," the woman said, peering through the glass. "If he wants to keep you alive, he'll back off, leave us be."

Shawn stirred in frustration. "I'm telling you I've got nothing to do with somebody named Harper! Just rode by to warn you about——"

"They're coming," Ma King said, paying no attention to Starbuck's words. "You get over there to the other window, Aaron—and make your shooting count. We ain't long on bullets."

"Yes, Ma," King said and hurriedly crossed to the opening on the other side of the door.

The woman, hitching at the gun belt she was wearing and which had gone unnoticed under her apron, stationed herself beside the cracked panes in the sash. Raising it slightly, she paused, turned half about, and swept the cabin with a frowning glance. Outside, Shawn could hear the quick pound of approaching horses.

"Where's Ollie?"

The surprise in Ma King's voice indicated that in the excitement of capturing a prisoner she had not noticed the absence of the rest of her family.

"Him and Dora went down to the shack," Aaron replied, and then ducked back as bullets began to thud into the log walls of the house and the rattle of gunshots filled the yard.

9 ～

"Goddammit!" Ma King said feelingly, "I told them to stay inside while Harper was hanging around."

Aaron rested the barrel of his rifle on the window's sill and pressed off a shot. He handled the weapon with an awkwardness that bordered on timidity.

"Went to get something—something Dora wanted," he said. "Aimed to be gone only a minute."

"She'll fool around and get Ollie and herself killed, that's what she's going to get," the woman snapped, opening up with her pistol.

The shooting outside was a continuous racket and a steady hail of bullets hammered at the thick walls and heavy door of the cabin. Glass shattered suddenly and Ma King jerked back, swearing lustily.

She brushed at the tip of her nose with the back of a hand. "We ain't hit a one of them yet! Guess I just can't set my mind to it with Ollie and Dora caught out there like they are. . . . Bet they didn't even take no gun with them."

Aaron shook his head. "Don't recollect," he said glancing around the room. "Didn't take the shotgun 'cause there it is. And Pa's rifle's laying on the bench."

"That Dora Clark ain't got a lick of sense! If that Harper bunch finds out they're trapped in the shack, they'll damn quick—"

Ma King's voice faded as she turned, resumed firing at the marauders. Starbuck glanced around the cabin; small, skimpily furnished with crudely built furniture, it was scarcely more than one room. A partition had been erected in the south corner to form a bedroom,

49

used, no doubt by Ma herself. Adjacent to it and on the same wall a double bunk had been built—serving as sleeping facilities for Ollie and Aaron. The opposite, rear corner was devoted to kitchen use. Where Dora, the girl mentioned, fit into the scheme and who she was Shawn had no way of knowing.

Glass tinkled again and through the thin haze of smoke that was beginning to fill the cabin, Starbuck saw Aaron draw back, look down at his left wrist where flying splinters had drawn blood.

"Don't know what this is all about, but if you'll turn me loose I'll give you a hand."

Aaron, injury forgotten and now taking the opportunity to reload, flicked a glance to his mother who made a negative gesture with her head.

"You can use another gun—"

King did not bother to look up but continued to feed cartridges into the magazine of his rifle.

"There's a half a dozen of them out there, and only two of you," Shawn continued. "They're going to realize that and when they do, they'll rush you."

Ma King wheeled angrily. "Mister, you're doing a lot of gabbling for nothing. Smart thing for you to do is shut your jaws until time comes for to figure out what I'm doing with you."

"Make him go get Dora and Ollie," Aaron suggested, stepping up to the window again. "Him a-walking with them'll keep Harper's bunch from shooting."

Ma King's eyes sharpened and a half smile pulled at her thin lips. "Now, that's a right smart idea, Aaron! They sure won't cut down on them with him right there in the way. You listening, mister?"

Starbuck shook his head. "Be a mistake. They don't know me. Be the same as one of you going out there."

Ma stared at him. "Can't you do nothing else but lie? Told you I wasn't swallowing that hogwash."

"Not lying—and if you're smart you'll listen to me. I'm not——"

"They're drawing back," Aaron announced through the acrid fog. "Reckon they're aiming to do some palavering—likely with this jasper, only he won't be showing up for the meeting."

The gunshots had ceased. Ma King, again reloading, stepped back into the room and took up a stand near Shawn.

"Turn him loose," she said, ducking her head at Aaron.

King propped his rifle against the wall and crossed to where Shawn sat. Leaning over, he began to fumble with the knots in the rope.

"You sending him after Dora and Ollie now?"

"Be a good time," the woman said. She waited until Starbuck was free and then, holding her pistol on him, beckoned him to the window. "You see that there little house at the end of the yard?" she asked, pointing.

Shawn looked through the jagged glass. It was the shack with the morning glories. He nodded.

"Well, here's the word with the bark still on it: you're stepping out that door and making a beeline for it. My boy and his girl are in there. You're bringing them back to me. That plain?"

"Plain enough but if you think I can do it without getting myself or them shot, you're loco," Shawn said bluntly.

Ma studied him with cold eyes. "I'm saying you can. Your friends ain't going to throw no lead at you."

"Not my friends——"

"All the time you're there in the yard me and Aaron'll have our guns pointing at you. Try running off and we'll fill you so full of bullets you'll weigh a ton. There ain't no place you can reach, once you're out there that we can't cut you down before you can get to it. You listening good?"

Starbuck shrugged wearily. It was useless to argue with the Kings, make them understand that he had no connection with the man they called Harper and his gang. Perhaps, if he could manage to cross the yard, gain the shack and return with Ollie and the girl, Dora, he might be able to convince them he was telling the truth. . . . But by doing so safely wouldn't he be proving their contention? He stirred again, realizing he was caught between a rock and a hard place.

"Now, when you start back with them, you keep

them to the inside. That way it'll be you walking betwixt them and your partners. You got that straight, too?"

"Won't make any difference. I'll look the same to Harper as your boy and this Dora."

"Don't forget what I told you now!" Ma King said, completely ignoring his words. "Try skinning out on me and you're a dead outlaw—hear?"

"I hear—"

The woman bucked her head at Aaron. "All right, open the door and let him out. I got to be standing here at the window so's I can hold a bead on him."

Shawn stepped up to the thick panel, halted. Anger and impatience were running through him at his failure to break down Ma King's stubbornness and make her hear what he had to say.

"Came by here to do you a favor," he said, deciding to make one more attempt. "Man named Cameron, up in Cimarron, wanted me to warn you——"

"Don't know no Cameron," she said, not taking her eyes from the yard. Evidently she was watching Harper and the riders with him, all of whom had pulled off to one side.

"He's a newspaper writer. Knows about you from the trouble your boys had with the law. Felt sorry for——"

"Ain't no need for nobody to feel sorry for us," Ma snapped. "Us Kings can look after ourselves. Always have, reckon we always will."

Shawn flinched as Aaron's rifle barrel pressed into his ribs, prodded him toward the door. He took a step nearer, halted, faced the woman.

"Can see that but the fact is there's a bounty hunter, name of Hillister, headed this way."

"Never heard of no Hillister either."

"He's after Aaron and Ollie——"

"Reckon we can handle him, too, was you to be telling the truth and he showed up. Now, goddammit, are you getting out there or am I going to have to wing you right here and now? I'm tired of you stalling."

Shawn swept Ma King with a look of disgust, swore under his breath, and reached for the door latch. Raising it, he drew in the slab panel and glanced out.

Harper and the others were in the tall brush beyond the yard and well out of range.

He shifted his glance to the shack at the end of the barren yard to his left. There was no available cover; the moment he stepped out onto the hardpack, he was in the open.

"Start moving," he heard Ma King say, and, taking a deep breath, he darted through the doorway and ran hard for the shack.

A faint yell went up as Starbuck legged it for the shack, but there were no gunshots. The distance was too great and shooting at him would be useless, but he knew that was not the way Ma King would see it; she would take it as proof that he was a member of Harper's gang and they had purposely withheld their fire.

He gained the small building, rushed through the door that swung wide to admit him. Closing it, he glanced at the young woman—only a girl in fact—standing in the center of the room. She was pretty in a quiet sort of way—even, tanned features, honey-blonde hair and level gray eyes that considered him gravely.

"Who're you?" she asked, her expression not changing.

"Name's Starbuck. Ma King thinks I'm one of the Harper bunch. I'm not but there's no making her believe it. . . . She sent me to get you and Ollie."

He looked beyond the girl to the man, one little older than himself, sitting at a table in a corner. He had the same red hair and blue eyes as his mother and brother, only there was an emptiness to him, a vacancy as if there was nothing behind the facade of family similarity.

Shawn recalled what he had been told of Ollie King, that he had been set upon by other convicts while in prison and severely beaten; it would have been better had they killed him, so John Cameron had said. He understood those words now; Ollie was a mindless imbecile staring out at a world in which he did not live but merely existed as a helpless vegetable.

"Can he understand what you tell him?" he asked, returning his glance to Dora.

She nodded. "Sometimes."

"Then explain that we've got to make a run for the house. Ma and Aaron will give us cover, but we'll be taking a chance if Harper and the others with him open up on us."

Dora frowned, touched the empty holster on his hip with her eyes. "Don't you have a gun?"

Shawn grinned wryly. "Ma won't let me have one. Like I said, she figures I'm one of the gang."

"You're not?"

"No, and I'd sure as hell like to find a way to prove it. . . . We've got to hurry—Harper and his boys could be moving in."

Wheeling, he stepped to the door, opened it a narrow crack. The outlaws had moved forward but were still in the brush. They appeared to be watching the shack, evidently unsure as to what was going on. He shifted his eyes to the house. Ma King, at the window, was beckoning angrily.

He swung back to Dora and Ollie. The younger King's face was slack, wooden, as he stared straight ahead. The girl nodded.

"I think he understands."

"Good. Once we're out there, run for the house fast as you can. I'll be on the outside, between you and Harper."

Dora's lips parted in a wan smile. She seemed curiously unafraid, considering the danger that lay ahead. "That sounds like Ma's doings, too——"

"Was. She gave me strict orders and I'm not about to buck her."

"I know what you mean. I've been around her for quite a spell now. Nobody's got the spunk to stand up to Ma."

Shawn again turned to the door, drew it partly open. The outlaws—he realized in that moment that he was thinking of them in that sense simply because Ma King had labeled them as such; they could be just ordinary citizens, or possibly even lawmen—were moving toward the yard. He swore softly. They had waited too long.

Taut, he stepped back, jerked the panel wide. "Let's go," he said. "Don't stop until you're in the house!"

Dora, hanging tight onto Ollie's hand, hurried into the yard, veered at once toward the cabin. Starbuck rushed to her side, and together the three of them ran for the squat structure at the opposite end of the clearing.

"Come on, Ollie—race me!" he heard the girl cry.

King laughed childishly, increased his speed. Over to the left gunfire broke out. Shawn threw his attention to that point. Harper and his men were spurring out of the brush, breaking onto the hardpack and firing as they came.

Gunshots began to crackle from the windows of the house as Ma King and Aaron laid down a covering barrage. The approaching riders, free of the hindering undergrowth, began to close in fast. Dust spurted around Starbuck's feet as bullets drove into the sunbaked soil, thunked dully into the dead stumps of trees beyond them.

But suddenly they were at the house, plunging through the door held open by Aaron. Sucking hard for wind, Starbuck whirled, hearing the loud pound of hooves in the yard only moments behind them.

He saw Aaron rush back to his place at the window, realized that Ma King's weapon had gone empty and the resulting lack of return fire was allowing the outlaws to come in dangerously close.

Snatching up his pistol from the table where Aaron had laid it, he crossed quickly to the window. Grasping Ma by the shoulders, he lifted her out of the way.

"Excuse me, ma'am," he said, and, crowding up to the opening, began to add his shots to those of Aaron.

"One's hit!" the older King brother sang out, looking over his shoulder at Shawn. "Your first bullet got one!"

Starbuck watched the sagging rider wheel away, leveled on the man behind him, and pressed off another shot. The outlaw yelled, clawed at his arm, and cut back for the brush.

"Another'n!" Aaron yelled. "Was the one they call Tex." He came fully around, grinned broadly at his mother. "Reckon they'll start thinking twice about us now, Ma."

Shawn faced about. The elderly woman, pistol now in the holster belted around her waist, was watching him. A soft, wondering look was filling her eyes. Beyond her Ollie sat numbly in the same leather chair that earlier had confined Starbuck. Dora, an old double-barreled shotgun in her hands, was crossing to the window where Aaron stood.

"Expect they'll make their big try now," he said. "Best we all get set to open up on them. . . . They find out there's more than just two guns against them, they'll likely back off—maybe for good."

Ma King broke out of her absorption. "You heard him," she said briskly. "Dora, you stay there with Aaron. Me and the stranger'll stand them off from this here window."

Shawn, his weapon reloaded, drew to one side of the opening, making room for the matriarchal head of the King clan.

"They're coming!" Aaron cried.

The cabin rocked with the blast of the shotgun and other weapons. Harper, sided by only three riders, slowed in the face of the murderous volley. At once the men with him swerved to the side, began to pull away. The outlaw leader, suddenly alone in the yard, yelled something, flinched as a bullet tore at the brim of his hat. Abruptly he wheeled and spurred off in pursuit of his followers.

"I reckon that's it," Aaron said, his voice filled with satisfaction. "They ain't going to try that again."

Starbuck turned, began to thumb fresh cartridges into the cylinder of his forty-five. Squinting through the acrid smoke haze, he touched each of the others with his glance.

"Maybe not, but just in case they do, I'd like to know first why I'm doing all this shooting."

11 ~

In the sudden hush that settled over the room, Starbuck dropped his pistol back into its holster and leaned against the wall.

Dora, eyes upon him, did not move, simply watched and waited. Aaron lowered his head, began to refill the magazine of the rifle while his younger brother, a wooden image in the cowhide chair, stared blankly into space. Only Ma King stirred. Folding her arms she met Shawn's gaze coolly.

"Maybe it'd be best was you to catch up your horse and ride on," she said. "Wouldn't be right dragging you into our trouble."

"Seems I'm already in it," Starbuck said, shrugging.

"You come in it of your own wanting—and I'm saying now I was wrong about you, and I'm saying, too, I'm sorry. And I'm thanking you for pitching in like you did—but there ain't no call for your staying around now."

Shawn studied the older woman. Her words were coming only from the surface, born of a strange mixture of pride and politeness. Inwardly she was hoping that he would not go.

"Never like to start a job I don't finish," he said. "Who's this Harper?"

He could see relief flood through both Ma King and Dora at his question. Aaron heaved a sigh, continued to work with his weapon.

"Outlaw," Ma said. "Him and the bunch with him are all outlaws. Expect there's sheriffs and marshals looking for the whole passel, but they're plenty smart.

Keep to the hills. . . . Rode in here about a week ago."

"Harper the only one you know?"

"Know them all," the woman said.

Turning, she took a leather pouch and a cob pipe from a shelf on the wall. Opening the sack, she pinched out a small quantity of the shredded leaves, began to tamp into the blackened bowl.

"Yessir, we know them all," she continued, digging into her shirt pocket for a match. "Paid us a visit here one day, bold as brass. There's one they call Dave Dismukes, and a Mexican—Gonzales. Another'n goes by the name of Tex Wingate——"

"He ain't liable to come again," Aaron broke in. "The stranger there winged him good."

"I'm called Starbuck," Shawn said.

"Then there's the one going by the handle, Georgia, a southern-talking fellow. Last one's Bill Drake——"

"Starbuck put a bullet in him, too, leastwise I think he's the one," Aaron cut in again.

"What do they want from you?" Shawn asked after a brief time, voicing the question that had been on his mind from the beginning. He could see nothing the Kings possessed that would warrant six men risking their lives to get.

Ma scratched a match into fire, held it to her pipe and puffed its contents into a glowing coal. Exhaling a cloud of smoke, she looked directly at him.

"Fifty thousand dollars."

Starbuck's jaw sagged. "Fifty thousand dollars! How —why——"

"They figure my boys knows where it's been hid. Was taken in a Wells-Fargo holdup."

Starbuck thought back, recalled what he'd heard in Cimarron about the King brothers and the reason why they had been sent to prison.

"Do they?"

"Hell no, they don't! Had nothing to do with it."

Shawn smiled. "Not what the law says."

The older woman glanced at him sharply. "You know something about it?"

"Was told Aaron and Ollie went to jail for a robbery. They spent a year of their sentence and then was

pardoned. . . . Harper and his bunch must figure it's
true, too, else they wouldn't be trying to find out about
the money."

"Only guessing. Showed up here first time, nice and
friendly as you please—but they was feeling us out
all along. Could see that. Then when we didn't tell them
nothing because we couldn't, they started getting nasty.

"Come in one day and found them holding fire to
Ollie's hand, trying to make him talk. I run them off
right quick and ever since then they been trying to grab
Ollie!"

"Looks like they could see that Ollie can't tell them
anything."

"They think he's just fooling, making out like he
ain't right."

"Harper told us he was going to make him talk,
or kill him trying," Aaron said, leaning the now-loaded
rifle against the wall. "What he'll have to do, too, because Ollie sure can't talk or nothing—even if he
knowed something. Them convicts fixed him up for
good."

"This Harper have any proof that you were in on
the holdup?"

"Nope, only thinks so because we was sent to the
pen for it. They're claiming we both had a hand in it,
that after it was over, it was Ollie that had the saddle-
bag full of gold while the rest of the gang suckered
the posse off into the hills. There was a shooting and
the others got themselves killed—leaving Ollie with
all the money."

"That the way it was?"

Aaron shook his head. "Was nothing like that, nothing to it at all. Ollie and me—we wasn't the ones in
on it, but there was a couple of fellows that claimed
they'd seen the holdup and they swore we was part of
the gang. We went to the pen on their say-so."

"They made a big mistake, them two that said it
was Ollie and Aaron," Ma King added, relighting her
pipe. "Maybe they looked like my boys but it wasn't
them. The law same as said so itself when it turned
them loose."

It was possible, Shawn admitted to himself. Errors

in identification had been made before by persons who, under the stress of excitement, believed they were seeing someone only to have subsequent facts prove them wrong; and likly it would happen again. . . . Still . . .

"What about the convicts that beat up Ollie while you were in prison? They must have known something."

"They was listening to rumors, that's all," Aaron replied. "Word gets in behind the walls fast sometimes, and part of that bunch who cornered Ollie the day we was all out building road, was due to be turned loose. Their time was up. Reckon they figured to find out from him where he'd hid the gold and go after it themselves soon's they got freed."

"Why didn't they try to find out from you?"

"Was Ollie that had—I'm meaning, that they claimed had it and buried it."

"But if you were with him——"

"Now, hold on!" Ma King broke in, frowning. "Way you're putting it, it's the same as saying Ollie and Aaron was mixed up in it!"

Starbuck brushed back his hat, cocked his head to one side. "Little hard to believe everybody was wrong; the law, the men who identified them, the convicts who wanted to find the money—and now Harper. Expect you've heard of the old saying that where there's a wet place there had to have been some water."

"Don't mean a thing where my boys are concerned. I know them—and they sure wouldn't get all clabbered up in something like that. Ollie's a little wild maybe—or was. I'll nod to that, but he'd never take part in no holdup. Aaron wouldn't either."

"Expect you can tell that from the way I handle a gun," the elder son said. "Never was no good at it."

"He's the worker of the family," Ma added. "Never had no time for nothing except working the place. Was Ollie that sort of took after his pa—in some ways."

Shawn, aware that Dora still watched him intently, and beginning to feel uncomfortable under the steady pressure of her gaze, glanced through the window to the country beyond. There was no sign of Harper and his outlaw friends. He would like to think they had given up but now, after hearing the reason for their presence, he had small hope.

He came around slowly, thoughtfully. Aaron had crossed to the kitchen area, had found a chunk of cold cornbread and was munching at it hungrily. Dora, at last breaking her engrossment, was moving to where Ollie sat. She halted there, began to fuss with his shirt collar. Ma King, however, had not turned away. Pipe jutting from her mouth, she met his glance head-on, a faint aura of defiance still clinging to her.

"This holdup, where'd it take place?"

"Colorado," Aaron said before his mother could make a reply. "Town called Enterprise."

"You there when it happened?"

"Sure was," King answered, and then glancing at his mother, checked his words. "Was there on business," he finished lamely.

Starbuck's shoulders lifted, fell. He wasn't getting all of the story; he was convinced of that now. But the need to know the truth was important. Their lives could depend on it.

"Think you folks had better face up to something," he said. "Harper's going to hit us again. I'm pretty sure of that, and this time there's a good chance we won't be able to stop him. Your ammunition's not going to hold out—for one thing.

"On top of that they're holding all the good cards. There's fire, for one thing. They can pin us down inside while they put a torch to the place."

Shawn hesitated, allowed his words to sink in. Then, "I figure our best chance lies in trying to talk to them, make them understand it wasn't Ollie and Aaron in that robbery—that it was somebody else."

Aaron tossed the remaining bit of cornbread into the wood box, settled back against the table. Ma King removed the corncob from her mouth, stared fixedly at the bowl.

"Ain't no use trying," she said. "Chet Harper won't listen."

"Why? He got a good reason?"

The old woman took the pipe by the stem, knocked

the bowl against the heel of her hand to loosen the dottle. "Just won't, that's why."

Aaron heaved a deep sigh, crossed to her side. "He's guessing, Ma, and he's coming close. I reckon he's entitled to the truth—helping us like he's done."

Ma King stared at the blackened tobacco lying on the floor at her feet. Finally she nodded, raised her lined face to Shawn.

"Aaron's right. We wasn't exactly telling you the truth—all of it, anyway."

12 ~

Ollie King stirred irritably, made a small, childish sound. Dora turned at once to the water bucket, and ladling out a quantity in the tin dipper that hung above, carried it to the man. Ma King watched, her expression unchanging as he clawed at the container, sloshed a part of its contents down his shirt front in his eagerness to consume it.

"You ain't some kind of a lawman are you?" she asked, finally.

Starbuck said, "No."

The woman's shoulders settled forward, and with a slight motion of her head, she started toward the kitchen area. In that moment a great weariness seemed to come over her and the tough bravado she affected appeared to melt, fall away.

"You tell him, Aaron," she murmured. "Time I was getting some eats together. Like as not supper'll be a long time coming here. . . . Dora, peel up a pan of spuds."

The girl wheeled at once, followed her to the table near the stove and began to help with the preparation of the past-due noon meal. Aaron, first quenching the thirst the cornbread had kindled, crossed to the front of the room. He pointed to one of the chairs.

"Might as well set."

Shawn waved the offer aside, continued to stand at the window. "Best I keep an eye out for Harper."

Aaron bobbed, sank into the chair himself. "Was sort of a accident, me being there in Enterprise," he said. "Went after Ollie."

"Then he was there?"

"Yeah. Never was much for staying around the place, was always slipping off, going to Santa Fe or Vegas or some other town. Was a fellow that liked to be where things was going on—which there sure ain't around here. Ain't never nothing but a powerful lot of god-awful work that never ends."

"You running any cattle?"

"Nope, sold off what we had. Just got the farming patch, the chickens, and one old cow."

"No horses? How do you do your plowing?"

"Oh, we got a mare. She's old, too, but she does pretty good. Sold Ollie's bay a while back. Was no need keeping him—and we was needing cash. Shame, sure was a fine animal.

"Anyways, I went up there after Ollie. He'd sort of teamed up with a couple other fellows, punchers riding north to Wyoming, where they aimed to take a job on some ranch. They'd first got together over in Elizabethtown, got all liquored up, and wound up later in Enterprise.

"We didn't know about that and Ma and Dora and me wasn't much worried. Ollie was always doing something like that, riding off and then showing up a couple of days later saying he was sorry and the like. Afterwards he'd settle down, do his share around here for a spell—leastwise 'til the itch got into him again."

"Then you got wind that he was in Enterprise—"

Aaron nodded slowly, seemingly listening to the crackling sound of grease turning hot in a skillet on the stove.

"Was more'n a week later and Ma was getting sort of worried. Me, I was getting mad, all the work piling up—the kind Ma and Dora couldn't do. Fellow rode by, said he'd run into Ollie up there and had a message for us from him. Said to tell us he was all right and he'd be home soon.

"Another week went by and no Ollie. Ma started getting her dander up then and after a couple, three more days, she sent me to get him.

"Found him right off—Enterprise ain't such a big place—but he wasn't ready to come home. Said he had a big deal a-stewing and if it worked out right he'd be ready to come back with enough money in his pocket to fix it so's we could plain forget this here place and get us a ranch that'd amount to something."

"Was like his pa that way," Ma King said, looking over her shoulder. "Always having big ideas and wanting to make things nice for me and the others."

"Big ideas is all it ever was—for both of them," Aaron murmured.

The older woman whirled. "Now, I won't have you bad-mouthing your pa like that! He was a good man, better'n most in some ways, and I won't let you go disrespecting him!"

"Ain't disrespecting him, only speaking what's gospel, Ma, and you know it."

Shawn glanced again to the empty, quiet land beyond the yard. No one lived without trouble, it seemed; everyone had a measure of problems, it was only that some had more than others. He had his—Ben, finding him and the settling of old Hiram's estate—all of which was being forced into the background while he took a hand in the Kings' affairs.

But he had grown accustomed to such interruptions and delays, for, try as he might, he was continually finding himself involved. He guessed he should care less about others, should turn a deaf ear to their adversities, and permit them to work it out themselves—capable of doing so or not. . . . But he could never ignore anyone who needed help; he hadn't been brought up that way.

"This big deal of Ollie's—was it the holdup?"

Aaron nodded. "Didn't know that right off, but that was it. Him and four other men he'd fell in with while he was laying around a saloon, they got word that a Wells-Fargo bank shipment was coming through. Was to be fifty thousand dollars in gold coin. . . . Totted up to ten thousand apiece, which sure is a lot of money. Well, they pulled off the robbery."

Startled, Shawn came fully around. "You saying now that Ollie was in on it?"

"He was, and it was just like everybody said. He was handed the money and him and some other fellow took off with it while the rest of the gang let the posse chase them off into another direction——"

"And got themselves killed," Ma finished.

Ollie King began to whimper softly. Dora paused, picked up a square of cornbread, placed it in his hand. He pressed it against his mouth, began to devour it wolfishly. The girl turned away quickly, resumed her duties at the cook table.

"Next thing I knowed," Aaron continued, "the sheriff come after me and took me off to jail. He had Ollie there, too, only they wouldn't let us see each other. Then a couple of men showed up, looked at me, and said yes, I sure was the one they'd seen ride off with Ollie and them other outlaws after the robbing was over.

"The sheriff started in then trying to make me tell where we'd cached the gold, and I reckoned from that Ollie'd hid it somewheres but since we didn't get to do no talking together, I was in the dark about what he'd told them.

"Wasn't 'til later when we was up before the judge that I found out Ollie was saying no to the whole thing and was claiming he wasn't one of the gang and that he didn't never see no gold."

"You believe him?"

Aaron shifted, scratched at the stubble on his jaw as he fixed his eyes on his brother. "I seen them that got killed and they was the ones he had that there big deal on with."

The cabin was warming from the fire in the stove and beginning to fill with the sizzling noise of frying meat and bacon and the smell of chicory.

"Don't quite savvy you," Starbuck said. "Seems to me you're not for sure he was in on it."

"He ain't," Ma King said.

"I reckon he was," Aaron drawled, quietly stubborn. "Ma just never would believe he could've done it, but I know better. Ollie had that gold, and he hid it somewheres. I figure he thought right up to the time we rode through them gates into the pen that we was going to be turned loose—only we wasn't."

"What about the man who was with him, if it wasn't you?"

"It dang sure wasn't me—and I don't know nothing about him! Ollie told me once he was dead. How it come to be he never did say."

Starbuck struggled to sort out the facts in his head, but he was having trouble. A lot of the pieces didn't seem to fit.

"Didn't Ollie try to clear you, make the judge see that you weren't the one with him?"

"Sure. Done his best, but nobody'd believe him. We was brothers and we'd been seen in the town together. And then them two coming and saying I was the one—we didn't have much chance of proving anything."

"How long were you in the pen before Ollie got hurt?"

"Eight—no was nine months."

"And he never told you what had happened to the gold in all that time?"

"Wouldn't even talk about it. Always put me off, saying the thing for us to do was work hard at what the jailers told us to do and not start no trouble. That way we'd be turned loose in a couple of years or so and we could go back to Ma and Dora and take up living where we'd left off."

"You think he had in mind to then go dig up the gold where he'd buried it?"

Aaron looked down at his hands. "What I would guess."

"But when those convicts caught him, beat him up——"

"They plain put a end to plans like that. Where he hid all that money nobody'll ever know. It's lost, gone for good unless'n somebody just happens to stumble on it."

Ma King had hesitated at her chores again, was studying Aaron from across the room. "All that's nothing but you thinking and guessing," she said. "Ollie never did come right out and tell you he done it."

"No, never did, but I know, Ma, same as down deep, you know. Only wish't he had told me everything so's I could go find that gold and take it back to the

Wells-Fargo people and get shed of all the trouble we're having."

"Should be able to make Harper understand," Shawn said. "A man can see that Ollie, whether he did it or not, won't ever be able to tell anybody anything. You said they tried forcing him, found out they couldn't. Can't see why they won't accept it and leave you folks alone."

Aaron King got to his feet. Moving to the door, he opened it and glanced out. "There's something you're forgetting, Starbuck. They think I was the man with Ollie, same as the law did—and they figure I know right where the money's hid."

13 ~

He finally had the whole story, Shawn thought. Everything now fit into place—particularly the reason why Chet Harper and his outlaw friends refused to give up and ride on. Failing to get the information they wanted from poor, addled Ollie, they had turned on Aaron.

"The truth helps," he said. "Can see better what we're up against."

Dora, in the act of setting food on the table, glanced up at him. "That mean you'll stay?" she asked, breaking her long silence.

"Changes nothing. Got into this and I'll see it through."

A relieved smile parted her lips. Ma King, bearing a platter of fried potatoes and sliced salt pork, flashed the girl a speculative look and frowned. "Reckon we can eat," she said, depositing the large stoneware plate. "You menfolks come on."

Aaron moved forward obediently. Shawn, making another sweeping survey through the window and seeing no indication of the outlaws, followed. Settling onto a chair, he watched Dora conduct Ollie to his place at the table, fill a plate, and start him eating, her features calm, her manner patient.

It wasn't much of a life for her, he guessed, helping himself to the food proffered by Aaron. Her time appeared to be occupied almost solely by caring for Ollie and tending to his needs.

The meal was eaten in silence. Starbuck, discovering himself hungry, relished the good if simple food, even to the black and bitter chicory coffee. When it was finished, Ma, more the motherly housewife than the hard-bitten, rough-talking old harridan he had encountered in the brush, waved him and Aaron back to the front of the cabin and, with Dora, began to clear the table and clean the kitchen.

Aaron, sinking once again into his chair, watched her with puzzled eyes. It was evident from his concern that she ordinarily didn't trouble herself with such womanly duties but probably left them to the girl; and such a change he found disturbing.

Shawn, giving it brief thought, realized there was a difference, and wondered, too. But it could be attributed to the novelty of having company even under trying circumstances, or it was possible that having another man in the house was triggering a release, one that freed her from the necessity of enacting the role as strong father-figure of the family.

"You going to try and do some talking to Harper?" Aaron asked as Shawn took up his position at the window.

"Costs nothing—and there's always the chance it might do some good."

"Just be wasting your breath," King said, searching his pockets for pipe and tobacco. "Sure do wish Ollie'd told me what he done with that gold. Be glad to tell him just where——"

"Be the wrong thing to do. Not theirs."

"Know that but I'd tell them anyway just to get rid of them, make them leave us be."

Dora had gotten Ollie onto his feet and was coaxing him into the bedroom in the corner of the cabin, where he could lie down and be out of the way if trouble returned. Ma King had finished her chores, was drying her hands on the apron she had restored to her waist.

"Expect that'd be the only thing that will make them pull out. They're going to believe what they want to."

Aaron, his pipe going, leaned back. "Expect you've seen a-plenty of their kind before."

"My share. World's full of Harpers—and they're all pretty much alike."

"Reminds me, when you first showed up you said something about bringing us word from somebody—"

"Man named Cameron in Cimarron. Wanted you to know about Hillister."

"Who's he?"

"Bounty hunter. Got it in his head that he has to lay every outlaw in the country by the heels and haul them into the law, dead or alive—doesn't make any difference to him."

"What's he want with us?"

"Thinks you and Ollie ought to be back in the pen."

"But the judge—and the Governor, they——"

"Your getting pardoned doesn't mean a thing to him. Still outlaws to his way of looking at it and he's loco enough to try and put you there again."

Aaron shrugged. "Once he sees Ollie and it's all explained to him, he'll maybe forget it."

"Not Hillister. Man can't be reasoned with. Catching outlaws is like a crusade with him—and he's dangerous. As soon kill as not."

"Sounds like you had some truck with him."

"Did—and I was lucky. Managed to talk hard enough to keep myself alive until we could get to the sheriff in Cimarron. He made Hillister turn me loose but that didn't end it. Tried to ambush me on the way here but I got by him. He'll still be hunting me."

Aaron frowned. "Why? If the sheriff told him you wasn't wanted, why's he still after you?"

"Wouldn't believe what he was told. Says I look like an outlaw because of the way I wear my gun—and that's enough for him. It'll be the same with you and Ollie. You've been branded and far as he's concerned that means you either ought to be behind bars—or dead."

King came forward in his chair. "You telling me that he'll try taking us back to the pen, or maybe even kill us if he has to?"

"Exactly what you can figure on. That's the reason

I stopped by here. Wanted to warn you about him."

Shawn became aware that Ma and Dora were standing quietly by, listening. The older woman, hands clasped under her apron, moved deeper into the room.

"Where's this Hillister now?"

Shawn nodded toward the window, at the country now beginning to soften as the afternoon wore on.

"Out there, somewhere. Probably hunted me for a time, then gave up and started looking for your place."

"Meaning he don't know where we live?"

"He'll find it. . . . I did."

Aaron shifted wearily. "Then we got him to worry about on top of Harper and his bunch," he said in a ragged tone.

Ma King crossed to him, laid a hand on his shoulder. "Don't fret, son. We can take care of him same as we can Chet Harper." Turning, she faced Starbuck. "Seems I'm beholden to you again—and I'm obliged. Not many folks would've bothered."

"Mad dog running loose is everybody's business."

Ma's lined features softened as a partial smile came to her lips. "Reckon your pa and ma can be real proud of you. They live around here somewheres?"

"Both dead. We had a farm in Ohio."

"And after they was gone you picked up and come west."

"Not just that way—came to find my brother. I've been hunting him for quite a time. On my way to Santa Fe now."

"He waiting there for you?"

"Could be. Don't know for sure. I've gone to a lot of places thinking he might be, but it's turned out I was wrong."

"Well, I'm sorry if we've caused you to maybe miss out on him. . . . Must be sort of lonesome-like traipsing around all over the country like you're doing."

"Used to it now—and someday it'll end. I'll find him."

"Expect you will all right," the older woman said in a gentle tone. "I'm hoping it'll be soon. Be a shame was you to waste your years and end up being old with no life left to live. Man like you ought to have a home—a family."

"Someday," Starbuck said, glancing through the window. "Aim to do—"

He drew up sharply, whatever he intended saying dying on his lips. Riders had appeared in the brush beyond the cleared ground.

"They're here," he said.

14 ~

Fear tore at Aaron King. Without conscious thought he came out of his chair in a quick lunge. Snatching up the rifle, he crowded close to the window.

From the corner of his eye he saw Ma shrug resignedly, and, disregarding the belted gun under her apron, take possession of the shotgun Dora had used and cross to Starbuck's side.

"They coming or waiting?" he heard her ask.

"Waiting," Starbuck said.

He saw her look past the tall man's shoulder into the yard. "That big one on the brown horse—he's Chet Harper. 'Pears he's lost somebody. . . . Tex, I reckon it is."

"He's the one Starbuck winged," Aaron volunteered.

Ma made no comment. After a moment he saw her step back. "What're you wanting us to do?" she asked, looking straight at Starbuck.

"Let them make the first move. It's their game; we'll call when the right time comes."

Aaron watched Ma turn to him, heard her sharp voice. "You got that straight? Don't do nothing until Starbuck tells you to."

In the quiet that filled the cabin he stared at his parent. Disbelief was running through him. To have her defer to another was a new and extraordinary experience. Always, about as far back as he could recall, hers was the word, the law, the final, irrevocable decision.

"All right, Ma," he murmured.

Doubt was threading his voice but the years of

subservience to her will were having their effect; if she wanted to let Starbuck handle things, he reckoned she knew what she was doing. Maybe it was best, anyway. Starbuck was a cool customer. He'd been around, likely had seen a lot of trouble. He'd know how to stand up to Chet Harper.

He wished he could be like the tall, hard-jawed rider. It would have pleased Pa. He'd wanted a man such as Starbuck for a son, instead he'd got Ollie and he'd got him—a slough-footed plodder who could barely ride a horse and was even worse when it came to handling a gun.

His place was in the fields. Pa'd told him that a long time ago, and he'd known the words were true. And with the same practical logic, he'd made the best of it, not minding too much when Ollie'd go tearing off for a hell raising in some town and leave everything for him to do.

When Pa died and Ma had stepped right into his boots, which she'd more or less been doing all along, he still hadn't thought much about it. Actually, he realized one day, he should have taken over as head of the family, being the elder son; but Ma hadn't given him the chance, had simply gathered up the reins herself and took charge.

He supposed it was right. He wasn't the strong kind, the sort who could be boss and get things done by ordering others around. And he was no hand to argue and fight; way he saw it, when there was something to be done, the thing to do was do it—not talk about it. It was easier than yammering and fussing and being responsible.

Aaron guessed that was the heart of it: he just didn't have it in him to accept responsibilities—except where chores around the place were concerned. He could do that and he'd been doing it just about all of the thirty years he'd been alive, but as long as he was being honest with himself he might as well own up to the fact that he wasn't even much good at doing that. While Pa was alive, they did have a ranch of sorts—a few head of cattle, a good stand of hay, a few hogs, horses and such, along with the prospects of doing better.

But after Pa died, things went down fast despite all he could do; it was like stepping onto a mudbank along the river—you started sliding and you couldn't stop no mater how hard you tried. Maybe it was his fault the place had turned into a starved-out, sodbuster's patch; maybe he should have set Ma down and taken over the way an older son was supposed to do.

Aaron shrugged as he stared morosely at the low hills beyond the yard. He could just see himself ordering Ma around, making Ollie toe the mark, and such. They would've laughed in his face. But it might've worked out. If Ma hadn't right away jumped in and made herself the boss, he would have been forced to assume the job as head of the family, and having responsibility thrust onto him, he maybe would have come into his own and amounted to something.

One thing sure, if that had panned out, he bet Dora wouldn't look at him the way she did; in fact, she probably wouldn't even be there with them—and he wasn't certain he liked that thought.

Stirring, Aaron glanced to where Ma and Starbuck were standing at the window, their attention on Harper and his men. An ease settled over him. There was no denying it was a relief to have someone like them doing all the thinking, saying what was to be done. . . . Still, if he had the chance to live it all over again and had his druthers, he'd like to at least try being his own man— be one who did the telling and not just the listening.

Dora seated herself on one of the chairs in the kitchen and settled her eyes on Ma and the stranger. The dishes and pans were all cleaned and put away and there was nothing to do now but sit and wait— and look after Ollie.

That was the routine her life followed—cooking, cleaning, housekeeping such as it was, and taking care of Ollie. It was not the life she had envisioned, and certainly not one she would have let herself in for had she known. Now, like a rabbit caught in a web snare,

she was trapped, unable to escape into a world bright
with promise because of circumstance.

It had been different in the beginning. Orphaned
at seventeen, she had made the long journey from the
plains of Illinois to Santa Fe, where she was to live
with her only remaining relatives, a childless aunt and
uncle who owned and operated a small store in the ancient Spanish and Mexican capital. To pay for her keep
she had gone to work at once in the establishment.

On the second day she was there, Ollie King had
ridden into town with several friends, and subsequently
dropped into the store, alone, to make a purchase. He
had stopped short when he saw her and from that
moment on could not take his eyes off her.

He finally did leave, only to return that same
evening, and under the disapproving glances of her
uncle, told her straight out that she was the prettiest
thing he'd ever seen, that he was in love with her and
never again would he be worth a hoot unless she
married him.

He was a redheaded, reckless, laughing man not much
older than she and said that he lived with his mother
and brother on a ranch east of the mountains. It wasn't
much of a place, he admitted frankly, but it had good
prospects and with her to fire him up he knew he could
turn it into a real home and a moneymaker.

On the fourth day she succumbed to his proposal,
agreeing also to wait until they got to the ranch before
going through the marriage ceremony. They could have
it performed in Cimarron, a town they were fairly near,
and he wanted very much to have his mother and
brother in attendance. It shouldn't matter to her, he'd
said, for after all, she had no close family to think
about; the aunt and uncle, who washed their hands of
the whole affair from the start, didn't count.

It took days for the shock of what she had come into
to wear off: a pipe-smoking, hard-swearing old woman
with a will of iron who made it plain that she hated
every inch of her because she had hooked her son; a
spineless brother who slunk about, tight-lipped, doing
chores on a place so hardscrabble poor that it was
below the level of even the worst tenant farm.

The wedding was out of the question for the time being; Ma King made that clear within minutes after they arrived and Ollie had announced their plans. There was too much work to be done. Things were way behind, thanks to Ollie's being gone, which, Dora gathered from listening to them talk, was an unpredictable frailty of his. Once they were caught up they'd all go to Cimarron and let the Baptist preacher get the job done.

Meanwhile, everything was to be kept decent, Ma declared, and had her two sons clean out the small shack at one end of the yard and fix it up as living quarters for Dora. After the marriage was performed, Ollie could move in.

It was all a terrible letdown for her, but she had made her bargain and there was no going back to Santa Fe and her aunt and uncle or, because of the isolation, to anywhere else. And so she fell into the servile system under which Ollie and his brother, Aaron, existed, soon impassively accepting the acid-tongued comments, directives, and rebukes of Ma King while she awaited the day when they would all make the trip to Cimarron, after which she and Ollie could at least live together.

But that never came to pass. Ollie, goaded by the old restlessness, mounted his horse one night when everyone was asleep and rode north—into trouble, and she never again saw the man as she had known him. He did write her a letter just before he was taken off to the pen and for that she would always be grateful.

While Ollie and Aaron were away serving their time, she stayed on with Ma partly because there was no other place to go, but mostly because of Ollie and the future they could have together if ever given the chance. And then when the pardons came through and he was back alive but, for all purposes, dead, she found herself facing the fact that if she was to have the life she now dreamed of, she must break away, find it for herself.

This hope was now stirring with greater vigor within her, brought to a shining glow by the man who had ridden into their midst with the thought in mind to warn Ma and Aaron of a threat, but who stayed on to lend them a hand.

Starbuck—tall, dark, cool-eyed, and steady-nerved, represented all that Ollie had not been: strength, courage, dependability, and with a knowledge of the world outside the tiny circle that imprisoned her—he could give her all that. And now as she sat watching him, the determination not to miss the opportunity began to crystallize.

She would offer him herself—everything, asking only that he take her with him when he rode out. If taking a wife was not in the scheme of things for him, then she would be his woman, hoping that love would finally come and grow and become a part of their relationship.

Failing that persuasion she would ask only that he enable her to reach the nearest town of any size, one where she could strike out on her own. The important thing was that she leave, that she put Ollie and Ma and grubbing, hungering Aaron with their starved-out cabbage patch behind her before it was too late.

But it would all have to wait until matters with Chet Harper were settled—and that would come to pass. Starbuck was a man—the kind who could handle anything.

15 ~~

"Just can't keep on calling you Starbuck," Ma King said, continuing to look through the window at the riders in the brush beyond the yard. "You got another name?"

"Shawn."

"Sounds Indian. There some Indian blood in you?"

"No. My mother was a schoolteacher. Once taught some kids from the Shawnee tribe. Liked the sound of the word, I reckon, and when I came along she made it into a name for me."

"Kind of pretty at that," the older woman said. "What do you figure Harper's up to?"

At that moment one of the outlaws pulled away from the others, angled toward a high mound of rock and brush at the edge of the clearing.

"Looks like we're about to find out," Starbuck replied.

"Harper's coming," Aaron announced unnecessarily from the opposite end of the wall.

"Let him. Probably wants to talk."

The outlaw rode in behind the buttelike rise, dismounted, taking care to not make a target of himself. Moving to the edge of the rocks that fronted on the cabin, he removed his hat, waved it overhead.

"You Kings there in the house—you listening?"

Shawn stepped to the door, opened it slightly. "We hear you!" he yelled back.

"Aiming to give you a last chance. Tell me where that gold's hid and we'll pull out, let you be."

"Can't tell you because we don't know."

81

Silence followed for a brief time and then Harper's voice came again. "That you talking, Aaron?"

"No. Friend of the family. Name's Starbuck."

"It's him I want to talk to. You keep out of this, mister."

"Aaron ain't got nothing to say," Ma shouted through the broken window. "Starbuck's doing the talking for us."

"You best forget the whole thing," Shawn added. "Aaron doesn't know where the gold is. Never did. He wasn't in on the holdup."

"Know better. He was there, all right."

"You just think so, like a lot of other folks did. Was somebody else with Ollie. Could be he looked like Aaron, but it wasn't him."

Once more there was quiet. Down in the field below the garden a meadowlark whistled cheerfully.

"How come you've stuck your snout in this, Starbuck?" the outlaw called finally. "You fixing it so's you can get that gold for yourself?"

"Told you—just a friend——"

"The hell!" Harper shouted scornfully. "You're after it same as me."

"If I was I wouldn't be hanging around here trying to find it. Get this in your head, Harper—Aaron doesn't know where that money is—only Ollie does, and you've seen the shape he's in. The gold's lost, cached somewhere, and it'll stay there until somebody stumbles onto it, turns it up——"

"That's a lot of bull!"

"It's the straight truth, and you better make up your mind to it and pull out. Any shooting or killing won't change anything—so forget it."

"Ain't about to, mister——"

"You pay attention to him, Chet Harper!" Ma shouted. "He's telling you the gospel truth!"

"And I'm telling you, old woman—I'm giving you one hour to send Aaron out here ready to talk! You don't, then we're coming after him."

"Done tried that a couple a times, ain't you? All it got you was some bullets. Be the same again."

"Maybe not. I figure a little fire'll do more good than bullets."

Ma King drew back, nodded to Shawn. "That's what you said he'd try—but I just never believed it. Is he just talking or do you think he'll do it?"

"Expect he will."

The old woman turned away, glanced around the cabin. "Sure would hate that," she murmured. "It ain't much but me and Cain built it ourselves—and it's all I got."

Cain . . . Cain King . . . He would have been her husband, Shawn guessed. Anger stirring through him suddenly, he swung back to the partly open door.

"Why don't you leave these folks alone, Harper? They can't tell you where that gold is—none of them!"

"Know better——"

"You don't know anything—you're just thinking they can—and I'll give you a bit of warning; you try burning down this place and there'll be some men die —you first of all if I can manage it!"

He knew he was probably wasting breath, that his words would have little effect on what the outlaws would eventually attempt. The odds were all against the Kings, and him, cooped up in the cabin as they were. Chet Harper had only to keep them occupied with part of his gang while he sent others to set fires that would quickly consume the cabin.

"Could be," the outlaw said, "there won't be no need for none of that—not if you show some sense. What say if I make you a deal?"

"Doubt if anything you come up with will interest the Kings."

"Ought to, spot they're in. . . . I look at it this way; there's enough gold there for all of us. You tell Aaron to take me to where they buried it and after we dig it up I'll hand over five thousand dollars of it to him. . . . Five thousand—that's a lot of money!"

"No doubt, but it comes right back to the same thing—Aaron doesn't know where it's buried——"

"And if he did, I sure wouldn't let him do it!" Ma shouted. "Why, I wouldn't trust you, Chet Harper, no farther'n I could throw a Missouri mule by the tail!"

"Better do some thinking on it, old woman."

"Ain't no need——"

"With all that much gold you could turn this dump into a mighty nice little farm—even get yourself a few head of cattle and start living like white folks——"

"Go to hell, goddamn you!" Ma King exploded suddenly, once again her old self. "I ain't listening, so you might as well quit the yammering."

"What about you, Starbuck?" Harper said then, calmly ignoring the woman's words. "You willing to make a deal?"

"My answer's the same as Ma's, and if you try pushing us, you're going to get some of your bunch killed."

"Not the way I see it, and I expect you'll be changing your mind after you've set on it a bit."

"Not likely."

"Just wait and see. . . . Now, I'll be back in a hour. You have Aaron ready to talk, or travel. Don't make no difference to me which. I figure I'm being good to you, offering to give you some of the gold like I am. But if you've still got your neck bowed, then we'll get him the hard way. I making myself plain?"

"Reckon you are!" Ma shouted. "Now, I'll make something plain to you—if you come back, come ready to die!"

16 ～

Starbuck wheeled, crossed to the back of the cabin. There was one small window high in the wall beyond the cook stove, and a plank door similar to the front entrance. Opening it quickly, he glanced around, swore softly.

Harper was smart. While he talked, two of his riders had moved into position. There was now one on either side of the house, sitting their horses well back in the brush, where they could effectively keep watch over the cabin and prevent anyone from leaving by the rear while still maintaining a surveillance of the front.

Reaching the barn or any of the structures adjacent to it was out of the question; the yard had been cleared of all brush of any size and a man endeavoring to cross would be at the mercy of the outlaws' guns. He could forget his thoughts of stationing himself in one of the outside buildings and being where he could set up a sort of crossfire should the situation deteriorate into a shootout—which appeared very likely.

It would be possible to slip through the doorway and, by keeping in the ragged shrubbery, make his way to the areas on either side of the cabin where the two outlaws were waiting, but there would be little gained by that. He might be able to disable one before the others became aware of his presence, and that small reduction of the odds hardly seemed worth the risk.

Shawn drew back, frowned, noting as he did that his sorrel, abandoned earlier when Ma King had taken him captive, was standing at the water trough near the well. The big horse had evidently tired of waiting and moved on of its own accord. It had halted, however, in an unsafe place, one where it would be in line with bullets fired at the house that went astray. But there was nothing he could do about it—only hope that the gelding, after taking its fill of water, would wander on into the barn in search of food.

Starbuck continued to stand in the opening, getting the lay of the land firmly established in his mind, and then reentered the room, closing the door and dropping the bar into place.

He did not mention the two outlaws on sentry duty, seeing no point in further alarming the Kings, but simply crossed over to the front and resumed his stand at the window. Harper and the remaining outlaws were no longer visible in the tall growth beyond the yard, but that they were there was a certainty.

He turned about once more, allowed his eyes to sweep the interior of the cabin. It had but the two doors and three windows—possibly a fourth if there was one in the partitioned-off square that made up a bedroom. It didn't matter; all were small and would not permit the passage of a man through them, being designed primarily for the admittance of light and air.

The place was much like a fort, and there was little doubt in Starbuck's mind that against bullets they could more than hold their own. Fire was a different matter; should Harper make good his threat to put a torch to the cabin, they could offer little if any defense.

He glanced around at Ma and Aaron King, at Dora. Each was silent, occupied at the moment with private thoughts. He wondered if they realized the seriousness of their predicament—decided they did but were spending no time in the consideration.

They were people accustomed to crisis, to facing calamity in all its various forms, be it an act of nature or man instigated. Disaster, danger, and utter failure were not strangers to them. In stoical silence they had weathered the howling, cruel winters, the scorching, drought-ridden summers, the onslaughts of disease—even man's hard-handed punishment for wrongdoing.

Now the object of persecution—this time by the

enemies of the selfsame law that had scored them in the past—they were accepting the offense with stolid resignation, seemingly reassured by the knowledge that they had survived before and would do so again.

Starbuck was finding it difficult to share their confidence. In an out-and-out battle with guns he would have few qualms; forted up such as they were they could give a good accounting of themselves even with restricted stores of ammunition. But fire—he shook his head, fully aware of their helplessness should the cabin be put to the torch. They would be pinned down, caught in a trap from which escape would be at the whim of outlaws guarding the doors with ready pistols.

"You think we ought to be getting ourselves set?" Aaron asked in a low voice.

"Not much we can do now but wait," Starbuck replied grimly.

17 ~

Ma paused at the doorway leading into the bedroom that had been hers and Cain's but now was only a lonely tomb of memories in which she spent the nights. Ollie, his mouth blared open, his body slack, looked like nothing more than a skin sack of bones. He had been a handsome boy, laughing and reckless and much the same as Cain, but wildness had brought an end to all that.

Turning, she glanced to where Starbuck and Aaron, coffeecups in hand, were sitting. Aaron was nervous—it was easy to see that—but Starbuck, his wide shoulders relaxed, his strong features composed, might have been a man with his mind occupied with nothing more than thoughts of his next meal. He was one to lean on, have deep feelings about—there was no denying that. Little wonder Dora couldn't keep her eyes off him.

Dora . . . Ma looked down at the empty cup she held, crossed slowly to the stove to where coffee simmered in its pot. Taking up the chipped, granite container, she refilled her cup and settled down at the table opposite the girl.

"He reminds me of my Cain," she said quietly.

Startled, Dora's eyes spread. "What——"

"Starbuck. Said he reminded me of my mister, some. You're a-wishing you could go off with him."

The girl stared at the older woman for a long breath, then nodded. "Guess I do, Ma. Maybe it's wrong, but I can't help feeling that way."

Ma King slid a glance over her shoulder at the two men. They were beyond overhearing.

"You come here to be Ollie's wife," she said.

"I know that—and I wanted to be, only it just never did happen. And now, coming back from the pen the way he is—there's no use, no sense in it."

"Reckon I understand."

Dora leaned forward, her features tense. "Do you, Ma? Oh, I hope so! There's nothing left for me here, no reason to keep on staying. I'd be wasting my life."

"What about Aaron?"

The girl frowned. "Aaron? I—I—"

"He's wanting you, too, maybe more'n Ollie ever did. He ain't much, God knows, but he's sure and he's steady."

"I never thought of him. Oh, I've caught him looking at me, sometimes trying to help, but I figured he was only being sorry for me."

"It's more'n that."

"But I don't love him, Ma—and I don't think I can stand it here any longer. I have to get away, find a different kind of life, one that's better. Maybe, if Ollie hadn't ended up the way he did and we'd gotten married, I wouldn't be feeling like I do."

"That you've got to get yourself a man?"

"Not so much that—it's that I want to go away, go where there are lots of people, do things, have things —see the big towns."

"All that ain't much good unless you've got yourself a man, too. Happiness comes when there's sharing. Don't amount to nothing if you're alone."

"I know, and I'm hoping Starbuck—"

Ma King raised her eyes to the window above the stove, a softness filling them as she studied the clean blue of the sky beyond.

"It's all right, girl. Ollie's my son but I'm a woman and I know what a woman needs—a strong man who'll make her feel like a woman, let her see that she's wanted. You're missing all that and I can't fault you none for fretting over it.

"Cain was that kind—big and quiet and full of strength and with a way about him that plain told you he could stand up to anything that come along. Just knowing he was around sort of made things all right.

"Nevermind he was a mite on the hard-living, hard-drinking side. He made me know I was his and no other man'd better even look slanchwise at me, else he'd break him in two. And when he roughed me up some getting his way with me, I knowed it was because he loved me. . . . There was a powerful lot of caring in his wanting."

Dora was staring at the older woman in amazement. This was a side of Ma she had not realized existed.

"You must have loved him a terrible lot."

"Reckon I did at that—maybe more'n any woman ought to love a man because it makes the hurt all the worse when the losing time comes. But I always figure we was going to live only once and it was smart to smell the roses while you had the chance. Life ain't never easy, especially for a woman, anyway—slaving and drudging to keep body and soul together, having young-uns and worrying about them while all the time you're holding onto your man, keeping him happy and a-needing you.

"But trying hard as you can it don't always last and when you lose your man something goes out inside you, like maybe somebody turned down the lamp. Things ain't never the same after that. Me, I had to step in take Cain's place, be him and me both. Aaron didn't have the gumption to take over and Ollie just plain didn't give a hoot. All he wanted to do was chase around, raise hell, have hisself a good time.

"Was right pleased when he showed up here with you, telling me you was going to be his wife. Maybe I didn't show it but it pleasured me just the same. Figured maybe he'd changed and was going to settle down, amount to something, but then he went and got all messed up in that robbery and spoilt everything."

Ma King paused, brushed at the sweat on her forehead. The low fire in the stove was making it warm in the cabin, but it was growing late and evening coolness would soon set in, bring relief.

"Expect I oughtn't to be talking to you this here way, me being Ollie's ma, but he ruint his life and there ain't no call to let him ruin yours. I'm seeing what's burning inside you, and like I said, I can't hold it against you."

"Then you'd understand if I went away with Starbuck?"

"Ain't saying I'd be real happy but I know what's chawing away at you. You've got the right to a decent life, which you ain't never going to have here with Ollie. Expect, was I in your shoes, I'd be thinking the same. . . . You sure Starbuck'll take you?"

Dora shook her head. "Aim to talk to him—ask."

"Well, he'll treat you good. Know that from just talking to him, but he won't marry you. Not ready yet. Got his mind set on finding this brother of his and he ain't got time for nothing else until he does. Like Cain that way—points his nose toward something and he won't quit 'til he's there."

"That's all right with me. Never had a man stir me like he does—even Ollie—but if he doesn't feel the same about me then I'll have to settle for just going with him."

"Like a camp follower, that it?"

"Maybe, but mostly so's I can get to a town."

"So's you can find work?"

The girl nodded, her calm face expressionless.

Ma shrugged. "Jobs ain't plentiful in this country for a woman—the decent kind."

"I'll make out."

"Expect you will—and you'll find yourself a man, too. With a little fixing up you can be right pretty."

"I'm glad you don't mind, Ma. I owe you a lot."

"Reckon you've paid your fare and you're entitled. Had my time. Wasn't long as I'd've like for it to be but it was what the good Lord laid out for me, I guess."

"I hate to leave you with Ollie—all that extra work——"

"We'll make out—Aaron and me. When this day's over and all the trouble's been settled, we'll just pick up where we left off, go right on living."

"Thank you, Ma," Dora said. "It means a lot to me."

"Know that. When are you doing your talking to Starbuck?"

"First chance I get."

"Want me to say something to him?"

"No, best I do it myself."

The older woman smiled. If she figured Shawn Starbuck correctly, he'd come to her and find out if she were agreeable to the girl's leaving, anyway. He'd not do anything behind her back.

"Be smart was you to wait until this ruckus is over," she said. "He's got his mind set on it now and he won't take kindly to having his thinking fogged up."

Dora frowned. "I'd like to know—get it settled."

Ma glanced again to the window. "Won't be long. Harper's hour is about gone."

18 ~

Shawn held the empty cup in his hands, considered it moodily. He had drained the last of the bitter chicory from it, was flinching from its harsh taste. Across the room Ma and Dora were engaged in low-pitched conversation while in the chair an arm's length from him Aaron sat in frozen silence.

From the bedroom in the corner came the sound of Ollie's measured snoring. He, at least, was out of it, had no worries. Whether they survived the day or not was immaterial to him, for his was a vague and shadowy world in which nothing mattered.

Restless, Shawn rose, stepped to the window. Still no sign of Harper but he guessed the outlaw would be making an appearance soon; the hour's slow, dragging minutes had about run their course. Wheeling, he settled again in his chair, this time facing Aaron King directly.

"Time's about up."

Aaron nodded, glanced at the nearby bench upon which had been piled all of the ammunition they had been able to muster. Beyond it the shotgun and two rifles leaned against the wall.

"Expect we can hold out for a while."

"Could be it won't be necessary—not with Harper talking fire."

"Keg of water there in the kitchen, and the bucket's most near full."

"The blaze will start on the outside. Be no chance to get out and fight it—Harper's already got two men watching from the brush, making sure none of us leaves the cabin."

Aaron's lips tightened. He frowned, stared at the floor.

"You sure you know what's shaping up?"

King bobbed his head. "Course I do."

"There'll be some dying before it's done with. Man ought to keep that from happening, if he could."

Aaron straightened angrily. "You saying I'm lying about that money—that I know where it's hid?"

"Not saying it——"

"Well, it's what you mean."

Starbuck shrugged. "Not just us two in this. We've got Ma and Dora to think about."

"I wasn't lying," King said doggedly. "Told the truth."

"Fair enough. Just wanted you to realize that it could cost us—all of us—our lives. . . . Don't mind losing mine so much if it's for a good reason, but throwing it away for a lie is something else."

"Was I knowing where Ollie hid that gold, I'd tell. Don't want to die any more'n the next man—and I sure wouldn't let Ma and Dora in for it if I could change things somehow. What's set you to thinking I was lying?"

"Harper. Seems plenty sure of what he's doing. All the talking we've done hasn't backed him off a bit."

"He's wrong—and I don't take kindly to be called a liar."

"Don't let it rile you. If you are, you'll likely end up dead as the rest of us. Be a cinch for them. They get this place to burning, all they have to do is sit back and pick us off when we come out."

"They kill me I sure wouldn't be able to tell them nothing—even if I knew."

"Probably won't kill you right off. Shoot your legs out from under you, maybe break your arms. They'll keep you alive long enough to get what they want."

Shawn was watching Aaron King closely from shuttered eyes. In his own mind he felt the man had been truthful, but Harper's stubborn persistence puzzled him. By this time most men would have concluded they were tracking the wrong bear and turned away; Chet Harper, however, was refusing to admit he was wrong. It was as if he actually knew the Kings were lying about the gold cache.

"You think maybe it'd help was I to go out there and lie to Harper, make out like I was willing to talk and then send him off to the first place I can think of?"

"Might work but only for a bit. Quick as he found out you'd lied it would go worse for all of you."

"Then what's the answer?"

"Already been given. Got to make a stand against him—only way we'll ever satisfy him."

Starbuck paused, shook his head. "Be the same even if you knew where the gold was. It's not Harper's and he has no right to it."

A load seemed to slip from Aaron's shoulders. "Then you're believing me when I tell you I don't know where Ollie hid it?"

"I believe this—that you wouldn't let Ma and Dora in for what's coming if you could stop it."

"Can bet I wouldn't! And I ain't in that big of a hurry to die myself. . . . Don't seem to be bothering you much, though."

"It does—just not showing, maybe. Lot of things I wanted to do before I cash in—got to do, in fact. Big reason why I'm not giving up yet."

"Don't see as we've got much chance, and way you've been talking, you don't think so either."

"Odds are plenty wrong, I'll admit that."

"Then what's making you think it ain't hopeless?"

"Long as we're breathing, we aren't beat. And this cabin's like a fort—plenty safe. Bullets can't get through these walls."

"But fire——"

"Thing we've got to do is keep Harper and the others backed off, not let them get near enough to get a blaze started while at the same time we'll be trying to pick them off."

"Can keep that up for a spell, but we ain't got bullets enough to last long."

"I realize that, but we'll take things a jump at a time. Could be something'll turn up that will change the picture. . . . Ma as good with her pistol as she makes out?"

"Plenty—and a lot better'n me."

"How about Dora?"

"Only fair. Knows how to shoot the shotgun and can use a rifle, but she ain't no crack shot."

"If she can aim, pull a trigger, and reload, she'll do. We'll put her at the back door, tell her if she sees anything move, to shoot at it."

"You want me at the end window, same as I was?"

"Good a place as any. I figure most of what'll go on will be out in the front—about the only way they can get at us. I'll take the door, leave the other window for Ma."

Aaron nodded. "Guess Pa knew what he was doing when he didn't cut windows in all the walls. Must've planned on there being times like this."

"Expect so. You remember him?"

"Some. Died when I was ten, or maybe it was eleven years old. Was a big man, did a lot of laughing and whiskey drinking."

"What happened to him?"

"There was an accident. He'd gone hunting for deer. Things was plenty bad and there wasn't much to eat—we was having a hard winter, worst that had come along since the fifties, I heard it said. He took his rifle and went back up on the ridge, about five miles west of here. Don't know for sure what went on but he got a deer and was toting it in.

"Somewhere he must've fell or maybe just dropped the rifle, because he was shot in the belly. He come on in anyway, lugging that big buck so's we'd have meat for the table. . . . Ma done all she could for him but he'd shed too much blood. Died that next morning."

"Must've been quite a man," Shawn said quietly.

"Yeh, reckon he was. Everything he ever done was for Ma, though. Me and Ollie, we didn't count for much; we was just no more'n a couple of the animals that run around the place. When them two were together it was like there wasn't nobody else alive in the world—only them."

Starbuck made no comment. The attachment between

his own parents had been much the same, a strange, powerful bond uniting two dissimilar persons, but they had found room to include both Ben and him in their universe. He shook his head thoughtfully. Being shut out, as had been Aaron and Ollie King, would be terrible.

"Aaron—you coming out?"

Shawn came to his feet quickly, touching the others in the cabin with his glance. "Reckon this is it," he murmured, and turned to the window.

19 ~

"Aaron King—you hear me?"

The deadening tension of waiting was over; now began the breathless tension of action. Starbuck looked into the yard. Again, Harper was behind the rocky mound. Two riders were visible beyond him—and there was the pair stationed at the sides of the house. . . . Five in all, counting Harper himself. The man wounded earlier was apparently out of it.

Twisting about, he glanced at Aaron. He was crowded up close to the window, features stiff, a whiteness around his mouth.

"Answer him—"

King started, swallowed hard. "Yeh, I hear you," he shouted.

"You ready to do some talking?"

Aaron turned questioningly to Shawn. Starbuck nodded. "Stall him—keep him busy for a bit while I do some looking around."

King resumed his position. "Ain't nothing I can tell you."

"Hell there ain't!" Harper's retort floated back.

Shawn drew up close to the square of shattered glass, threw his glance out beyond the end of the house. He could not see the outlaw. Frowning, he moved to the opposite side of the sash, probed the area on that, the north part of the yard. There was no one to be seen there either. He gave that thought. Had Harper changed his plans, or had the two outlaws moved in nearer? Could they at that very moment be starting their fires?

". . . Told you I don't know where that gold's hid. Was Ollie that done it, not me."

With Aaron's words beating in his ears, Starbuck wheeled, started for the rear of the cabin. Ma King, rifle in her veined hands, stood beside the kitchen table seemingly awaiting his orders. Dora was nearby. He paused, bucked his head at the older woman.

"Get to the window—keep an eye on that pair in the brush."

Ma, lips compressed, immediately moved to the front of the cabin. Shawn snatched up the shotgun, and holding it by the barrel, passed it to the girl.

"Want you back here," he said, and stepped to the back door.

Dora followed him closely. "Keep to the side," he cautioned, and hunching low, opened the thick panel slowly.

On hands and knees, Starbuck worked his way out onto the narrow stoop to where he could see the brushy flats to either side. A sigh of relief escaped his lips. The outlaws had moved in closer—but only a short distance. Evidently, if such was to be their job, they were awaiting a signal from Harper before lighting torches and setting fire to the cabin.

Pivoting, Starbuck returned to the doorway, the beginning of an idea slowly forming in his mind. Harper, either overconfident or being one man short, was not bothering to post a man in the back yard to watch the rear of the house; and it could be he was simply relying on the pair stationed at the sides to keep it under surveillance. In any event, it offered possibilities—a ray of hope.

Once more inside the cabin, Shawn faced the girl. "Don't think they'll try coming in this way, but stand here where you can watch the yard. You see anything move, shoot."

Dora smiled, took a position at the edge of the door frame. Starbuck recrossed the room to where Ma King stood, peered through the upper half of the glass. The two men in the brush had not moved; Harper was still behind the mound.

"Through talking!" The outlaw's voice was sharp,

impatient. "You're going to make me find out the hard way. All right, up to you. . . . Was only trying to treat you decent."

"Decent—hell!" Ma King shouted. "You don't even know the meaning of the word, Chet Harper!"

"Know what I want—and I aim to get it."

If he was to do anything, he was fast running out of time, Shawn realized. The outlaw would not be held off much longer. Checking his pistol for loads, he looked down at Ma.

"One way maybe I can stop this before it gets going. . . . From the outside."

The older woman wagged her head. "You can't go out there—alone——"

"Spotted the pair Harper's got waiting at the sides of the house," he continued, bypassing her words. "Think his plan is for him and those two over there in the brush to come in shooting. While they're keeping us busy, the others'll slip up from the sides and start the fires. Can block that by getting to them before Harper gives them the signal."

"Risky——"

"Good chance I can make it by keeping low and dodging in and out of the brush clumps."

"But there's two of them. You do manage to get to one, there's still the other'n."

"Reason I'll have to move fast—and I can't see staying in here like rabbits in a trap and letting them roast us alive without putting up a fight."

A brightness came into Ma King's eyes as a tight, grim smile cracked her lips. "Way I'm looking at it, too. You want me to try sneaking up on one of them?"

Starbuck shook his head. "Better if you'll stay in here, help Aaron. Keep Harper talking long as you can. Need all the time you can buy me."

Aaron said: "What if they open up on us before you get back?"

He hadn't realized King was listening. "Shoot back— don't worry about me, I'll look out for myself. Pretty sure I can stop one of them before he can get a fire going, the other one will depend on luck. . . . I'll face up to the problem when it comes."

Wheeling, Shawn struck for the back entrance in long strides. Ma King's voice followed him.

"Good luck—son."

He grinned, dropped to a crouch, touching Dora with a look as he moved by her.

". . . Waited long enough!" Harper's hard-edged words came from the direction of the mound. "Can see you're just putting me off. You ain't listening to my offers."

"Just that we don't figure we can trust you," Ma answered.

"Trust me—what the hell you want me to do, put it in writing? Give my word—"

Starbuck eased through the doorway, paused on the outside. Pressed flat against the rough logs of the house, he put his attention on the outlaw to his left. The man had dismounted and worked in closer to the cabin. He was poking about, evidently searching for a dry bush or other suitable bit of brush that would serve as a torch. Shawn grunted in satisfaction. He had been right about Harper's plan.

And he was having a bit of luck. From ground level the outlaw was less likely to see him as he probed around than had he still been up in the saddle.

Pistol in hand, Starbuck took a deep breath, flung a last look at the man, back momentarily turned to him, and rushed to gain the first stand of cover. He reached it, hunkered in tight—and then whirled, gun ready, as a sound behind him caught his attention. Anger and surprise rocked him.

It was Dora.

"What the hell——"

"Wanted to be with you," she answered in a low voice. "Have to talk——"

"Talk!" he echoed in an exasperated whisper. "What the devil's wrong with you? Not the time or the place. You ought to be inside helping Ma and Aaron."

"Nothing I could do—and Ma said it would be all right. . . . No need to watch the back door with you out here."

"Maybe, but you can get hurt—shot."

"Wouldn't matter," Dora said in a worn voice.

Shawn gave her a close, wondering look, felt a stir of pity. Something was disturbing the girl, something deep down and serious—but whatever it was would have to wait. He glanced to the outlaw. The man was standing a few steps in front of his horse, face turned to the mound behind which Chet Harper crouched.

"Stay here," he said. "We'll talk later."

Starbuck again checked the outlaw, reassured himself that the man's attention was centered elsewhere, and, bent low, hurried on to the next large clump of sage. He halted, aware immediately that Dora, like a small, silent shadow, was at his heels. He swung to her, furious.

"Told you to wait!"

The girl's calm features did not alter as her gray eyes met his, held steady. "I'm afraid—by myself."

He swore under his breath, turned back. The outlaw was still waiting for word from Harper. He had kicked loose a fair-size snakeweed, was holding the dry, globe-shaped bush in his left hand. The right was evidently ready with a match.

Starbuck swore again. He had hoped to reach the man, overcome him with a minimum of disturbance so as not to alert the others, and thereby have time in which to double back and take care of the rider on the opposite side of the cabin. His chances for accomplishing this were fading fast; he was now not only hampered by the presence of the girl and would necessarily have to be extra-cautious, but Ma and Aaron had about come to the point where they could stall Harper no further.

"I'll have to move in on him fast," he said, pointing at the outlaw as he tried to make her understand. "Stay here—this time I mean it. Things could go wrong—and he could start shooting."

Dora shook her head. "Only if I have your word you won't leave here without me."

"So that's it!" he said, anger narrowing his eyes. "You think I'm running out on the Kings."

"I—I had to be sure."

"You went to a lot of trouble for nothing. I'll be around until this is all over."

She nodded. "I'll wait," she murmured.

Starbuck turned away, cast a brief look at the outlaw still facing the opposite direction, and moved quietly toward the next bit of cover. Well beyond, at the edge of the yard, he caught a glimpse of Chet Harper once more in the saddle, cutting back to where the remaining outlaws had positioned themselves.

Harper would give the signal for starting the fires when he rejoined them. At that same moment all three would break out, close in on the cabin, firing their guns as they came while the two men on either side of the structure, taking full advantage of its blind walls, would rush in and lay their blazing torches.

That accomplished, their orders undoubtedly then called for them to swing in behind the cabin and cover the back door with a continuing hail of bullets. Thus all those within the house would be effectively pinned down while the flames raged unchecked.

Shawn gained a thick clump of rabbit bush, moved quickly on to a stunted cedar, and halted. The outlaw was no more than a wagon's length away—a tall, blond man. Dismukes, he thought Ma King had called him.

A pistol shot racketed through the late hush. Harper had reached the pair in the brush, was sounding his signal. Dismukes bent forward. A small flame flared in the shelter of his cupped hand. Starbuck, pistol gripped by the barrel, lunged forward, no longer restrained by the need for caution and silence.

The outlaw wheeled at the sound of his approach. His eyes spread with surprise and a yell formed on his lips—but died as Shawn's heavy weapon smashed into the side of his head with a dull thud, dropping him to the ground. Snatching the outlaw's pistol from its holster, he threw it far back into the undergrowth and took up the briskly burning ball of snakeweed. It would be wise to let Harper think all was going as planned.

Holding it to his right in order for the boiling smoke to afford him a screen, he trotted toward the cabin. Reaching the structure, he dropped the flaming brush, being careful to place it a safe distance from the tinder dry wall.

Wheeling at once, he doubled back to where the outlaw lay. Spread out where he had fallen, Dismukes would likely be out of it for several more minutes. When he did recover his senses, he would have neither weapon nor horse and could thus be counted out of the action.

Seizing the reins of the bay the outlaw was riding, Starbuck headed for where he had left Dora. The girl came to her feet as he drew near. Her cheeks were flushed and her eyes bright from excitement.

"Stay low—out of sight," Shawn warned. "Want them to think I'm Dismukes." He continued on without hesitating, striking for the rear of the cabin, as Dora, quickly grasping the idea, crouched low on the opposite side of the horse.

"Got to stop the man on the other—"

His words ended abruptly as smoke rose up from the north side of the cabin, began to stream into the sky. He was too late. The fire had already been started.

Only vaguely aware of the steady thunder of gun-shots coming from the front of the structure where the Kings and the outlaws were maintaining a continuing exchange, Shawn released the reins of the horse, which veered away immediately, and started for the opposite corner of the cabin.

Abruptly the rider assigned to that side broke into view. It was Gonzales, the *vaquero*. He was hunched over his saddle, swarthy features set. Their eyes met at the exact same instant. Gonzales' hand swept down for the pistol on his hip. Starbuck snapped a hurried shot. The *vaquero* jolted, buckled, clawed at the outsized horn of his heavy Mexican hull as the horse reared, spun, began to trot off to the left.

Shawn gained the corner of the house, turned. The clumps of brush Gonzales had bunched against the wall were burning fiercely. Small tongues of flames were beginning to appear on the dry logs.

He rushed ahead, hearing the pound of hooves and the hammering of guns still in progress on the hard-pack fronting the cabin. Ma and Aaron were apparently matching the outlaws shot for shot. Gagging, choking on the dense, black smoke, he reached the pile of blazing weeds, began to kick it clear of the wall, scatter it. Jerking off his hat, he fell to beating out the dozen or so small fires that were finding purchase on the logs. When the last was dead, he wheeled, ran hard for the brush at the upper edge of the open ground.

He could be seen from the yard, he knew, but he was gambling that Harper and the two men with him would be so occupied they would not notice his passage. Also, layers of smoke from the now-smoldering clumps were drifting across the clearing, affording him a measure of cover.

Starbuck reached the thick growth of sage and rabbit bush, threw himself full length into it. There was little wisdom in going back into the cabin and simply adding his bullets to those of Ma and Aaron. He would do far more good from the outside if he could take a position opposite the structure, set up a crossfire. Once the outlaws realized they were caught in the middle they would quit—but he needed to circle around, get behind the mound of rock from which Harper had done his talking.

Raising himself cautiously, Shawn glanced about, seeking a route that would enable him to reach that point without detection. Motion near the back of the cabin caught his eye. He swore angrily. It was Dora, racing through the haze, to join him.

21 ~

She paused before him, breast heaving from the effort of running. Starbuck reached out, seized her by the wrist and roughly drew her down beside him.

"Why the hell didn't you stay in the cabin?" he demanded. "You trying to get yourself killed?"

"They couldn't see me," she replied as her breathing evened off. "Anyway, they're too busy with Ma and Aaron—and you promised we could talk."

He stirred irritably. "What've we got to talk about?"

"Me," she answered quietly.

"You've picked a hell of a time to do it," he snapped, and glanced toward the yard.

Harper and his two riders were wheeling in and out, throwing ineffectual shots at the Kings, safe behind the thick walls of their house. The outlaw would be wondering about the fires, cursing his ill luck because both had apparently failed to touch off the structure, impatient for Gonzales and Dismukes to try again.

"What's on your mind?" he asked curtly, turning back to her. He was anxious to let her have her say, get it over with, since there seemed to be no putting it aside. If it had to be, there would come no better moment, as the outlaws were doing no damage.

"I want to go away with you."

"Said that before—and I want to know why. Your place is here."

"Was here," she corrected. "Ollie's the same as dead now. We'll never get married."

So that was it. She had come to the King place

intending to be Ollie's wife. Before the marriage could be performed Ollie had gotten into trouble—trouble from which he emerged a hopeless misfit.

"Have you talked to Ma about going?"

Dora nodded. "Just a bit ago—before the outlaws came."

"She agree?"

"Said she wouldn't blame me if I did. Said she could understand that I had nothing to look forward to with Ollie and that I was entitled to have a decent life with a man who would love me and take care of me."

"Must have cost her a lot to tell you that."

"Well, she did. Ask her yourself. . . . She knew I was going to talk to you about it."

Starbuck fell silent, his eyes on the hardpack fronting the cabin. The shooting had ceased and the three outlaws had ridden in behind the mound, probably to discuss the failure of the fires and wonder what had become of their missing partners. In the abrupt hush the mournful plaints of a dove, oddly out of place in those moments, drifted in from the trees to the west.

"Still doesn't seem right, somehow."

"Why not? We were never husband and wife—and if it were me in the same condition, he'd leave me in a minute! Was always going off anyway without giving me a second thought."

Shawn gave that consideration, shrugged. "What do you want me to do?"

"Just what I've said—take me with you. I'll go anywhere, do anything you say. We can be married——"

"No," he cut in, flatly and decisively. "Not in the market for a wife."

"Even if she could give you everything you ever wanted?"

"No, not even that," he answered and then became quiet as the full import of her words registered on him. "Not sure I know what you mean," he added, finally.

Dora faced him coolly. "Means exactly what it sounds like—everything you want; me and what comes with me."

Shawn, again silent, stared at the girl. She had a

strength and will he had not suspected, that the quietness of her had hidden.

"Suppose you could give up the search for your brother, could find a fine ranch and settle down, become a cattle grower—get rich and powerful?"

"Can't see that ahead—not for a while———"

"But suppose you could, wouldn't it make you change your mind?"

"No—"

Dora's mouth drew into a petulant line. "Why not? What's wrong with me? Don't you think I'm pretty enough?"

"Not that. Just that I'll get what I want the way a man usually does—by working for it."

"That would take years. Why waste them when you could have it all now?"

Starbuck shrugged impatiently. "You're talking bosh! Even if I was interested, how could you—"

He paused, realization like a shaft of light freed by his own question, flooding across his mind. He grasped her by the arms, drew her close, stared at her intently.

"Just now came to me—how could you do all that for a man?"

"I can—and would for the right one."

He shook her roughly. "How?"

"I—I know where the gold's hid!"

Starbuck's jaw tightened as anger rushed through him. "You know—and you let Harper and his gang make war on the Kings!"

"I wasn't afraid for them after you came—and besides, why should I give it to Chet Harper just so's he'll leave them alone? He and his bunch will go away as soon as they decided Aaron doesn't know where the money is, anyway."

"But in the meanwhile there'll be some killings over it, maybe even Ma———"

"Not likely."

"No? You think they're playing games out there, using cotton balls for bullets? I've already shot one man."

"A Mexican—an outlaw."

"A man just the same, and before this is over with,

there'll be more go down. Stand a damned good chance of stopping lead myself—while all the time you're sitting back with the key, with the thing that can stop it!"

"It's my gold. Ollie sent me a map in a letter he wrote me before they took him off to the pen. Told me to hang onto it until he came back. It's no good to him. The whole fifty thousand dollars won't help him one whit—so it's mine."

Shawn shrugged wearily at such reasoning. "Wasn't Ollie's in the first place. . . . Ma know about this, too?"

"No, of course not. But if she did she'd tell me to take it and run—do what I'm intending to do. Ma's a woman. She know's what a woman's up against in this country, believes in grabbing what she can and hanging onto it."

"Doubt that, Dora. She wasn't talking about the gold if she said it."

"I know Ma King pretty well—and I think she'd feel the same way about it. She lost her man, had to slave to keep herself and her boys alive. Still doing it, in fact—but she'd be practical about the money."

Shawn looked out across the yard to the mound of brush and rocks. The outlaws had not moved. "You've been around Ma a lot longer than I have and maybe you know her better. Could be I've misjudged her—but that's neither here nor there. The gold's not yours. It has to go back to the people it belongs to—Well-Fargo."

"No—never!" Dora said in a quick, firm way. "I'm offering it—a share of it—to you if you'll take me to where it's buried and help me get it. After that, if you don't want me, all I'm asking is that you see me to some town where I can be on my own. . . . If you're not willing, I'll make other plans."

"Go get it by yourself?"

Dora's shoulders stirred. "I'm not that simple-minded. I'll need help—a man's help."

"Which will mean taking in a partner."

"That's what he'll be."

Starbuck smiled at her. "Not much choice around here. Got anybody in mind?"

"Chet Harper."

He stared at her incredulously. "You think you can deal with him? He'll agree, sure, but once the gold is in his hands you'll never see him or it again! Truth is, you'll be lucky to get out of it alive."

Dora looked down, bit at her lower lip. "That's why I wanted you, Starbuck. I know I can trust you."

He shook his head. "Count me out. I want no part of it, and if I've got anything to say, the map will go to Wells-Fargo——"

"But you don't," she cut in, abruptly cool. "It's mine and I'm going to keep it, and if you turn me down, I'll think of something else—either chance Harper or maybe I'll just go it alone, let it stay where it is until someday I can find the right man who'll see things my way."

"He probably won't be hard to meet——"

"And don't think you can leave here and go running to some lawman about it," she broke in. "I'll be gone by the time he could get back."

"If any of us leave here," Starbuck murmured, again shifting his eyes to the outlaws. He drew up sharply. They were filing out from behind the mound. Evidently they had concluded something had happened to Gonzales and Dismukes, were now changing their plans.

"If so, it won't matter. The gold wouldn't do me any good. . . . Nobody else will get it either."

"Odds are mighty good that's the way it'll work out," Shawn said, eyes still on Chet Harper and the two men with him.

Dora gripped his arm suddenly, looked up into his grim face. "Starbuck, think about it again. Don't say no! There's so much we can have, so much good life ahead of us if you'll take it. With all that money we can have everything we ever wanted—go to all the places we've dreamed of visiting."

He did not respond, simply continued to watch the outlaws.

"It can be on your terms. If you don't want me for a wife, then take me as a woman—I'll be happy and satisfied."

"There'd be no happiness," he said. "We'd always

be thinking about that gold—where it came from, how we got it. You can't build anything good on that kind of a foundation."

"But we could—I know we could! And we can leave here right now while everything is quiet. Your horse is in the barn. I can use the one Dismukes was riding."

"And just forget Ma and Aaron, and all this trouble?"

"They'll be all right. Harper won't hurt them when he finds out Aaron can't tell them what he wants to know."

"Can believe that. It's the in-between that worries me—the time when all the shooting will go on before he decides Aaron doesn't know."

"Then why can't we have Ma tell him—after we've gone—that we've got the map—"

Starbuck wasn't listening. The outlaws were swinging in toward the cabin. A rifle blasted the hush, sending up a chain of rolling echoes. The man to the left of Harper flinched, then laughed.

"I'm getting in behind them," Shawn said, his features tightening. "Aim to stop this before it gets any worse. . . . Best you stay here."

Dora shook her head stubbornly, smiled. "I'm coming with you. I still think you'll change your mind."

22 ~

Starbuck cut back through the brush, circled toward the mound. Harper and the men siding him had now halted a distance below it, eyes on the figure of Dismukes, walking unsteadily across the flat. The outlaw, hat in one hand, was holding a wadded bandana to his head with the other. There was no sign of the *vaquero*.

Shawn gained a hedge of waist-high sage to the north of the rocks, halted. Dora, never more than a step behind him, hunched close by.

"Maybe they'll give up now," she said tautly.

"Doubt it," he replied. "Fifty thousand is a lot of money—and Harper's not the quitting kind."

"It can be yours—ours."

He turned, looked down at her. "Don't start that again!"

"But why? Don't you want a lot of money?"

"Nothing wrong with that. Would be a fine thing having all you needed and being able to do what you've always wanted to do, but there'd be no peace inside me. I'd always remember that I had no right to it."

"Just having it makes it your right. Out here you have to look out for yourself, take what you can and hold onto it. There's such a thing as not being practical—of being too honest."

A half smile pulled at Starbuck's lips. "I don't think so. You can't be too honest or just a little honest. Either you are or you aren't."

Harper and his men had now pulled off to the south edge of the yard and intercepted Dismukes. They were

113

grouped before him in a half circle while he talked, apparently relating what had occurred.

"Time we got into those rocks," Shawn said. "Things are going to bust wide open here in a few minutes."

Turning, he dropped farther back into the feathery, blue-gray undergrowth, and, keeping low, trotted the remaining distance to the tumbled mass of brush and rocks.

Climbing halfway to its summit, Shawn drew in behind a large boulder and swung his attention to the far side of the cleared flat. Dismukes was walking slowly on toward the dense brush to the east; Harper and the others were separating, one man curving in to the south wall of the cabin, another angling for the opposite side—following a course that would bring him close to the mound—while the outlaw leader himself moved cautiously on a direct line for the front of the squat, log structure.

"You come too close, Chet Harper, and I'll shoot you off'n that saddle!"

Ma King's voice crackled through the afternoon sunlight.

"Ain't never killed a man yet but that ain't saying I can't!"

Harper pulled up. "You ain't done much good so far—and I expect you're 'most out of bullets. . . . Better trot Aaron out so's I can talk to him."

"Tired of telling you—he ain't got nothing to say. Now, take your bunch and get out of here—you seen what happened to Dismukes, and the Mex ain't around no more, either."

"Makes no difference."

"Well, it ought to. Starbuck's still out there somewheres and what happened to them's going to happen to the rest of you unless you move on."

"I ain't worrying about Starbuck, whoever he is."

"You better be—only three of you left."

Shawn watched the rider slanting toward the mound with narrowed eyes, striving to guess the path he would take—one crossing in front of them, or one behind.

"He's the one they call Georgia," Dora said in

a low voice. "Other one heading for the back is Bill Drake."

"It's Georgia we need to think about," Shawn replied. "Likely be some shooting when he gets here. Want you to ease down behind those rocks. Be safe there."

Dora gave him a quick, hopeful look. "That mean you've changed your mind about me and——"

"Just don't want you hurt," he said, shaking his head.

Her shoulders sagged, and, turning about, she crawled into the hollow a yard or two below where he crouched.

Georgia, eyes on Harper, bore in steadily. It made no particular difference to Starbuck which route the outlaw chose; to him it was simply a matter of being prepared to act. He hoped he could take the man without gunplay; shooting would immediately draw Harper and Bill Drake, whereas eliminating the man quickly and quietly, as he had Dismukes, would enable him to remain unhampered, free to move about and in good position to further lower the odds.

The outlaw drew near, veering slightly left. He had elected to cross in front. Starbuck, hunched low, fell back, hurriedly circled the formation, and gained its lower end. Gun still holstered, he waited behind a shoulder of granite, poised to spring. Georgia moved up, came abreast—passed by.

Starbuck threw himself from the corner of the rock. His fingers caught at the man's arms, locked around fabric of his shirt. Throwing his weight to the side, he dragged the outlaw from the saddle.

They hit the ground solidly as Georgia's horse shied away. Cursing savagely, the outlaw struggled to get at the pistol pinned beneath him. Shawn pulled back, swung a blow at the man's jaw—missed.

"Hey—over here!"

The yell broke from Georgia's mouth before Starbuck could prevent it. He lashed out again at the outlaw's head, but the man jerked aside again, rolled to his knees. On beyond him, Starbuck could see Harper coming up fast, ignoring the shots directed at him by Ma and Aaron as they sought to help.

Georgia's hand flashed down, came up. The slanting rays of the sun glinted off the pistol clutched in his fingers. Shawn lunged to his left, fired, all in one single motion. Georgia rocked back on his haunches, hung briefly, and toppled.

Starbuck spun to face Chet Harper. The outlaw leader, now in range, snapped a bullet at him. Shawn flinched as it grazed his arm, struck the granite behind him, and noisily sang off into space. Dropping to his knees, he triggered a shot at the onrushing man, swore as the lead went wide.

He threw himself full length, taking what cover he could find. A second bullet ripped through the cloth of his corded pants, seared a stinging groove across his thigh. Cursing, he steadied the weapon in his hand, pressed off a shot.

Chet Harper yelled, buckled. His horse, suddenly without a firm hand on the leathers, swerved, began to lope toward Georgia's mount, which was standing head up, ears pricked forward, in the brush a hundred yards or so farther on. The outlaw, one arm dangling loosely at his side, gripped the horn of his saddle as, bouncing like a rag doll, he fought to stay upright.

Shawn, feeling the warm, stickiness of blood trickling down his leg, drew back into the rocks. Thumbing cartridges from his belt, he reloaded quickly. There was still Bill Drake to account for. Pistol cylinder full, he circled to where Dora waited, climbed on to the forward edge of the mound as she eyed him anxiously.

"You've been shot!"

"Only a scratch," he said, dismissing her alarm.

Turning toward the cabin, he came to sudden attention. Drake was moving toward him, arms raised, palms flat to show he had holstered his weapon. Shawn rose to full height, and, gun leveled at the man, waited for him to get near. . . . Evidently Drake wanted no more of it, was quitting.

"Don't shoot!" the man called as he approached the mound. "I'm leaving."

Starbuck nodded coldly. "Pull your gun—let it drop."

Drake, face shining with sweat, reached for the

pistol on his hip. Lifting it carefully with the tips of his fingers, he allowed it to fall.

"Now move on," Shawn snapped. "Get your friends and ride out—and keep remembering I'll be standing here watching everything you do."

Bill Drake bobbed his head. "Was ready to go a hour back, only Harper wouldn't listen. Way I seen it the Kings was telling the truth."

"They are. They don't know where that gold's buried."

The outlaw mumbled something, jerked a thumb in the direction of Harper, still in the saddle. His horse had halted beside Georgia's.

"Aim to catch up the bay and take him to Dave so's he'll have something to ride. That all right with you?"

"All right—"

Drake clucked at his mount and moved on. He came alongside the sprawled figure of Georgia, paused to look down. After a moment he shook his head.

"Old Georgia was wanting to pull out, too, same as me, but we just couldn't make Chet listen. . . . You see he gets a burying?"

Starbuck nodded, watched the outlaw ride on, reach Harper and the stray horse. Drake, leaning over, gathered up the reins of the two animals, and, with the outlaw leader clinging tight to the horn, led them off toward the brush where Dismukes had vanished.

Shawn heard the light crunch of gravel as Dora climbed up beside him.

"I—I guess it's all over."

Gaze still on the receding outlaws, Shawn holstered his weapon. "Finished," he said quietly.

She moved around to where she could face him directly. "Do you still feel the same—about me and the gold, I mean?"

"Nothing's changed."

A small sound escaped her throat as she looked away. Then, "Are you going to tell Ma about me having the map and knowing all the time where the gold's buried?"

He was silent for a time, finally shrugged. "No, that's up to you."

"Then I can keep it?"

"Have to decide that for yourself. You're the one who'll have to live with whatever it is you do. . . . Come on, best we get back to the house. Could be Ma or Aaron got hurt."

He took the girl's hand to steady her, and together they climbed down from the crest of the mound and headed across the flat to the cabin.

23

Starbuck slowed his step, an uneasiness moving through him. He had expected the cabin door to swing open when they drew near, see Ma and Aaron standing there, hear them sing out. The offhand statement he'd made only a few mintues earlier to Dora concerning the possibility of the Kings being injured abruptly assumed solid reality.

"Something's wrong—"

He broke into a run as he muttered the words, and, ignoring pain in his leg, hurried on. The girl kept pace with him. They reached the structure. Extending his hand, he grasped the latch, flung the panel back, and rushed into the dim interior.

"Ma?"

In that same fraction of time Starbuck pulled up short. Ma King was standing against the wall. Next to her, arms raised, was Aaron, and, facing him as he entered, a pistol in each hand was, Luke Hillister.

A gasp of fear broke from Dora's lips at sight of the towering, black-bearded man. Impulsively she caught at Shawn's wrist.

"Who——"

"The bounty hunter—the one I came to warn you about."

Hillister, eyes like glowing coals in the basket of his dark face, motioned to Starbuck, directed him to turn about.

"Sure wasn't looking to find you here, too, bucko," he rumbled in his deep voice as he stepped up, lifted Shawn's weapon from its leather. "Reckon I got me a real passel of prizes this time. . . . You get out of the way now, missy. Just stand there by your ma."

Starbuck pivoted slowly, seeing Dora cross the room quickly to the side of Ma King.

"You've got no call coming here, Hillister," he said angrily. He was blaming himself for his own carelessness. If he'd stopped to think instead of pounding up to the door like some wet-eared kid—

"No? Ain't these folks the Kings?"

"They are, but they're not wanted."

Luke Hillister wagged his massive head. "I know better'n that. Was them that done that robbing up Colorado way."

"Not saying it wasn't, but they went to the pen for it."

"Out now, ain't they?"

"They were pardoned—served all the time the law figured was needful."

"Law was wrong," the bounty hunter declared stubbornly. "They still got to pay. Wasn't right they was turned loose, and I aim to——"

"Listen to me, Hillister! The law's through with them—doesn't want them back—same as it doesn't want me."

"Ain't sure of that, either."

"You ought to be!" Starbuck snapped. "You saw the Cimarron sheriff look me up. You heard him say I wasn't an outlaw."

"Hell, old Bart Trueman don't know nothing. I'm betting the next sheriff I go to'll be real glad to see you, same as he will the Kings. . . . Where's the other boy?"

Starbuck sighed in disgust. He'd known it was useless to try and reason with Luke Hillister, but he had to make the effort. Turning away, he glanced about the cabin seeking an idea, a means for overcoming the bounty hunter. The rifles and shotgun were propped against the wall near the bench where the spare ammunition had been piled. His own weapon was tucked under the waistband of Hillister's pants.

Wait . . . Hold off, he cautioned himself. *You'll only get yourself and some of the others hurt if you try any-*

thing while he's holding those two cocked pistols on you.

Ma King, elbows bent, hands folded under her apron in womanly fashion, touched him with her eyes, then let them move on to Hillister.

"You're wasting your time, mister," she said. "The law ain't after my boys."

"I am," he answered flatly. "Where's the other'n?"

"Reckon you'll just have to find him yourself. I sure ain't telling you."

"Suits me," the bearded man said, his broad, thick shoulders stirring.

Hillister backed to where Starbuck stood against the door. Motioning again at him with one of his weapons, he said: "Get over there with them others."

Shawn crossed slowly, nerves razor sharp, muscles taut; if he could somehow throw himself to the side, snatch up one of the rifles—get to the hidden knife in his boot.

"Don't you go trying something cute," Hillister warned softly, reading his mind. "I only got to squeeze a trigger and you ain't got no head!"

The bounty hunter laughed at the sound of his own words, cackling in an odd, broken way. In the breathless quiet that filled the cabin, Starbuck glanced at the Kings and Dora. Aaron, arms still held aloft, and the girl were rigid, fear drawing their features into harsh, flat planes. Ma's sun-browned, lined face was expressionless, but her eyes were sharp, calculating.

Reaching the wall, Shawn stepped in beside Aaron. Luke Hillister holstered the weapon he was holding in his left hand, opened the door. Then, taking a step to the side, he gathered up the two rifles and the shotgun in his hamlike fist, carried them to the opening, and flung them into the yard. That done, he kneed the panel closed.

"That's so's you won't get no ideas," he said, grinning at Starbuck. His dark, heavy-lidded eyes swept the cabin, halted on Ma King. "Ain't you got no rope in here, missus?"

"Out in the barn," she replied cooly. "You want it—go get it."

The bounty hunter favored her with a hard grin. "Trying to trick me, eh? Well, you ain't about to. I know what I'm doing."

Shawn watched the bounty hunter edge toward the bunks built against the wall. He had slipped in through the back while Ma and Aaron were at the windows, busy fighting off Chet Harper and the others, he guessed. Likely it had been all the shooting that had attracted him to the cabin and divulged the location of the family.

"This'll do good as rope," Hillister said, jerking a blanket from the top bunk. Bunching it in his hand, he tossed it to Starbuck. "Get busy tearing that into strips so's—"

Luke paused, his gaze reaching through the opening that led into Ma's bedroom. He grinned widely, exposing his strong teeth.

"Well, what d'you know! Here's that other boy—a-hiding under the covers like a scared little rabbit!"

"You leave him be!" Ma shouted.

Careful to keep his weapon leveled at them all, still grinning, the bounty hunter leaned to the side, grasped Ollie by the ankle and dragged him off the bed.

"Get up little rabbit—and get in here!"

Ollie struggled to a sitting position and stared blankly around the room. Hillister swung his leg, kicked him brutally in the ribs. The younger King recoiled in pain, cried out.

Ma surged forward, eyes blazing. "Cut that out! Can't you see he don't know what you're saying? He ain't right in the head!"

She halted as Hillister threatened her with the gun. The bounty hunter reached down, caught Ollie by the arm and jerked him upright, shoved him stumbling toward the others. Dora caught him by the hand, pulled him in to her side.

"You got that blanket tore up?" Luke shouted, turning his attention on Starbuck. He was suddenly angry, his eyes raging, his mouth trembling as he spoke. "Get to doing it so's we can get out of here. I'm tired of fooling around!"

"Be dark pretty quick," Shawn said in a voice

pitched to calm the violence boiling through the bearded man. "Why don't you figure to stay here 'til morning, have a bite to eat—rest?"

"Hell with waiting!" Hillister screamed. "I'm taking the three of you right now soon's——"

"You ain't taking nobody—no place!" Ma King cried.

Her hands came out from beneath the apron. In one she held the old Navy Colt, overlooked by Hillister when he took a rifle from her. She triggered the heavy weapon fast but the cloth of the apron had snagged on the hammer. The bullet thudded into the wall behind the bounty hunter, missed narrowly.

Luke Hillister fired in the same moment. Ma staggered back as the load smashed into her, drove her to the floor while the cabin rocked with the blasts of the two guns overridden only by Dora's screams.

Starbuck leaped forward through the layers of smoke, hurling the blanket into the bounty hunter's face as he did. Hillister brushed it aside, endeavored to avoid Shawn's rush. He failed and the two men came together in a solid collision. The impetus carried Luke backwards, slammed him against the wall. Starbuck rebounded, struck out with his balled fist.

The blow only grazed Hillister's jaw, evoked a stream of curses. The bounty hunter swung his pistol at Shawn's head, caught him high on the neck. Starbuck went to his knees, instinctively rocked to one side. A knee smashed into his shoulder, knocked him out of the way. He looked up. Aaron King, Ma's pistol in his fist, mouth blared wide in a cry of anguish and hate, eyes blazing, stood over him.

The Colt began to blast. Once . . . Twice—several times until it was empty. Luke Hillister, as if pinned against the wall, hung there, half bent, his huge body jolting each time a bullet struck him. When the deafening thunder had finally ceased, he remained motionless, bearded face tipped down, and then abruptly his massive body toppled to the floor like some giant tree felled by a mighty wind.

Shawn drew himself upright, stepped to the door, and opened it to thin out the drifting clouds of acrid, choking smoke. Turning, he crossed to where Dora and Aaron knelt beside Ma King. Beyond them Ollie had found a chair, was sitting down.

The girl, holding the older woman's head in her lap, looked up at Starbuck as he hunched beside her.

"Ma's dead," she murmured, voice breaking. "She—she said she loved me—and called me daughter."

Shawn looked away. After a time he slipped his arms under the slight body and stood up. As he turned for the bedroom Aaron stepped in close, his arms extended.

"Let me have her," he said tightly, "She's my ma."

Starbuck released his burden, fell back, watched King carry the still figure into the makeshift room and lay it on the bed. A bitter thought pushed into his mind: Aaron had found himself at last—but it was too late. Ma would never know.

24

Starbuck folded his arms across his chest, and, leaning against the thick-trunked old cottonwood growing in solitary majesty on the slope rising before him, lowered his head. Farther up the gentle grade a square of whitewashed stones outlined the King family cemetery. The lone grave within its boundaries now had a companion.

The night before he and Aaron had nailed together a pine coffin, and then, with the morning sun slanting down from a clear sky, they had laid Ma, clad in her one Sunday dress—a crisp, black satin trimmed in yellowing lace—beside the man who had meant so much to her.

Well before that they had buried Hillister and Georgia in a place some distance from the area. Shawn had scratched their names, such as he knew them, into headboards and driven them deep into the soil to mark the location. Aaron had felt that neither was entitled to the smallest commemoration, but Starbuck performed the chore, anyway; outlaws undeniably, they were still men and, despite their imperfections, their passing should be noted.

Aaron had taken the death of Ma hard, but it also had changed him, turned him from a passive, ineffectual man to one of firmness and decisiveness. It was as if the loss had jarred him from the apathy of indifference, causing him to finally assume the role he had avoided.

Starbuck raised his eyes as the last words of the familiar prayer being quoted by Dora reached him. Motionless, he watched King, one hand gripping the arm of his brother, turn from the grave and start down the slope. The girl stepped in beside Ollie, took his other arm, and together the three approached Shawn.

"Reckon we've done the best we could for her," Aaron said quietly, halting. He released Ollie, allowed Dora to continue on to the house with him. "Hard to find the words so's I can say how grateful we are."

"No need."

"There's plenty need. Most men would never bothered to do what you done—especially did they know who it was they were helping. . . . Us Kings have always been plenty short on friends."

"Maybe you never gave folks a chance. Man has to go halfway himself. Can't expect others to do it all."

"Could be you're right—and things are going to change some. Aim to see to that." Aaron paused, stared off across the rolling hillscape. He seemed unwilling to look at Starbuck as he voiced his question.

"You taking Dora with you?"

Shawn frowned. "You know about that?"

"Ma told me. Said she was set on being your woman."

"Her idea—not mine. Happens there's no place in my life for a woman—not yet, anyway. Would be only a matter of helping her get to the next town."

"Then you ain't wanting her?" There was a faint hoarseness to Aaron King's voice.

"Like I said—just helping."

"She know that?"

"Made it plain as I could." Starbuck considered the man intently. "Dora means a lot to you—can see that."

Aaron shrugged despairingly. "Just wish you wouldn't take her——"

"Neither here nor there with me. Leaving it up to Dora."

"She never had nothing here 'cepting hard work, so I can't blame her for wanting to go. . . . I'd change all that, was she to stay—make it all up to her."

"Might try telling her that."

In his mind Shawn doubted it would mean anything to the girl. She felt cheated by life, and now with the promise of the gold Ollie had hidden away at her disposal, she had visions of enjoying all the good things she believed had passed her by.

"Maybe she wouldn't listen. Always wanted to talk to her, say things, but she was Ollie's girl—and I didn't think it'd be decent—even after we come back from the pen."

"It would've helped if you had. Nobody ever took the time to tell her how they felt, that she was loved and wanted. . . . Something you can fix right now," he added, ducking his head at the girl moving slowly along the path as she returned from the cabin. "I'll be saddling my horse. Time I was heading out for Santa Fe."

He cut away from the slope, slanting through the dappled shade toward the barn where the sorrel was stabled.

"Starbuck—"

At Dora's call Shawn halted. He nodded at King still standing under the cottonwood, head bowed, hands locked behind his back.

"Aaron wants to talk to you."

She paused, studied the lonely figure briefly as interest brightened her eyes, and then turned back to Starbuck.

"Are you leaving now?"

"Soon as I get my horse ready. If you're riding with me, get your things together."

She crossed to him, her features calm, set. "You'd take me with you?"

"If that's what you want."

Dora smiled, seemingly pleased with the knowledge. "Thank you," she murmured, "but I've changed my mind. I'm going to stay."

Wordless, he stared at her.

"I'm not sure why. Something Ma said, I guess, or maybe it was you—or him," she added, glancing again at Aaron. "He's changed."

"He'll do fine now."

"I know—and I'll help him," she said, and extended her hand. "Goodbye—"

He took her fingers into his, felt the edges of a folded piece of paper in his palm, frowned.

"It's the map," Dora said. "I'm asking you to give it to the law. . . . I don't want the gold."

Starbuck slipped the creased sheet into a pocket, smiled. "It's the right thing to do. It could never buy you what you really want."

Bending forward he kissed her lightly on the forehead. "So long," he said, and continued toward the barn and the waiting sorrel.